The Rewards of Excellence . . .

"Young _____ 'we need pilots _____ one might have _____ but what you di_____ do you know th_____ less than 0.1 percent of all our recruits even catch sight of that dreadnought before it destroys them? There has never been a trainee who has successfully attacked it, until now."

She paused, and I wondered at the things that were being revealed here. My eyes sought her figure.

"And therefore," she said, and lust and euphoria flew straight out the window, "we assign you now to Experimental. There you will fly the most advanced fighter in our fleet, the spearhead we will throw at the Whole should hostilities break out, as most of us believe they will. And some day, you will have the honor of leading the first wave of battle; it will be a grim day for the Whole. My congratulations to you; rank and salary will, naturally, increase."

"A grim day," I repeated in an inaudible croak.

"Young man," the admiral said, "men
... older like you. Your reflexes alone ...
gun. We brought you to this board, but ...
with ... and in the Advanced Attack—"

DON WISMER

A ROIL OF STARS

This is a work of fiction. All the characters and events portrayed in this book are fictional, and any resemblance to real people or incidents is purely coincidental.

A Baen Books Original.

Baen Publishing Enterprises
P.O. Box 1403
Riverdale, N.Y. 10471

ISBN: 0-671-72040-6

Cover art by Debbie Hughes

First printing, February 1991

Distributed by
SIMON & SCHUSTER
1230 Avenue of the Americas
New York, N.Y. 10020

Printed in the United States of America

To
J. Gary Nichols
Librarian and Friend

Introduction

The story of how we of the Polar Cloud forestalled absorption into the Wholeth Empire has never been properly told. I tell it now for many reasons: my children and grandchildren, my place in history, my imminent death, among others. I have never been the most humble of men, though at one time I was, I think, the most cowardly, carnal, and impulsive, as you will see. But what I did changed our society beyond anything we had ever imagined. Blame me, praise me; we rule ourselves, and that's the gift I gave.

A note on sources: in reviewing my wristcom notes from those days, I have been tempted to cast myself in a more favorable light, though even a river of whitewash could not have concealed the active folly without erasing my part altogether, which vanity forbids. As it stands, most of my story reveals me to be a poltroon, a craven seeker of status, a rakehell, and a brownnoser of the first degree. For this I apologize, mostly to those I have harmed, many now alas gone and beyond my hunger for forgiveness.

In portraying Celia (Lee) D'Ame, who should be awarded the title Heroine of the Polar Cloud or some such, I have relied mostly on what she told me herself during our brief association, extrapolating her motives without daring to enter her soul; she declined several attempts to induce her to interview, and threatened suit should I proceed; she can sue my corpse.

The actions of the other great woman in the story, Selah Maja, I report by inference; she still lives, still serves the one who is now the Wholeth Lord. But she is twelve thousand light years away, and further than that in any wish to deal with me.

As for Kel Kellem, Lee has his files still, and I have retained a copy. He truly loved her, I think; may G-d rest his soul.

—Ryne Sangre

Part I:

The Cloud

Prologue: Ryne

I sat in a two-seater, copilot to my right; a sandy-haired fellow named Randy Slader. All around us was the blankness of interspace, but emergence was only seconds away. I checked the instruments: weapons charged, thrusters in top working order, communications operational. *It's only a simulation*, I told myself. I glanced at Randy, and he smiled nervously back. Somewhere, deep in the blankness where only instruments could detect, a hundred others waited like we, our ships howling through inconceivable distance, the enemy moments ahead.

FLARE! The fire of transition blew away around us, and we emerged into real space. At once the instruments went into hysteria. The images came at me like a firestorm, and we hurtled toward disaster.

There, ahead of us, was a grey-green planet, a typical outrider on the fringe of a solar system, local sun glinting like a backlit diamond in the far distance. A large moonlet, and two or three dozen tiny ones, were scattered in near space like buckshot, and a tenuous ring around the planet besides. And, coming over the north planetary pole was a fleet, as large as ours, of enemy ships. Larger.

My bowels dissolved. *It's only a simulation!* my mind screamed. An explosion flared far ahead as one of the enemy blew grapeshot into space; at our acceleration, if we ran into such a cloud of metal, we'd be torn to bits in seconds.

Again I looked at Randy, but he was staring intently ahead, nerves of steel apparently, listening to the readouts and trying to anticipate the targets our flagship was choosing for us. I felt a jolt; our two-seater had let fly an impact bomb, at exactly the moment the computer-plotted trajectories demanded. There would not be a lot for us two humans to do at this stage. From the habit of a lifetime, I looked around for escape.

Suddenly there was the most full-spectrum sound I had ever heard, and the cowling above our heads was ripped away as if snagged by a meat hook. The air in the tiny cabin erupted into space, and I felt my ears pop. An emergency membrane leaped out of the console and enveloped each of us, and I remember thinking: that tears it; we're goners for sure. One of their long range weapons had hit us, obviously, and I had no clue what it was. In a moment, probably, it would be academic.

DAMAGE DAMAGE DAMAGE, the readouts screamed. Then computerized control gave way, and the ship was in my hands. A small battlewagon was close at hand now, and the flagship was ordering us in to attack. Off the port side, the large moonlet loomed like a cratered, icy hell.

Again I looked at Randy, and . . .

Whatever had torn our cowling away had pierced the emergency membrane on his side. He was clawing frantically behind him, where there was stored another emergency pack for situations just such as this. But he was losing; his skin was swelling—I could see the blood erupting through his fairness and freckles—his eyes were popping out, and he seemed to be swelling like a balloon as the vacuum of space sucked at him. Then suddenly he screamed, though of course I could not hear it, and I saw his gaping, distending mouth, red and yellow fluids erupting suddenly from it. . . .

I screamed then, too. I looked away. I looked anywhere else. *Simulation*. . . . That moonlet! Randy . . !

The battlewagon seemed to erupt in fire; it was throwing the works at us. I had no idea how many other fighters were heading for it; we could have been all alone, for all I knew. I gibbered, expecting at any moment to have my organs press through my skin as the air departed around me.

With a wail of terror I wrenched the fighter away from the battlewagon and shot in low orbit at that pock-marked, blessed moonlet. Perhaps behind it . . .

Prologue: Lee

On their last night together, Kel Kellem and Celia D'Ame walked arm in arm up a low hill that overlooked the Institute. Four large moons had risen and were bathing the purple foliage of the black planet with a gentle glow. There was something about the moonglow which reacted against the vegetation, bringing forth an iridescence and transforming the landscape to a crawling and quiet kaleidoscope of soft color. Though it could not be seen from space, at such times the black planet was not black anymore, but was one of the most beautiful nightscapes among the planets of the Polar Cloud.

Kel and Lee walked along a grassy path, climbing a low hill to the north of the outer gate where a farm pond sat in a natural hollow between two higher and steeper hills. Below them the Institute rested like a group of sugar cubes in the still, bright night. There were beast-noises too, and things that were not insects exactly but something that made similar sounds and were similarly difficult to identify. A quiet, soft, alien night, on a world where man did not originate but where he somehow belonged.

They sat against the curve of a "tree" and watched

the moons wheel down, one by one, below the horizon. All at once an arm of the galaxy lay scattered like chalk across the lower reaches of the sky, while on the edge of their vision the rim stars of the Cloud itself hung in a faintly curving haze. For a long time they said nothing; there were no words for them at this time and in this place.

At length a beast no bigger than a human hand leaped out of the farm pond and fell back with a ragged splash. They were startled, and the spell lifted and faded away, like a ghost in the comfortable night.

Kel touched her on the arm, but when she turned toward him he was still looking over the farmstead, his expression lost in the vanished moonlight.

"So you're leaving tomorrow?" he asked, his high-pitched voice flat and dead.

Lee shifted uncomfortably.

"We need a ship," she said at length. "A good ship, not just some lifeboat from a second hand yard. Something that can take the Roil and survive. Something that can get us there in the first place. There's no ship like that here, and none on the planet where I come from."

And now they could see the Roil, low in the sky away from the Cloud, somewhat toward the galactic arm. It seemed like nothing more than a smudge of white, perfectly round, pale as the belly of a dead cod. The violence of it was not visible in any way. It might have been a white balloon a couple of light hours wide, sitting placidly stillborn in the live night sky.

"They're in there, somewhere," Lee said softly as she looked at it. "Ten years ago my parents fled the Wholeth fleet and disappeared in there, and the Whole never found them. And no one even cares, here in the Cloud. I alone . . ."

"And I," Kel said earnestly, his hand on her shoulder, trying to look into her shadowed eyes. "But I'm a paper scientist, a historian and analyzer of facts that other people gain. I don't know ships at all."

She grimaced slightly and glanced at him, and he was as lost in her as he had been the first day he had seen her, the first time she had looked his way. For she had come to the black planet looking for someone like him, someone who knew all there was to know about the Roil.

"Yes, I think you do care," she said, almost wonderingly. He kissed her then, long and slow, savoring each touch, each nuance, filing them in his memory.

Her eyes were open; she stared at the night.

The next day she went to the central spaceport of the black planet and took passage for Sigma Radidiani. She would find herself a ship, any way she could.

Chapter 1

War it was, and I wanted nothing to do with it. The Wholeth Empire has been rediscovered a bare thirty years before, and the Cloud was only now mobilizing as a unit, for the first time in its twelve hundred years. We all knew from childhood history that somewhere, "down there," in that flung-out galactic arm, was the place that we had escaped so long ago. But we never thought much about it, assuming that the old ways had broken down and gone into chaos, and that the old worlds had forgotten us. We were too busy fighting among ourselves to worry about it. We should have—worried, I mean.

The Roil revealed us. That fuzzy patch in the sky did us in, for our scientists couldn't let it alone, and they blundered into an expedition of similar Wholeth busybodies and that was that. The Whole then knew that up there in that big globular cluster, a human civilization reigned. And we knew that the Wholeth lords still held the galactic arm in a grip of velvet steel.

And we also knew that they wouldn't let it be. The idea of a people apart from the Whole . . . well, they could not abide by it. And so even as their first diplomatic fleets arrived, bringing veiled threats, we began to prepare.

The trouble was that there was no single government in the Cloud when the encounter at the Roil occurred; we had been warring among ourselves for centuries, and it took the idea of the forced worship of the Wholeth Lord to bring us together. At least we of the Cloud were used to war, revelled in it (I except myself) and trained our young people in all aspects of it, from unarmed combat to strategies involving fleets of starships. It was only blind luck that the Whole was so stagnant, so bureaucratically hidebound, that the thirty years it took us to unify, took them to get around to paying us serious attention. But they weren't in a hurry; they saw things as carrying a certain inevitability. All things would merge, in time, into the one and glorious Whole.

It was enough to make you sick.

I was drafted out of a profession that I had entered with a single thing in mind. My planet was closer to the center of the Cloud than most in the cluster, and so I never saw the Roil or the galaxy in my night skies, and probably wouldn't have noticed them if I had. I had eyes for only one thing, and that is understandable when you realize that I was twenty-three years old. I was going to be a psychologist, I thought, and meet a lot of open and vulnerable women.

Perhaps if I had parents to whom ethics and religion were more than words in a dictionary. . . Ah, well. Now I know. The twenty-twenty vision of ninety-some years. . . . (I'll try to keep such observations to a minimum. During those long-ago days, I was thinking no such thoughts. It's not easy now to admit these things, you see.) My parents had been professional animal breeders before one of the internecine wars had killed them. Like most artists they had lacked any form of morality, and I had inherited it.

I wasn't doing very well at the university when the call-up came; whenever I role-played, psychcom on my wrist, with one or another of my female colleagues acting as the patient, I couldn't seem to avoid making suggestive remarks. This got me into considerable trouble, and it was rather a relief to find an induction notice in my message file one day, even though soldiering was near the top of my list of things to avoid.

The type of psychologist I had been aiming to be, I soon discovered, was of little interest to the service. I had been planning to become a Roamer, a psychfile specialist who wandered about, striped psychcom prominent on wrist, attracting patients who needed some little word, *ad hoc*, for just a moment on the street perhaps, from a sympathetic and trained personality. There was a good living in it, since the insecure always pay well. But the military of the Cloud were not to be found wandering about; they were in high training, and needed nothing so effete as a kind word (or pinch on the bottom). The central, federated government was as ruthless as all its constituent parts; every soldier worked long hours at karate and the like, and those who couldn't handle it were mustered out, or worse.

Now, I've already pointed to some of my many deficiencies, but there was one thing I did particularly well in those days: react. No doubt this was part and parcel of my cowardice; I was like a bird, looking frantically around to see where danger lay, and when it came I could move beyond the speed of light, so it seemed. This served me particularly well in one-on-one combat, as long as it was controlled by an instructor; I had no idea how I would do in a real fight, a street fight, and never wanted to find out. My reactions were so fast that the boot camp folks earmarked me as, of all things, a fighter pilot. I was appalled, but even then I knew better than to grovel. What happens to grovelers, I had found out early in life, was always worse than what happens to the insincerely brave.

It was in boot camp that my political consciousness began, not of my own choosing. In between twenty-mile hikes and fifty thousand-mile space walks and black belt training, the trainers drummed at us all manner of propaganda against the Whole. I remember one time sitting in a gigantic, crowded classroom, sleepily admiring the fine wisps of hair on the nape of the neck of the woman in front of me, when the instructor said: "The Wholeth women have emasculated their menfolk." This jarred me awake. The instructor was a lantern-jawed lieutenant named Riley.

"I didn't mean that literally," he said, attempting a smile to hideous effect. "But the matriarchy keeps the secret of genetically-derived psionics to itself. Any man that attempts power among them has his mind erased, or worse. In all of the empire's history, the only exception has been a few sycophants who have ingratiated themselves with the Lord herself, usually sexually, for the Wholeth women are not immune to carnality, their propaganda notwithstanding." *Super*, I thought remotely. "And often such a man lets power rise to his head, eventually to offend the Lord and fall. It is a pattern that has occurred over and over, and its fallout reaches into the lowest strata of the Wholeth worlds. Men are not kings in their homes; women are. If a man steps out of line, beds another woman for example, the wife reports him to the nearest Wholeth temple, and the man's mind is tinkered with, and he'll never betray his wife again, or think a rational thought again."

The woman in front of me yelled: "Serves the bastard right!" I jumped. The lieutenant frowned, and tried to continue:

"Women dominate officialdom too," he said. "Good for them!" another female voice shrieked from across the classroom. The lieutenant went on through clenched teeth: "Only in their military is there a semblance of equality. When there is military talent, male or female, they have the good sense not to interfere with it, though it is a shock to women entering from regular Wholeth society to see men in assertive positions. With the power I have to demote *you*, for example," he said, glaring at us, trying to catch the eyes of the women.

By the time he got to that point, though, I was losing interest. *I'd never meet anyone from the Whole, female or male*, I thought, fool that I was.

Another time, we all assembled while the trainers tied a woman to a plasteel post and then shot her dead. Then they had each of us shoot a dampened blaster at her, one after another, standing in line and waiting a turn at the weapon, until there was nothing left of the corpse but a smoking puddle. "So do we do to cowards," they told us. "War is imminent, and this one tried to desert. If any of you harbor any such thoughts, conceal them well. Or you will end up like her."

I concealed like crazy from then on.

When I emerged from boot camp, barely in one piece, I was shipped to the great warship base on Sigma Radidiani, one of the rim stars of the Cloud. Fighter pilot—there was a certain status to it, I admitted to myself, and occasionally my brain would turn to the women who no doubt would flock to such stalwarts of the Polar Cloud. But such fantasies were fleeting; mostly my thoughts were on combat and on atomization in deep space, and I spent the greater part of my trip plotting methods of reversible self-mutilation.

Let me set the scene: Sigma Rad was in its boom stage then, the fighter base taking up half a continent, with people from virtually every one of the nine thousand Cloud planets milling about pretending that they knew what was going on. From the shuttle, coming down, it looked like a million square mile parking lot, with buildings and landing fields and thousands of entrances, gaping like open mouths, to underground hangars where most of the firepower hid. Sigma Rad was only one of more than a hundred such installations scattered among the rim stars; but it was the most important, the place where the most advanced machines were deployed. As we came lower, the haze of the atmosphere blurred my view of the horizon from the porthole, and the pavement seemed to dance in the distance like a burning pizza under Sigma's bloated sun.

I looked about at my fellow recruits, and as usual when I'm in a crowd, felt as alone as on another planet. For they were young, mostly, younger than I, eager shiny faces, black and brown and red and white and every shade in between, from planets hot and cold. Some were from worlds where no human life would ever survive unaided, people to whom it was a major trauma to be more than four feet from a respirator. Half of them, at least, were from the nobility, for most of the Cloud's planets had been set up as hereditary fiefdoms of one kind or another by the earliest settlers. But what struck me most was their banter, their assumption that they were embarking on something great and honorable and brave, instead of what they were actually doing, leaping into a meat grinder.

I had one of my rare spasms of pity, and then the devil intervened, and I noticed for the fiftieth time the shape of a raven-haired young woman, two seats over on my left. She was the product of an oxygen-poor world, and was blessed with a deep chest which enhanced the other features with which nature had endowed her. I think I'll name her Sexina, I thought huskily.

"Er," I said, bending past the squat fellow between us as much as the seat belt allowed. His name was Jame Torrester, I had found out earlier, from the jungle planet Riv, and that's all I knew about him, or cared; he was male, you know.

I had noticed that he had carried on a discussion with Sexina earlier without the need to fondle her. I had thought at the time, in high jealousy: *the man looks like a frog.*

"Er," I said again, "your name, please. What is your name? I've got to see if it matches your, your, er, face."

"Get your elbow off my knee," Torrester growled. The siren broke off her conversation, which I had interrupted, with a fat blond across the aisle, and turned her vivid brown eyes on me. She caught the direction of my gaze, and glanced down at her jutting mammaries. That was always the trouble back then; I could not control my eyes. She looked back at me.

"You're drooling," she said. My hand flew to my mouth; it was possible for sure; it had happened before. But there was nothing there. The blond laughed, the raven one frowned prettily and turned back to her, and Torrester turned a broad shoulder between me and the women. I sank down in my seat, hoping I could melt through the crack between the cushions. Red flaming face; I should have been used to it.

Torrester had pity on me, for just as the shuttle touched down, he murmured, just loud enough for me to hear: "She is the Honorable Contessa Cassia Glane of Spandor, my friend, sent by her noble family for martial training. If you get within a light year of her, let me know."

I flashed a watery grin at him. He regarded me with ice-blue eyes, into which there came a softening when he saw the wavering around my lips.

"Did you ever think," he said, almost to himself, "that every type of behavior can be observed, and learned?"

"I beg your pardon," I said indignantly. I was, after all, a psychol in training.

"Watch the successful ones, and pretend you're them," he said, his voice just above a whisper. "I see that you dabble in self-hypnosis. Would you share with me, my friend, the current submessage?"

Now I was amazed. He could see the student's psychcom I still wore on my wrist, and everyone had an audio implant in the mastoid processes of each ear, radio-linked to whatever wrist unit he or she carried. But not everyone used subliminals; he must have inferred, from the hunger in my face and the striped psychcom itself, that I would be trying anything to gain control over myself and everyone else.

Yet a submessage is a private thing, and I hesitated to share it with anyone. He simply sat there, and looked at me; I felt a bump and looked out the port; we had landed on a circular platform, which was already sinking into the ground. We would be interrupted any moment, and I always sought every advantage, and what was the harm? He seemed a likeable fellow, and heaven knew that likability was what I needed just then.

I told my wrist unit to render itself audible in Torrester's earpieces, and it did. Here is what Jame Torrester heard that day, the message that played beneath the ambient sound level, over and over, all day long in my ears:

I am confident.
I am attractive to women.
I am loveable.
I am like a magnet.
I need comfort and attention.
I am popular with women.
They want to be with me.
I am sexually attractive.
I am the image of masculinity.

The recording went on for several minutes while
the shuttle settled into dimness. Finally, Torrester
said, "Variation on a theme. Tell me, my friend: has
it worked?"

"Absolutely," I said, trying to puff up my chest.
"They can't keep their hands off. Why, just two
months ago . . ."

"Or," he murmured, "does it keep you in a lather
all the time, so that you think of nothing else?"

"I think of nothing else anyway . . ." I began, but
again he interrupted me.

"Advice: concentrate on relating with everyone,
both sexes. Let the sex part take care of itself; don't
even try anymore. And stop drooling all the time."

My hand shot to my mouth again, and he chuckled. Then he seemed to sink into himself again: "I
was once you," he breathed. "And it didn't do me
any good."

"Here," he said then, "I'll dump my subs into
your unit; listen when you wish, but don't use them
yourself. You know how personalized subs have to
be. But maybe they'll help."

He did it, but I had no chance then of listening.
The shuttle bay doors flew open with a crash, and
we all began to fumble with our seat belts. My eyes
sought, and found, the raven woman, but she never
once looked my way.

Chapter 2

The cratered moonlet shot in jagged landscape under me, while behind me the battle raged, and next to me Randy's body froze in a ghastly contortion. The flagship screamed, the readouts read me damage reports, and all at once I rounded a high mountain range and found myself facing the most frightening thing I had ever seen. For there in front of me, a Wholeth dreadnought was rising into the space, thrusters flaming, shields down to pour all its power into lift-off.

The enemy ship was as at least a mile across, though I was not calculating measurement at the time. It bristled with every form of armament mankind has yet devised, and probably some that the Cloud knew nothing about. Its computers must have seen me, since in seconds I would impact it amidships. My racing brain saw electrical pulses swivelling turrets, pointing them at me. . . .

In blind panic, I gave it everything I had: laser bursts, torpedoes, grapeshot, impact bombs. My reactions were so fast that from sighting to assault, less than a second had passed. It was only my quickness that saved me, for even as I emptied the little fighter of every bit of destructive power it possessed, I wrenched it upward and away from the giant enemy, praying loudly (screaming, actually) and giving myself ten gees, though I would have tried thirty if the fighter had had it in her, and killed myself in the process.

I saw a sudden flaring reflection in the membrane as I began to black out from the acceleration, and looked down at the rear screen. My disbelieving eyes saw the great ship begin to break up. Fire was splitting it open; great gouts of flame were leaping from holes in its skin. Then, in one final spasm, it tore itself apart, and blew itself all over the moonlet and the space around in a gigantic fireball.

And . . .

"We find your actions inexplicable," the woman, clothed with more braid than fabric, said. I was standing before an admiralty review board. The woman speaking: Admiral Palla Belanger. Four others, two women and two men, sat with disciplined smiles behind a long, curved table, facing me as I stood rigidly, sweat beading my forehead.

"Inexplicable," she continued, "except for that unknown faculty that great fighter pilots possess." The others nodded sagely. *They* understood what she was talking about, at least. "A precognition perhaps," she said, "a feeling for what is about to happen. That is why we put humans in computer-controlled ships at all, for though they can take manual control in a damage emergency as you did, they are mainly there to use their gut instincts, to feel what is coming and anticipate it."

My guts, I thought, had been letting loose with a vengeance at the time. But they didn't know what my state of mind had been. All they knew was that I had caught a Wholeth dreadnought in the act of lifting, just about the only time such a ship is unshielded and vulnerable to fighter attack. And then, too, they reasoned, hadn't this fellow intuited somehow that it was hiding there, ready to outflank us? It was the only explanation, for in the light of the event, no one could reasonably accuse me of deliberate flight, could they? I hadn't been on Sigma Rad more than six weeks, and now I had blundered into this.

Why, why, why hadn't I been able to keep in mind that it was only another one of the endless simulations we trainees were put through? The whole thing had taken place in a closed chamber the size of a coffin. Randy Slader hadn't even been there; he'd probably been across the yard in another chamber, watching my image die in the holography around *him.* I didn't care that I had done something apparently heroic; I was thinking about how they would interpret it and what they would assign me to next. Perhaps I did have some sort of precognition; I knew to the soles of my boots that no good would come of it.

Admiral Belanger frowned down at the amorphous crystalline readout in front of her, hesitating over what she saw. Even in my distraction, I noticed that she was one of those trim women of perhaps fifty who probably ran five miles a day and had six or seven black belts, and hadn't gained an ounce of cellulite or other lard on a figure that would have enriched a backport whore, though the whole effect was marred by a face which resembled a bent shovel. She had a daughter too, I remembered, one that was completely unlike her, that fat blond on the shuttle that had been talking with the would-be paramour I had nicknamed Sexina. I had seen the blond here and there in my off hours, accompanied by a civilian barmaid she had befriended somewhere name of Celia D'Ame, a looker in her own right. But of Sexina I had seen nothing, and I had been looking, believe me.

Perhaps, I thought, I might make something of my brief acquaintance of the daughter of this flinty woman, and avoid combat duty thereby, somehow.

"What puzzles us," the admiral grated on in a voice like a chain saw, "is a series of claims you have made with the medical authorities in the weeks you have been on Sigma Radidiani: asthma, drug abuse, flat-footedness, venereal disease, mental disturbance. At first we saw these as tactics to escape the service, and were preparing to either demote you to the medical corps where you could use your psychol background, or execute you as a coward. But one of your crewmates has been trying to convince us otherwise, a Trainee Jame Torrester, who has insisted that you suffer merely from a mild hypochondria. In view of your performance in the Advanced Attack Fighter Test, we are prepared to accept that interpretation at this time."

The admiral paused and looked up, and if I hadn't felt my still lips with my tongue, I would have thought that she was observing lip movements that mirrored my thoughts: a silent and thorough string of curses directed at Jame T as an interfering, obnoxious, goodie-two-shoes. The medical corps . . . I might have escaped combat duty altogether! The other admirals were looking doubtful; cowardice made more sense to them, perhaps. Cowardice . . .

"Do you have any comments to make on this record?" Admiral Belanger asked, looking at me with eyes the color of speckled granite, but with less life in them.

I had prepared for this one, and had thought I would break down dramatically and throw myself at their mercy. But the remark she had made on cowardice was beginning to sink in. "Execute you as a coward"—that gave me pause; I remembered the bubbling red puddle at boot camp.

"Homesickness," I croaked at last. "It will pass. But as to the Test, anyone could have done it."

A crack developed in Admiral Belanger's face; she was attempting a smile. I saw the others relaxing too, the tightness easing from their faces. I had said something that fit one of their fondest stereotypes. The aw-shucks hero I was now, if a little eccentric; in a moment, I thought, I could have them eating out of my hand.

"Young man," the admiral said, "we need pilots like you. Your reflexes alone might have brought you to this board, but what you did in the Advanced Attack—do you know that less than 0.1 percent of all our recruits even catch sight of that dreadnought before it destroys them? There has never been a trainee who has successfully attacked it, until now."

She paused, and I wondered at the things that were being revealed here. My eyes sought her figure. Forget her daughter; what kind of influence could I gain with mama?

"And therefore," she said, and lust and euphoria flew straight out the window, "we assign you now to Experimental. There you will fly the most advanced fighter in our fleet, the spearhead we will throw at the Whole should hostilities break out, as most of us believe they will. And some day, you will have the honor of leading the first wave of battle; it will be a grim day for the Whole. My congratulations to you; rank and salary will, naturally, increase."

"A grim day," I repeated in an inaudible croak. Then I recalled Jame Torrester; perhaps I could return the gesture he had done me, and meddle in his life.

"Can," I asked, trying to be bluff and hearty, "my friend Jame Torrester be assigned to that unit too?"

The admirals looked at one another. "I don't see

why not," one of them said. "We'll look into it."
Then I had an inspiration:

"And perhaps my friend, Trainee Belanger (I didn't know her first name, I realized with sudden horror), who is, I understand, related to you?"

Sudden anger leaped into Palla Belanger's eyes, and I quailed back before I saw that it was not directed at me, but at an image in her mind.

"My daughter," she said, fairly hissing it, "is a slug. She is barely qualified to draw the breath of life. She . . ."

The admiral recollected herself, glancing at her colleagues around her. "On the other hand," she mused, "perhaps it would be good for her. . . ." Then: "Dismissed," she said; she was addressing me once again. "But before you go, give us all the honor of shaking your hand." She smiled a smile that would have shattered every piece of glass on the planet. She reached for my hand.

It must have felt like a rotting mackerel, from the expression on her face. Hers felt like a limb from a tree, with the bark still on.

Interlude
Recorded Report
to: Celia D'Ame
from: Kel Kellem
(Love ya!)

Of the Roil, the earliest record we have comes
from the massive Cloud library, accessible on-line by
all Cloud citizens through interspatial holography. It
dealt with an incident some 605 years before, well
before the Cloud emerged as a political entity. The
record was a fragment from a time when all of Polarian space consisted of widely separated confederations, each jealous of its own sovereignty and yet
carrying on a trade that made many wealthy and a
few more powerful than any earth-bound barbarian
had ever dreamed.

There was a ship called *The Defiant*; it was a
trader gone out from our globular cluster solely to
see the Roil. On board was a fledgling astronomer,
the son of a wealthy man who could afford to see to

26

it that his son made a name for himself by the close-up study of the peculiarity in space.

The trader had come close and studied the Roil, weaving in and out of its crests and valleys of tenuous, superheated gas like a flying fish skipping over the waves of an unusually turbulent sea.

Data was sent and received, and days went by until *The Defiant* was ready to turn around and come back home. For deeper into that gravitational maelstrom the ship's captain refused to venture, and there is no record that the astronomer boy importuned to any great extent. Closeness to the Roil bred awe, and fear.

And then *The Defiant* ceased to be.

At least that was the effect of it. For an interspatial transmission stopped in midstream one day in a sudden gulf of exploding blackness, and ended for all time the wealthy man's ambition for his astronomer son.

When at last I (Kellem) viewed that last transmission across the centuries, I understood it no more than dozens of analytical experts had over many, many years.

For there was that routine view of the Roil, if a kaleidoscopic, stop-motion rippling of violence could ever be called routine. And then like a black funnel, a darkness rose up so suddenly that even the finest time-stop resolution could not define it, and the signal was ended as if an axe had cut it in half, leaving the outward-speeding image in front and, behind, nothing at all.

Chapter 3

For nearly three months, everything went along famously. Diddling with the experimental ships turned out to be child's play; their mortality had been exaggerated. In fact they were as safe as modern computer-directed design (CDD) could make them, which was safer than mingling in mixed company, as I was soon to discover. The machine they let me play with the most was the OB IV, a two-seater somewhat like the simulation image, but with a roomier cabin—it was actually possible to get up and move about a little, and there were such features as a head, and a tiny galley.

Various kinks had to be worked out, though. The engineers had been able to install a full range of shielding in a fighter-size machine for the first time, working wonders of miniaturization. But the shields had to be aligned exactly with the firing of the weaponry, raised and lowered in precise synchronization to allow the shell, grapeshot, or whatever to pass.

Early in testing, I was in near orbit around Sigma Rad, fired a shell, and discovered that the shield was dropping a fraction of a second too late. If it hadn't been a dummy shell, I wouldn't be dictating this today, for if a shell is fired while a shield is still up, it impacts the shield from the inside, and the explosion is held within the shielded area, consuming the spacecraft.

Once the fighter is gone, the shield is gone, too late.

For the hundredth time I yearned, as every pilot did, for a one-way shield which would allow particles and shells to pass through from our side, but let nothing come through from the other. The scientists were working on it, they said. They had said it for years.

Several times Admiral Belanger invited me to soirees, where I would stand holding a drink in one hand and eye all the women in the room. Apparently I was some kind of exhibit, for both men and women would talk to me on the subject of fighter ships, and almost nothing else. Most of her guests were from the aristocratic classes of a thousand planets; I fit in not at all, and if I were perceived by her as a potential lover, I never saw it, though I looked. I was a promising trainee and nothing else. And her daughter never showed up.

As the weeks went by, and once I realized that the service protected its experimental pilots, and as long as war clouds were on the distant horizon, I actually enjoyed myself. True, within a few weeks I had a sexual harassment complaint lodged against me, but being around Jame Torrester was beginning to tell. The admiral had assigned us as roommates (which I had definitely not requested), and since within days the froglike fellow had become a popular figure around that part of the base, I could feel the charm rubbing off on me.

One day I listened to his submessage, and here's what I heard:

I help people.
I like myself.
I work on goals every day.
I treat all persons, whatever rank, with dignity.
I see the divine in every man.
I see the divine in me.
I make each day count.
I learn from mistakes.
I let guilt come and go as I need it.

And so on. Knowing how powerful daily repetition of anything is—it's why religious people tend to succeed, because they repeat positive messages to themselves all day—I still was put off by Jame's sub. Where were his immediate needs? I had always understood subliminals as an avenue of braggadocio, of wish fulfillment, of gaining something.

I fiddled with mine a little nevertheless, adding this line: "I act cool at all times." I knew better than to use a clause such as: "I never let emotion show," though that was the meaning. Negatives don't work with subliminals; they only implant the ideas you're trying to avoid.

"I don't understand what the admiralty saw in me, to assign me here," Jame told me one day as we were lounging in our cabin just before supper time. "But I like it. I cannot remember when I've learned more about interspatial engines."

I regarded him narrowly; he was lying on the lower bunk, gazing upward at the underside of the mattress above. It seemed to me that his sense of priorities was entirely wrong.

"Perhaps it's your girlfriend?" I told him, for he had no trouble at all attracting women, despite his squatness of body and grossness of features.

I went over to the mirror on the far wall. I had been thinking of redoing my image again in my eternal quest for personal magnetism. "If I had a girl-friend like that, I'd feel pretty good too," I said.

"Lee?" he said, taking me at my word as he always did. "Yes, she's a good woman insofar as I can tell, though there's something hidden in her that I cannot seem to ferret out. I like her, but she is angry with me most of the time because I won't take her on a ride on one of the fighters—strictly against regs, you know." That was typical of him, the stickler.

"I'll bet you ferret every chance you get," I said, examining my nostrils in the mirror. "What do you think if I slicked back my hair and shaved the moustache?"

I became aware that the silence had meaning in it. I turned toward Jame and found him frowning at me.

"If I 'ferret' with her, as you call it," he said slowly, "it's my business. Ryne, my friend, your obsession is unhealthy. Male/female is a part of life, not the essence of it."

I felt my face getting red again. "It's not part of it for me," I said hotly.

"And because of that, you've made it the focus of every waking moment." He shot me a glance with those clear blue eyes. "Don't you think that such an imbalance feeds itself? Do you think women want to get closer to someone whose entire being is taken up by tumescence and release?"

"Why not?" I grumbled. "If there's me among the males, there must be one like me among the females, too. I'll worry about balance once there's something to balance."

"Take a sex suppression drug, then," he said. "Most soldiers do."

He let my sudden silence lengthen, and then chuckled. "The cure seems worse than the disease; perhaps you *like* this state of constant tension?" He sighed. "All I can do is repeat, my friend: just forget about it, and nature will take its course." He linked his hands behind his head and kept staring at the bottom of my mattress. I realized all at once that he had taped a booksheet there, and was staring at the image of each page as it appeared and replaced itself in the timed sequence that he had selected.

"Dammit," I said, my frayed nerves gone. "All you can do is study? I am dying of sexual deprivation, and you work on interspatial mechanics?"

But he took no offense. He never did; it was one of the things so maddening about him.

"And that's another thing," he murmured, still looking up. "You have no thought for tomorrow, such as what you're going to do once this war is over. I'm going to set up a service business for the new generation of cheap interplanetary vehicles we're developing right here. You've got to set goals and work toward them, my friend Ryne. What are you planning for, Roaming with a psychcom and seducing every flighty female you meet?" I nodded. "You'll be thrown out of the profession in weeks. You're letting this thing wreck your whole life. I have half a mind to buy you a backport whore and let her work you over for a few days, and then once you're wrung out, try to force some sense into your head."

"I thought of that," I said mournfully. "It worked sometime for me at the university; it was the only way I could get any studying in. But then I had to take a year off to fight a disease I caught. Anyway, there aren't any whores on Sigma Rad; the MPs shoot every one they find."

"It saves you from folly," Jame said. "Listen, Ryne, Lee and I are going out tonight; why don't you come with us and get drunk or something? That's a whole lot better than wandering around the grounds flashing that ridiculous psychcom at every skirt you see and getting kneed in the groin half the time."

I felt a twinge of memory down below, and turned back to the mirror. I had decided to slick the hair and keep the moustache. "I suppose so," I said humbly. Humility being out of character, I added: "Ask Lee to bring Sexina with her, ok?"

"Who?" he asked sharply, sitting up. I didn't answer.

It was to be one of the pivotal evenings of my life, though I didn't know it then. But first, something intervened.

Meals were served in a large hall, an old hangar actually, converted because its internal wiring had become inadequate for modern equipment. The brass tried to honor us test pilots by giving us table-cloths and human waiters and waitresses, but the effect was marred by the loud echoing hollowness of the metal building. There is something sterile about a dining room whose ceiling is eighty feet high.

To make it worse, the brass used every meal to give us a speech, bring us the latest military news, tell us about some new technical marvel, exhort us to be good soldiers, do our best, etc. ad nauseam. The hollowness of the room made every amplification echo like a bowling alley, and half the time we couldn't understand anything that was said, which was a blessing as far as I was concerned.

Now, as I sat shovelling it in with Jame, Randy Slader, and a half dozen others, Vice-Admiral Oul Chester stepped up to the podium, and we knew it was morale time again. We all groaned.

"Pass me the coffee," Rik O'Rourke said across from me. "I'm going to drown myself in it."

"You'd float on top," said Claire Hevel, a cherry-haired looker to O'Rourke's left. Unfortunately, she was the one who had filed a claim against me, and I was avoiding looking her way for fear she'd add another count to it.

We were wrong about the prissy vice-admiral; it was newstime. Usually one of the staff adjutants delivered the news, and it was uncommon enough for a vice-admiral to do it that we quieted down and listened.

"There is movement on the diplomatic front," he began in that sonorous, preachy voice of his, "which you can read in the on-line files. Affecting us here is an imminent visit by the newly-designated Ambassador to the Wholeth Empire, who will pay us a courtesy inspection prior to embarking on his descent across the Gulf to the galactic arm. He is, you may recall, the Vice-Regent of the Cloud, eleventh in like to the throne itself, Sir Anthony Palin-Marek. He and his retinue will arrive on Sigma Radidiani in four days time. Various ceremonies are planned in which some of you will have a part, so please pay close attention to your on-line files, as schedules will vary from the routine."

This interested me about as much as the latest research in crop dusting, but then he said something that made me sit up and take notice.

"The Vice-Regent's assignment coincides with ominous reports from Intelligence regarding the gathering of a Wholeth battle fleet at the Outer Archipelago, which if you recall is the closest Wholeth-inhabited planetary system to the Cloud, a small island of stars jutting out from the galactic arm. There are also reports that one of the Lord's inner circle has been sent against us, though who it might be cannot be determined. We know that she and her daughters possess powers far more extensive than the average Wholeth paranormal, yet we also know that she never leaves her empire, and her daughters are all less than eleven years old. So who of unusual power could she send? We don't know.

"Since tachyonic holography loses itself in static before it reaches even halfway across the 12,000 light year Gulf separating our two civilizations, our information is fragmentary, yet is seems at least as if some military action is planned. This follows certain reports from the black planet and its Institute regarding a breakthrough in one-way shield technology. You pilots can appreciate the value of this; were you able to maintain shields permanently, firing through them from your side but with nothing allowed to pass from the other, then you would have no vulnerability during lift-off or during the discharge of weaponry. It would be a tremendous advantage over anything we imagine the Whole to possess." He paused, adjusting the microphone, which was doing its usual bad job.

The assembled pilots seemed stunned. The breakthrough had actually come? It was difficult to believe, but when the vice-admiral took his glasses off the end of his nose and said, "We'll be installing one-way shields forthwith, beginning with the most advanced of the fighter ships," a loud cheer rose up to the metal ceiling and rocked the room. I cheered as loudly as anyone; a one-way shield was another barrier between myself and death.

"The black planet," Jane murmured to my right. "Lee has friends there; she lived there before she moved to Sigma Rad. But she never mentioned anything about shield research; all she ever talks about is the Roil."

"She's a waitress," I hissed, "not a military analyst. Now shut up and listen." The relief I had felt at the shield news had died quickly, and now my innards had begun again to churn out bile. A Wholeth battle fleet could only mean one thing: action, and soon, and certainly involving the best pilots among the military of the Cloud. What had Admiral Belanger said about the honor of leading the first wave of battle? Why don't we simply join the Empire, I thought desperately? It would be better than being blown to oblivion in deep space. (Notice how my thinking was

confused back then. I was comparing my own death
with the subjugation of nine thousand planets and
trillions of people. Now, seventy years later, death
holds no further terror for me, but it is because I've
lived those seventy years. If every young soldier
avoided combat with such energy as I had back then,
there would be no more war, on either side. If, if,
if. But that's not the way it is, G-d help us.)

In any event, my intestines were protesting so
actively that I barely heard the rest of it, yet it had
great importance for me later. The vice-admiral said:
"What is of particular concern to us is the visit last
week of a Wholeth ship to the black planet itself.
The ship, of peculiar golden cone-shaped construc-
tion, set down at the edge of the Institute and
claimed diplomatic interaction, wanting to talk with
those who had studied the Roil. The occupants of
the ship were a woman who called herself Selah
Maja and claimed to be the newly-appointed Governor of the Outer Archipelago, and her pilot, one
Restor Kalil. Her claim was verified by an interspatial query to the Wholeth embassy at our capital on
Tyghe's Planet. This Maja person, who seemed to
be alone except for the pilot, very odd for a ship
that size, spoke with various scientists we sent in,
none of whom have knowledge of the work in the
classified area of the Institute; the spy devices we
sent in with them revealed nothing. We acted with
caution, for as an appointee of the Wholeth Lord,
Maja is almost certainly one of those paranormal
woman that they breed, and we could not expose
our knowledgeable people to mental probing. She
invited the Director of the Institute, Gaim Fannet,
on board, and we had him decline."

The vice-admiral cleared his throat, and it came
over the sound system like a volcano erupting, rat-
tling dishes all around the hangar. After an embarrassed moment, he continued: "Then, in the dead

of night on the third day, the ship suddenly lifted
off. What concerns us is the possibility that information somehow reached that ship from the Institute,
though we detected no electromagnetic transmis-
sions to or from it, and certainly observed no unau-
thorized personnel. Wholeth women cannot read any
minds not in their immediate presence, and Maja
never left the ship. But while the ship was there,
security telltales in the Institute were disturbed. If
it was a spy ship, then it used methodology opaque
to us. We're closing the black planet to tourist or
'diplomatic' visitation from now on, because of the
uncertainty this woman has caused."

"Why didn't we just blast her out of the sky?"
someone yelled, a breach of discipline. The vice-
admiral scowled.

"We tried," he said grudgingly, "once it lifted.
But it was unusually fast, and didn't let its shields
down for a moment once in space. We should have
atomized it on the ground, perhaps, but she was a
high official in the Wholeth court, and the ship carried the Wholeth Lord's colors on its insignia and in
its transmission codes. That sort of provocation we
were not willing to inflict on the delicate diplomacy
going on between the Whole and the Cloud.

"But I have not come to the worst part," the vice-
admiral said, his voice so sober that we craned to
listen. "After the golden ship left, thirteen of our
scientists . . . well, they lost their minds, is the best
way of saying it. They were babbling idiots by the
time the Wholeth ship reached interspace. Now the
question bedevils us: how did Selah Maja do it? It
is as if she, or someone else, left the ship and wandered around the Institute at will, but we kept a
constant stream of visitors interacting with her and
Kalil, and nothing of the sort occurred. She is not
one of the Lord's daughters, so presumably does not
have unusual paranormal powers: invisibility, machine

control, that sort of thing. So the question is: how did it happen? And the lesson is: stay away from Wholeth women."

Claire Hevel turned toward me and said, "Hear that, Ryne?" Everyone at the table smirked, and I squirmed. "And your mother," I said feebly, but I couldn't put any strength into it because of her claim against me. She smiled grimly, and Oul Chester said: "On the diplomatic front, it would seem that the latest Wholeth gambit will be to claim that an alien civilization is pressing upon the Empire from the other side of the galactic arm." The room erupted into hoots and catcalls. My mind, veering away from Claire Hevel, thought, alien civilization indeed: in all of mankind's exploration, almost no sign of any other civilization had yet been found, confounding the predictions of old-time astronomers. The exception was here in the Cloud, for the stars of globular clusters tend to be old compared with those in a galactic arm, and on certain airless planets we had found the faintest traces: lines of rust in the soil, for example, certain compounds where they should not be. But that was all, and nothing in the galactic arm itself.

"They call these aliens the Onn," the vice-admiral said, "and are doing all they can to express fear and confusion to us. We have no reason to believe them; and even they claim that they have not been able to holo Onnish ships, much less capture a live Onn. Humanity, they intone, is facing a common threat; if the Whole is swallowed up, the Cloud will be next. We've heard it all before."

It's their excuse for the recent rise in diplomatic interaction, and for the formation of a battle fleet, I thought. We point to the fleet, and they say: heaven forfend that we would use this unconquerable armada against the Cloud; no, we are throwing ourselves at the Onn in lonely, suicidal struggle to save humanity from alien domination. Join us; if you do not, you betray humankind.

Right.

There was an excited buzz around the room, drowning out the next news item the vice-admiral intoned—something about a crop failure on some of the coffee planets, a sharp rise in spot prices, and how lucky we were that the Admiralty cared so much about us that it spent the extra money anyway, and so on. The vice-admiral turned then to other news, and capped the performance with a homily on patriotism, which gagged me, though the bile of fear was doing a good job all by itself.

Now I need *to get drunk*, I thought. But the real action was yet to come.

Chapter 4

Jame took me to the same bar where his girlfriend Lee waited on tables. She was just leaving her shift when we arrived, and when she sat down at the table, there was still a sheen of sweat on her high forehead, for she had been in and out of the kitchen for hours. She smiled at Jame, and there seemed to be real affection in her hazel eyes.

I had seen her before, since I notice every good-looking woman I see anywhere; but now, up close, I was enchanted, and forgot the oncoming war. Enchantment comes upon me easily, but there were good reasons for it in the visage of Celia D'Ame. On top of the high forehead was a shock of long auburn hair, the kind that changes color from red to brown depending on the light. It was parted in the middle and had been braided down the back while she worked, but she had shaken it free and some of it hung over her right shoulder in deliberate disarray. Her skin was fair, and her eyes too seemed change-able in color, now green, now brown, depending on the way she held her eyebrows at any particular time. She was tall and met Jame eye-to-eye; I was a few inches taller and was thinking: *just the right size.*

Her figure? I noticed it, of course, and it was moderate, the kind of shape you see on most leggy women, rather subdued everywhere, yet carried with grace and purpose, the inhabitant constantly aware which pose produced which effect on which people around her. Certainly she was aware of the effect she was having on me. She held out a cool hand when Jame introduced us, and commented: "Ah, yes, Ryne Sangre. Kitty Belanger told me about your conversation with the Contessa. Most amusing; I understand you were there, Jame?"

Her voice was low and husky; Jame shot me a glance, his thick lips twitching, and said: "Oh, he's not a bad fellow once you get to know him. Top pilot, you know; flies Old Bonecrusher, the most advanced fighter we have, and loops rings around the rest of us."

I was grateful; I truly was. Something of my self-centeredness quivered before Jame's magnanimity. I was surprised, however, on the effect of his words on Lee D'Ame, for she seemed to soften like a snowball in July. Her eyes were interested when they looked at me now, and I hadn't seen that in a woman's eyes more than once or twice in my entire life. I thought it was my newly slicked-back hair.

"You fly Old Bonecrusher yourself," I said to Jame.

"Ah, yes, but not as often as you, or as well," he said.

Lee broke in: "I want to see this Bonecrusher," she said silkily. "Jame's told me something about it, and I am intrigued. And now you . . ."

"Regs, my dear," Jame said, patting her hand fondly.

She frowned, bantering: "Phooey on the regs," she said. "What good are they if you can't bend them once in awhile?" Then, compounding the illogic: "For little old me?"

She goes from aristocrat to tease like an actress, I thought.

"But here is Kitty herself," Lee said, moving sideways to make room for the chair next to her. And with that, the admiral's daughter came up from behind me, circled the table, and sat down with a thump.

This, I hadn't expected. I had guessed that I would drink about a gallon of witslap rye and stagger back to our cabin, while Jame and Lee went off somewhere and did whatever they did, which hurt to think about. Now . . . Had it been a deliberate setup by Jame Torrester, that foxy old goat? Even now, I don't know if I should thank him, or hunt him down and blow him away.

"Hello again," she said, looking squarely at me. She was blond and overweight, as I indicated earlier, not the fatness of the truly obese, but maybe forty extra pounds which she carried with assurance, even arrogance. Her face, with its almost invisible eyelids, was as fleshy as Jame's, heavy-lidded and pouty, but underneath I caught a glimpse of that flat bone structure so prominent in her mother. She regarded me with half-closed, pale blue eyes, and I thought to myself that she could have been a looker if she had wanted to. Certainly she had a figure, lots of it, and with a little self-discipline, perhaps . . .

Who am I to be invoking self-discipline, you may ask? Well, I can see the flaws of others, tolerant though I am of my own.

"Hello yourself," I said. Jame grunted, and Lee smiled at her.

"We were just talking about that time on the shuttle," Lee began. Jame cut her off.

"Let's order drinks, shall we?" he said.

"You're a pilot now, aren't you?" Kitty said. Her voice was not near the rasp of her mother's, though it could have been if she had let it.

"The best," I said modestly. "And you are too."

"Thanks to you, I understand," she said. Jame raised an eyebrow. I cut in. "My guess was that you and your mother didn't communicate a whole lot." She seemed to consider this, the pouting lips pressed sideways, as if pinched between invisible fingers.

"My mother and I have differences," she said at last. Then, with sudden heat: "I've been her little soldier for twenty years."

"It's bad enough as a big one," I said dryly. Jame and Lee laughed, but no change came onto Kitty's puffy face.

"Why, then?" she said finally. "Why ask for me before an admiralty court, when the last time I saw you I was laughing at you?"

Good question, I thought. This woman didn't dance around a subject; she zeroed right in. I didn't want to tell her that it was a life habit of mine to try to get in good with any authority over me, and that I had had some vague thought of using her connection with her mother. That I was dead wrong was also not unusual; I was often unprepared for what ensued when I set about manipulating people.

"I wanted to meet Sexina," I said honestly enough, "and you seemed to know her."

"Sexina?" she asked, eyes widening.

"The Honorable Contessa Cassia Glane of Spandor," I said.

She laughed suddenly, and I had to admit that it was a wonderful effect. Without her habitual pout, her face was alive, though again I am predisposed to a favorable opinion of anyone female and unattached. Then, too, I was already sexually charged, both by habit and by my earlier consideration of Celia D'Ame.

However, Kitty overdid it. She laughed until tears were rolling down her face, with Jame looking on with a puzzled expression, and Lee staring into the green-filled glass in front of her as if it were a crystal ball.

"She thought," Kitty gasped, "she thought, she thought, she thought you were the lowest . . . *thing* . . . she had ever encountered. Oh, I loved it. Here you were, an unknown untitled nobody, leering over her, who might look twice at a Grand Duke, maybe. And you . . . you . . . call her 'Sexina'? Oh, how I would like to tell her that; she'd rave for hours, and probably call on her father's bodyguards to break both your legs, or worse!"

"Tell her," Lee urged. I shot her an alarmed glance.

"I can't," Kitty shrilled, and hiccupped; she was beginning to recover. "She moves in circles beyond those of a mere admiral's daughter. She's somewhere on the base, though I have no idea exactly where."

Good thing, I thought. I can't say I had enjoyed listening to all this, but I did enjoy watching her. For one thing, her bodice was shaking nicely. With alarm over broken legs subsiding, there was budding in my mind again the thought that it couldn't hurt to know the admiral's daughter, no matter how severe the rift between them. Hadn't the admiral agreed to let her with me into Experimental? She wouldn't have done it if she had wanted her out of the way. (I had cause to revise this reasoning later.)

When Kitty died down, Lee started to talk about the Roil with Jame, who seemed to have a wealth of knowledge about it, gleaned no doubt once he had realized her interest. He had the knack of listening, and as she went on and on, I found my eyes mostly staring at Kitty's cleavage as it swelled out of her snow-white outfit. I gathered absently that Lee's mother and father had been swallowed up by the Roil somehow, while on a mysterious mission to the galactic arm for the nascent Cloud central government. They had been spies, it seemed. Lee was obsessed by it.

We drank steadily, and once, as I tore my eyes upward to Kitty's, she smiled faintly at me. My hopes soared; it was all I could do to keep from reaching over and squeezing and yelling: "How about *that*?"

The possibility never occurred to me that Kitty's thoughts were a mirror-image of mine. All her life she had tried to coax a little affection out of that ramrod of a mother of hers, and had alternated between desperately trying to please, and just as desperately trying to distance herself. That's why she kept out of shape, I was to know later; it galled her mother as almost nothing else could. But now, and probably not consciously, the notion was circulating in her: here is a pilot my mother particularly admires. What if. . . ?

Finally, we left Jame and Lee and weaved back toward my quarters, and I found myself pulled beyond them and into her own. Her skin was as smooth as a baby's, and she didn't seem fat anymore, just big and hungry and delicious. She was strong under her overlay of flesh, and utterly tireless, and utterly ruthless. Later we lay against one another and she cried soulfully and clung to me, and I wondered contentedly, in euphoria but with a twinge of unease, what I was getting into, so to speak.

Interlude
Recorded Report
to: Celia D'Ame
from: Kel Kellem
(Thinking of you. . . .)

The next record is a product of the Cloud Intelligence Service and seems to be reliable. It says that some 495 years ago another ship came spinning out of interspace into the vicinity of the Roil. It was a one-seater and the pilot was Wholeth, one of their most famous figures in that colorful time, when the Cloud was yet unknown to the Whole. The man was the Lord's Consort, one of many to be sure, but named Chief Consort posthumously and mourned by aristocracy and common citizen alike.

The man's name was Crestor Falon, and his title during his life was Stead, though ruling over no particular sector of the empire. Some said that he himself held some of the paranormal powers of the Wholeth lords, but none said it aloud and I found the fragment only in learned Polarian studies of that particular time.

No one was really clear as to why Falon had headed for the Cloud. One Polarian speculation suggests that he had had a falling out with the Her Lordship over a sexual infidelity, and was at the time hotly pursued by armed forces who were following a hidden interspatial transmitter that Falon had not so far been able to find. It must have been somewhere on the hull; triangulation as a means of fixing the location of a tachholo emission was useless, but when a transmitter broadcast the surrounding starscape whenever a ship entered real space, computers could fix a position. Falon had had no choice but to stay in interspace and maybe find himself somewhere in the intergalactic void when he emerged, or hop from system to system, keeping just one step ahead of the pursuing ships which had to wait for the report from the computers which worked, although very quickly, slowly enough to cause a delay.

The Roil was rumored to distort interspatial transmission from certain anomalies in Wholeth astronomical records; the experience of the Polarian *The Defiant* was unknown among the Whole of the time. In any event, Falon had apparently had nothing to lose, and he had circled the Roil close in, spinning his ship on its axis with dizzying speed, perhaps trying to confuse the watchful eye of the pursuers' computer.

The transmission was distorted not at all. It showed clearly, when slowed to minimum speed, the uneasy false horizon of the Roil, the wheeling starscapes above, the pseudopods of the Roil reaching up like clutching fingers around which Falon's ship skimmed and straightened again and again.

And it showed a blackness reaching up, so quickly that the Roil itself was blotted out in an instant and replaced by the background static of a signal suddenly cut off.

The Lord had honored Crestor Falon, apparently missing his ministrations and perhaps uneasy that the truth of the celebrated man's presence at the Roil would cause popular unrest. She had also sent a battalion of scientific crews to the Roil and gone over it with a fine-toothed comb, at least as much as such a thing could be done in a place that was gravitationally opaque. Three ships were lost, not like Falon's ship or *The Defiant*, but by collision with dust or rock or wrenched apart by some gravitational violence whose nature could not be well defined. But of a leaping blackness, nothing was found, no theory advanced to explain it, no trace of Falon or his ship ever found.

For ten years the Lord had doggedly sent ship after ship, scientist after scientist, to the Roil to dig for the man that she may have loved. And there was nothing, and at last she grew weary and withdrew her crews and declared the Roil off limits to all her people, an interdicted tombstone to Crestor Falon. It was when her descendant finally lifted that interdiction 460 years later, that the Wholeth and Polarian scientists blundered into one another at the Roil and contact began.

Chapter 5

It was a pale and ghostly remnant of Ryne Sangre that reported for duty the next day. Jame met my bloodshot eyes with a quizzical lift of his brow as I staggered into the duty room. Kitty wandered in only moments behind me, the indiscreet ninny, looking as fresh as if she were ready to run five miles right along with her mother. She tried to wink at me, and I fought for the strength to wink back.

If I weren't exhausted enough, the next few hours brought me back to full awareness of the near future, the war, and the possibility that I would not survive it. All the pilots from every unit on Sigma Rad were ordered to the survival training unit and outfitted, and the fact that man-to-man weapons were being implanted in me did more to alleviate constipation than would have a quart of magnesium citrate. I was in a blue funk when I left the survival area in a ground car, haunted by the violence done to my body that day and what it implied, and barely thinking about the night before. It shows where, despite my daily obsession, my true priorities lay.

Underneath each of my fingernails, the surgeons had imbedded a tiny crystal, "wired" into nerves which I could control via a sort of instant biofeed-back. The crystals in my left hand functioned as short period blasters of one-second duration. The ones in the right hand were stunners, again one shot per digit.

If I ever had to use the things, and I prayed that I would not, the blasts would blow the tips of my fingers away—not as far down as the bone, but certainly enough for pain and lots of it. The trade-off was that the implants were almost detection-proof.

The other area of implant was my chest, in which they had installed a tiny signal transmitter, so that if I were crash-landed, they could locate me, or my mangled corpse (so my thoughts went).

Finally, they had redesigned my pilot boots into the weapons of the diplomat, in case I was captured alive. Each boot, synthetic leather as soft as satin, had woven into its underlying fabric a series of fibrous ultaprocessors interwoven with long bundles of resonators. They were sound weapons; by varying a nerve signal, amplified to the faintest possible radio signal by the tiniest implants of all, I could produce anything from a nerve-shattering blast to an ultra-sonic hum, which would set the teeth on edge and control the emotional tone of a group.

One of the shoes, the left one, had an additional built-in module that would emit an odor so nauseating that it would clear a room and confuse any enemy (who, I thought, would probably burn me down for using it).

Why not blades in my fingers and toes, lasers in the buttons of my coveralls, etc.? Waste of time, too detectable, the experts said. Who am I to say? I had no intention of using any weapon they gave me.

No sooner had I returned to Experimental than I was summoned to the offices of Admiral Palla Belanger. Oh, oh, I thought, for I was in too unsettled a frame of mind to curry her favor through my usual toadying.

Muddled as I was by neurotic apprehension, I assumed she wanted to discuss the piloting of the experimental ships; but as it turned out, she was more concerned with the piloting of her daughter.

"I understand that you and my daughter Catarina have linked forces," she said without preamble as I was ushered into her spartan offices, halfway across the million-square-mile starbase. As she stood, ramrod straight, behind her desk glaring at me, I groaned inside; I had had no idea that she had a personal network of some kind keeping watch over her Kitty. The idea had been to be known to this iron woman as befriending her daughter, not ravishing her.

"Yes," I said feebly. "A fine person, your daughter. She . . ."

"Silence," the admiral said sharply. Her speckled eyes carried light for a change, but it was the light of fever, and I shivered.

"I have two things to say to you," she said. "The first: tell your roommate to stay away from that obsessed nuisance Celia D'Ame. She's been pestering us for ten years to run a suicidal mission to the Roil, and we're tired of hearing it."

I opened my mouth to protest that Jame's affairs were, unfortunately, no affair of mine, but she cut me off. That topic was over; now for the meat.

"I would not have chosen the likes of you as a lover for my daughter when there are thousands of more noble young men on this base," she went on without a break, her voice as harsh as a sandblaster.

I was shocked, and dared to say: "May I remind you that the last time I saw you, your attitude was entirely different?"

She snorted. "That was duty," she said. "This is personal. You may be a hot star pilot, but the visibility of your lusts has disgusted every decent female on this planet."

This shocked me too. I had had no idea that need could yield so universal a self-defeating effect. Of course, I could see the reactions of the various women around me, but that the entire sex was intrigued only by those whose libidos were concealed, that was baffling.

"I like your daughter," I said desperately. "She has many noble qualities. She . . ."

"Name one," the admiral said, and as the silence lengthened, she added, "other than prowess in bed."

"She worked to become a pilot," I said at last, guessing frantically, "to be close to you."

Again the admiral snorted, but this time there was less conviction in it. I saw something relax in that shovel face, and for a moment, I hoped. But then it hardened again, and she said, "No. I have had too many disappointments with Catarina to buy that, even for an instant. She wants ease, and hopes to get it through association with me. I tell you this because when she invites you to the Vice-Regent's reception two days from now, you will know that it was none of my doing." She was practically growling now, her chain-saw voice on low throttle, moving relentlessly ahead. "Fleet Admiral Shela Rankin knows of my daughter's presence here, and assumes that I would welcome the honor of an invitation. Since I cannot tell her otherwise, I must put up with it, but you should know, and you should tell Catarina, that I do not welcome it, or you, or her."

"Invitation?" I said, confused.

She grimaced, as if she had bitten into something. "You will get one. My daughter has hers by now, and who else would she invite as an escort but the one she thinks is somehow a favorite of mine, and whom she has therefore seduced?"

"We were together only one night!" I exclaimed

before I could stop myself. She said nothing, only stared fixedly at me with those eerie granite eyes.

"And," I said, dredging up abject injured innocence, "I had believed that you respected me through my piloting, if nothing else."

She smiled, the stiff face cracking without the faintest hint of friendliness.

"I gave you the benefit of the doubt," she said. "Perhaps you were only lucky. Perhaps you were running away. Perhaps you do have real precognition. I don't know, and I don't care. There's only one way to find out, isn't there? And that is in combat, and that you will see very soon now, if Intelligence has any credibility. I look forward to it."

Well, my insides started churning again. I waited, unable to speak, but she had evidently finished, and sat down rigidly at her desk and looked away. I turned to leave, and as I reached the door, my back to her, I heard her speak, softly, as if she cared not whether I heard: "I loved my daughter once. Now she distracts me from the war, from peace of mind, from duty. I cannot allow it to go on."

I left her then, hating her, hating myself, and hating Kitty too.

For the rest of that day, wild thoughts dominated my brain: stealing Old Bonecrusher and hightailing it to a deserted inhabitable planet (virtually impossible to find), deserting to the Whole (which would probably shoot me out of hand), crashing the fighter lightly (how do you do that?). I didn't see Jame, and so did not tell him what the admiral had said about Lee; that was far from my thoughts that evening. I would have stayed shivering on the upper bunk all night, and certainly had no desire to further work on Kitty, but she herself came for me, and the novelty of being invited by a woman went to my wildly spinning head, and I went. Almost without a word she brought me to her cabin and tried to repeat the night before. I said nothing of my meeting with her mother, mostly because I didn't want her to emote all over me. My vigor was not as it could have been; in fact, it never was. Nevertheless, she didn't complain. Not then.

And at the critical moment, I found myself wondering who was watching us; were there hidden cameras inside the bedroom, perhaps? A wilting sort of a thought; it was all Kitty could do to bring me to recovery.

The third day, the day before Palin-Marek's visit to Sigma Rad, I dragged myself to the duty room, and there received an order to take the OB into orbit, and assigned as my copilot was none other than Trainee Kitty Belanger. Coincidence? I didn't think so; somehow, I thought, she had wangled this with her mother.

I had it exactly backwards.

"This is a test of adverse flight conditions," the flight instructor, a tall dignified sort of fellow named Pascal Tortelli, told us as we entered the underground hangar where the fighter rested. "We rarely permit this one, and I'm frankly surprised that the Admiralty should risk the OB IV on it. You two watch closely, for your detection screens and artificial gravity will be off throughout the test, as if damaged in a firefight. You'll have to let conditions lead to response; that is what this test is all about. Oh, yes: we have installed the new one-way shield equipment, so you'll be shielded from beginning to end. Good luck; you'll need it."

This sounded ominous despite the welcome news regarding the shield, and I looked about the hangar for a way out, but personnel were everywhere, and besides, I was one of the best pilots on the base. Wasn't I? Kitty tried to catch my eye; she was in fine fettle, raring to go, and didn't seem to notice the sheen of cold sweat on my face. Tortelli smiled at us in professional encouragement and shook Kitty's hand. He took hold of mine and frowned; it must have felt to him like a slab of raw bacon. I followed Kitty into the OB, and a towmotor led us to the platform deck, which rose smoothly to the surface of the fighter base. Then up we went into the reddish sky, anti-inertial engines allowing the planet to throw us away.

I looked over at Kitty. She drew her pouting lips apart in a smile, and reached over and pinched me on the thigh. "Ever try it in orbit?" she said coyly.

I nearly gagged.

"Didn't you hear Tortelli, you crazy bitch?" I ranted. "Something's due to happen up here, and we might never reach ground again."

She shrugged, and seemed unsurprised at my insult. Perhaps she had heard it many times before, from people more important to her than I. "So what can happen?" she said. "You're the best pilot in the fleet. I know; my mother told me, and everyone says so." She settled back languidly, large breasts pushing against the fabric of her flight suit and the shoulder strap that belted her down.

I groaned. I took hold of the wheel, which was shaped much like a groundcar's emergency steering wheel, round as a ring. We were just reaching stable orbit and could feel the change to zero gravity coming upon us as the ship's acceleration faded. The planet hung below us like a dusty balloon, filling over half the forward viewplate. We were still on automatic, but I knew that if I moved the wheel back or forward, control would switch instantly to me and the ship would respond. I let go as if it had sprouted steel needles.

We waited for full zero gravity, but it didn't come. For whatever reason, we were being held into a particular orbit, but accelerating nonetheless. I stared at the instrument readouts, and listened to the running commentary coming from the ship's central processor. The base still had control, and there was nothing yet for us to do.

"At any moment they'll turn control over," I babbled. "Then something's going to happen, and we don't know what. Watch your long range screens for enemy drones and especially for incoming missile dummies and the like. Are the screens up yet? We've got to prepare for anything." My eyes were darting frantically over the little cabin, wondering if they had planned to blow a hole in the cowling to make the simulation truly realistic. I remembered the image of Randy Slader, and shuddered. We had emergency membranes too, but I didn't trust them, no more than I trusted anything or anyone.

Kitty watched her readouts and said cheerfully: "All detectors are now disabled. Ryne, I think this bucket seat reclines into a couch. We could manage it if you . . ."

"Forget it!" I yelled. My readouts showed what hers had, that the base had switched off our long and short range detectors and we were now blind. "What if there's a cloud of grapeshot ahead, for G-d's sake? There's no way we could avoid it now; we'll be torn into bite-sized chunks if they plan something like that."

"They won't," she said placidly. I saw with a start that she was chewing on something, against regulations during combat flight. "Think about it, Ryne. An admiral's daughter, and one of her favorite pilots, placed in real danger? Not likely. Anyway, the OB's shields would stop anything like grapeshot, especially now that it has the new one-way unit. Come to me."

Oh, G-d! I thought. My eyes were everywhere, trying to guess what they were about to do. Where was precognition when you needed it? I groped hysterically in my mind, and found nothing there but terror.

"Kitty, she knows about us," I wailed. "And she doesn't like it."

Kitty sat up straight. "She knows?" she said. Her eyes narrowed, and something seemed to pinch her lips together; her habitual frown returned. "Of course she wouldn't like it," she said slowly. "I've often wondered how she brought herself to the love-making that produced me."

"Kitty, forget about that now, will you?" I shouted. "Watch out the cowling; we've got to anticipate what they're doing to us, or we're dead meat."

"I don't think she'd kill us, even so," Kitty mused. I was climbing the walls of my mind, and still nothing. "There's got to be something there still, for me. She could not be so . . ."

"Kitty, drop it. Tell me all about it if we get out of this. Right now we . . . KITTY!" I screeched the last word, for directly ahead of us something had appeared through the transparent cowling. I first saw it as a dot, but in an instant it was hurtling upon us. I had the confused impression of a tumbling mountain, bare and jagged, and . . .

Kitty screamed, and I threw my hands forward, an instinctive act, warding off the threat with my bare arms. There was a violent lurch and we were thrown back into our cushions, and I believed that time had stopped, that we were impacting that object and that I was feeling the ship as it crushed into atoms. Something gigantic filled the cowling above our heads, and I heard a bass pitter-patter and then a deafening clang. I waited, arms rigidly outstretched, hands around the wheel.

And then, wondrously, there was empty space in front of us and we were diving into the planet, sitting placidly below, while above us, almost faded away already, was a glimpse of the tumbling thing.

Kitty screamed again, for the planet seemed to be rushing up at us, and I realized that I had forced the ship into a steep dive by pushing forward on the wheel. I drew it back slowly, and the acceleration lessened as the ship sought a lower orbit. Kitty sobbed, and I looked over at her and saw tears streaming down her face. I would not have been surprised if my eyes were as wet as hers, for I was shaking with the ague of salvation. We should have been dead, and we both knew it.

It had been a meteoroid, one of hundreds that any planet has in orbit around it. This one was unusually close in, and the pattering and clanging I had heard must have been outriding pieces of debris. The base had thrown us at it, and only the sheerest chance had saved us. For when I had thrown out my arms, I had jammed the wheel forward, and we had skimmed the tiny asteroid so closely that it had seemed a world of its own, above our heads. If we had impacted, all the shielding in the universe wouldn't have helped us. The ship would have survived, so powerful is the shielding, but we would have been smashed into pulp by deceleration and inertial effects.

And now, as I shook, a new thought: had it been chance that I had hit the wheel, or had it been the action of a reactive fighter pilot? Or had it been fear alone, instinctive warding-off alone?

Or: had Palla Belanger risked her daughter, yet believed I would pull us out of it? Or had she wanted to kill us both? My self esteem dictated the latter; yet what if. . . ?

Traces of courage were beginning to rise in me, though I did not know it then. As for Kitty, she was still crying, and wept all the way to landfall, for she had no doubts at all: her mother had tried to kill her, and any love she had had was now dead.

Chapter 6

They didn't bother to call us before a review board this time; we both found citations in our on-line files, when next we looked. "Capital job!" Tortelli had enthused when we brought the BC IV to a stop on the platform. "Just leave her right here; she'll be ready tomorrow for the Vice-Regent, don't you worry. Now you two go off and celebrate. You've done something that only the best pilots can achieve." What happened to the worst pilots, he didn't say. Kitty and I staggered off and shuddered in each other's arms in her cabin, made love with unbelievable passion, then shuddered for awhile again.

"She wanted to kill me," Kitty said hopelessly. I had to agree that it was a possibility. I remembered what the admiral said as I left her office the day before.

Our near escape affected me with a certain fatalism, and I no longer had faith that I could escape the imminent war. Perhaps this was what made my lovemaking so intense, I don't know. So long deprived, I was starting to depend on Catarina Belanger. It worried me; it did not fit in with my image as man about town, or starbase, or wherever.

Finally, Kitty sent me home: "I want to be alone," she snivelled. First, though, she invited me to the Vice-Regent's reception as the admiral had predicted. I accepted, and I didn't tell her what the admiral had said to me about it. I didn't have to; she knew her mother's attitude already.

Torrester eyed me cynically as I crawled into our cabin, and commented: "Is it all that you expected?" I didn't answer, and slept as if a hundred dervishes danced on my brain, demanding satisfaction.

The next day, the news that a subaltern named Caryn Spacek read us during breakfast brought me to a further low.

"Hear, all you assembled," she said, always the dramatist, "that reports of an enemy fleet are confirmed. Many of you will meet it first hand in the immediate future; the rest of you, envy them. Your turn will come."

I groaned. Claire Hevel glared at me from across the table, and grated: "What did you say?" I babbled out an assurance that she had not been the subject; she scowled and said something obscene. I should file a claim against *her*, I remember thinking. Naw; it wouldn't wash; nobody would believe it.

Later that day, the inspection by Vice-Regent Sir Anthony Palin-Marek went off on schedule. The Experimental pilots stood in a line before their ships, sweating in rivulets while the red sun of Sigma Radidiani blazed overhead, and Palin-Marek whisked past in a ground car, waving one foppish hand at us as he commented to his strawberry-haired companion, no doubt to the effect that it was all so common, don't you know. I had seen his viz in an on-line news file, and I can't say I had liked anything about him. He looked too much like me, right to the slicked-back hair, except that he seemed bored with life, which I most certainly was not.

I did not envy him. From Sigma Rad, he was due

to head for the Outer Archipelago of the Wholeth Empire, there to present his credentials and be escorted on to the galactic arm, to the presence of the Wholeth Lord herself. Whether his was strictly a ceremonial office, I knew not then, though now I believe it was. Were the Wholeth paranormals to pick his brain, I now know, they would have found practically nothing. He was a useful tool to the confederated assembly of the Cloud for exactly that reason.

One thing he did that day, however, was to have a great bearing on my future and, indeed, the future of the entire Cloud: he ordered the admirals to grant everyone on Sigma a twenty-four hour leave in honor of his visit, except for essential operational personnel. Partly this was to enable as many beautiful invitees, male and female, as possible to attend his reception, the one to which Kitty had invited me, for he was a notorious roué. Partly it was to assert his power, and the result of it was that all the experimental ships were left topside on the tarmac, to be lowered the next day by maintenance crews weary after a night of carousing. A fatal error, said Polar Intelligence in its official report; the salvation of the Cloud, as it turned out.

So as Radidiani descended in the planetary west, I hied myself to Kitty's quarters and collected her, and we hummed by groundcar toward Fleet Admiral Rankin's spread near the geographic center of the starbase. Kitty had stared at my formal uniform, which I had not worn since I had encountered the admiralty court, and had sighed contentedly: "There's hope for you, after all," she told me. "Thank you," I had said, wondering what she was talking about.

Even now, after all these years, I can see her in her youth, smell her, nestling against my left armpit in the back seat of the groundcar, lips pressed together and hair the scent of jasmine. For a moment I loved her, the admiral's daughter. I understood her, I thought; she had given me more of herself than had any woman, and understanding is the cousin of love.

The fleet admiral was fond of antiques. That was the first impression the official quarters conveyed. Every place one looked, from hallway to alcove to vast open space, there were wooden end tables and commodes and chiffonniers, all stained a dark brown, nearly black, with figurines and knickknacks and chachkas spilling all over them.

It was impossible to determine, without an electron microscope, whether each piece was real earth-bred wood or not. My guess was not, but I was cynical. We ascended a broad marble staircase, and the fleet admiral's bewhiskered husband greeted us at the top, turning to an aide to figure out who we were, then welcoming us as if we were favorite grandchildren. I grasped Kitty's forearm and dragged her inside, as she seemed inclined to pass the time with the fellow while dozens of groundcars were lined up behind us, disgorging more distinguished passengers than we.

I ushered her through the entrance of the main hall, and we found ourselves at the head of another broad staircase, down this time, looking across the heads of a gigantic chamber where human waiters and waitresses fawned over notables, and pockets of dignitaries expressed informed opinion to one another while they guzzled like fish and looked around for more important groups to belly up to.

"Pilot Trainees Catarina Belanger and her escort, Ryne Sangre," a loud voice announced. I jumped as if stuck by a needle, and a hundred eyes glanced up at us. Kitty seemed to grow taller and glared back at them, then took a firm step forward, pulling me off balance. I put my foot down and found that the floor was gone, and then the foot hit in a bone-jarring stagger on the first step. But my reflexes brought me out of it, and anyway by that time all the eyes were looking elsewhere, since we held no interest to any of them—we had no potential for increasing either their rank or their income. Down we went, Kitty moving in stately fashion like an ocean liner, and I worked to keep up without looking like I was being dragged.

Nearly at the bottom step, I caught sight of someone I had thought I would never see again, for far across the room near one of the serving tables was a knot of servicemen, and in the middle, looking petulant and bored, stood the Contessa herself, the Honorable Cassia Glane of Spandor. Her jet black hair was piled in a bouffant and her face was deeply colored with cosmetics, and she looked as if she were on fire, face in flames and a gout of oily smoke pouring from her forehead.

Kitty saw her too, and turned to flash me a delighted smile. "Sexina!" she stage-whispered. "Shut up," I hissed.

If I were lucky, the Contessa would have no memory of me, or at the least would not recognize the starved creature on the shuttle. Kitty had done a lot in the last few days in removing the hungry lines from my face and mind, though I can't say I was yet aware of it. I only hoped that Kitty would suppress any mischief she might conceive vis-a-vis the Contessa. Behind us, the loud voice announced that Duke and Duchess someone-or-other were gracing us with their presence, and then we were in the midst of the crowd, and by the time we had moved fifty feet I had snagged three drinks from passing waiters.

Kitty drew more attention than I had expected. For one thing, Admiral Belanger, on overall charge of operations, held real power on this planet, second

probably to the fleet admiral herself, though not
officially so, and this was her daughter. For another,
Kitty's formal bodice was low-cut enough, and her
figure overly full enough, to draw attention from the
captains and commanders and admirals and diplomats, most of whom were half soused. Soon the affair
became for me a series of leering encounters, as dignified gentlemen peered down her front and offered
inane remarks regarding the political situation, to
which Kitty responded grandly, throwing back her
shoulders, and I stood alongside sipping on whatever
was at hand.

At length, one of the Galahads took her by the
elbow and led her away, telling her that he must
confide something privately about her mother. I, left
standing there, watched his hand slip down her
nearly naked back as they pressed through the
crowd. Oddly, I felt no pang of jealousy; the fellow
better watch himself, I thought at the time; he was
playing with a volcano.

And then, in came The Vice-Regent of the Polar
Cloud, Sir Anthony Palin-Marek himself. The crowd
fell silent as he was announced, for power was entering the room, whether likeable power or not. He
strode to the head of the stairs, arm-in-arm with his
strawberry-haired filly, and then paused grandly,
striking a pose he must have seen in a historical
painting, left hand on hip, the other on the hilt of a
ceremonial sword, left foot back and aside, knee
slightly bent, right foot straight forward, eyes staring
over the crowd, whiskers bristling. I barely suppressed a giggle. The strawberry one stood beside
him in sway-hipped fashion, and I think that most
of the eyes were on her, though it would have
insulted Palin-Marek no end had he known.

"I hear he's thinking of delaying departure until
the intent of the Wholeth fleet becomes clear," I
heard an admiral with a pencil-thin moustache com-

ment to a captain on my right. The captain, a fish-
faced man of perhaps fifty, frowned. "I hope not,"
he said. He said nothing more, leaving the admiral
to infer whatever he wished. I sidled up.

"The Wholeth Fleet? What's it going to do?" I
asked them. They considered me, noting my trainee's uniform. The captain snorted and looked back
up at Palin-Marek. Then a startled look came into
his aquatic eyes, while the admiral said, rather
kindly, "No one knows. You may see action soon
though, if the diplomats' guesses are any good.
Excuse me, now; I see my wife." And he moved
away, leaving me with a sudden gnawing in the pit
of my stomach.

I turned slightly to move on and found the captain's nose an inch from mine. The frown was gone,
and in its place a fatuous smile. "Say," he said alco-
holically. "You would not perchance be kin to yon
Vice-Regent, would you, my boy?"

I was puzzled for a moment, then I got it. He had
noted the resemblance I had seen out on the airfield
and in the news files, accentuated now by the formal
uniforms and grooming. I looked back up at Palin-
Marek, who was descending elegantly down the
stairs, and yes, there was a resemblance. His moustache was fuller than mine, and his eyes a greyer
color, and he seemed more strongly built, but certainly the jawline was there, and the shape of the
eye sockets, and the cheekbones, and the slicked-
back hair.

I winked at the captain. "No one should know," I
said in a hoarse whisper.

He smirked in conspiratorial fashion, and said,
"Boy, you just leave it to me. In the meantime,
should you need anything, the name's Stoner, Fleet
Captain Garner J. Stoner. Come see me; we'll get
acquainted."

He seemed inclined to continue the conversation,

but I caught something out of the corner of my eye. I reached out and grasped Stoner's hand and said, "Thank you, sir. I will," I lied. Then I turned and took three steps forward and stared.

The Honorable Cassia Glane was standing four feet away against the edge of one of the serving tables; I had blundered her way after all. The group of young men had dissipated, and she was talking now in a desultory fashion to two tough-looking customers who were dressed in some exotic livery, the colors of some noble house, their faces the same flame-red as the Contessa's. What had caught my attention, and had previously been obscured by the crowd when I first had seen her, was the fact that the upper part of her gown was only just this side of transparent. As I have said, controlling my eyes was a real problem in those days. Kitty had only dampened my libido, not destroyed it, and now it raged suddenly up at the sight of this woman's splendid honeydews, and unlike Kitty she carried not a single extra ounce on the rest of her.

The lower portion of her pale cream gown was more conventionally opaque, with a train dragging on the floor, heaped around her concealed feet and the cat's-paw leg of the heavy wooden table. My steps had taken me to the corner just across from hers, and to my right stretched a damask yellow tablecloth covered with crumbs and discarded dishes.

It must have been the drinks that washed caution away that evening. I forgot all about avoiding this woman as I viewed her gigantic orbs, and as a result, history repeated itself for me, and the history of the Cloud changed for all time.

She caught sight of me, and once again her gaze followed mine to its targets, and then she glared up at me and said: "Sir, again I find you drooling in my presence. Pray begone, as it annoys me." And she turned back toward the two hulks, who fixed me with their handsome eyes and looked as if they could bend steel beams for fun, and eat ball bearings for breakfast.

The Contessa didn't condescend to move away, merely turning her back, and the two moved protectively to her elbows, their shoulders pointed in my direction, heads turned away, haughtily ignoring me. But my reaction was much different than it had been on the shuttle. I wasn't embarrassed, not this time. Instead I was furious. No doubt it was the alcohol, but I was tired of dismissive glances from people of rank, and might have kicked her shapely backside, which I was now regarding, save for the two Hercules next to her. Then my eyes strayed from her bottom to the train of her gown, and an idea was born.

Sidling a step forward, I watched their heads, but they were looking resolutely away, having dismissed me from their attention. I dropped my right hand, grasped hold of the middle of the narrow end of the serving table, and lifted it up three inches.

The satiny gown obliged by stirring where its train was pressing against the table leg. I didn't even have to pull the table forward; the train sagged a fold or two under the leg all by itself, and I let the table quietly down. The Contessa hadn't moved, nor felt the stirring at her feet. I slipped backwards into the throng, and began to put distance between myself and her.

"My dear Contessa," I heard someone boom out behind me.

"George!" I heard her lilting voice say, "what a pleasant surprise." And then, rrriiiipppppppppp as she took a step forward, and a shriek.

I felt a jolt of enormous satisfaction as hubbub grew up behind me, dying to look back though I didn't dare, and all at once someone had me by the elbow, and I looked in alarm and found that it was Kitty. Her face was lit by what first I thought to be drink, then realized was hilarity mixed up with fear. The commotion behind us grew.

"I saw that, Ryne Sangre!" she hissed out of the side of her quivering mouth as she led me away, smiling at passers-by as if we were on an aimless stroll. "Can't you keep away from big bosoms for a minute?" She seemed inclined to break into peals of laughter, and then, suppressing it, said: "Don't you know who those gorillas with her are? They're her bodyguards, sent by papa to save her from herself. You're in trouble, Ryne Sangre. They'll know who did it, and I fear for you."

My ear-to-ear grin faded. "How could they know?" I said doubtfully. "The gown snagged on the table, that's all. She deserved it, Kitty. No one should wear something like that."

"Around people like you at least," she said. "No, they'll know, Ryne. She is from a vindictive noble house, and wars have begun over more imagined slights. We'll have to watch out, and if you see any sign that they're coming at you, you send that woman the most abject apology ever written in the history of the universe, and hope that she takes pity on an untitled sex-crazed commoner and settles for it. G-d help us if she won't."

I noted the "we'll" and "us"; she was throwing her lot in with me. Perhaps they will not dare to monkey with the consort of the admiral's daughter, I thought hopefully.

And then we were face to face with Admiral Palla Belanger, and the laughter died in Kitty, while worry grew in me.

The admiral was speaking sharply to some hapless grey-haired woman in an ornate uniform; then I saw that it was the fleet admiral herself, Shela Rankin. Kitty's mother saw us, and I thought her shovel face would fold up. Then she forced out a smile, and beckoned as the fleet admiral turned toward us.

"Fleet Admiral Rankin," she said formally. "My daughter, Pilot Trainee Catarina Belanger. Her escort, Trainee Sangre."

Kitty bowed, and the fleet admiral held out a gracious hand to me. I took it, not knowing what to do with it. I bent over it and pretended to slobber, and apparently it was the right thing, for she took it back and didn't even wipe it on her jewelled uniform.

"So pleased you could come," she purred. Kitty forced out a smile, and I bowed again. The uproar back of us had died down, thank heaven, so that I was able to bring some slight concentration to the women in front of us.

"I must say, Catarina, that you have ensnared a handsome young man," the fleet admiral said graciously, and I warmed to her. She was older than Kitty's mother, and had a fineness of features that made you forget her age and try to see what was in her eyes. *This is nobility itself*, I thought drunkenly. I'd make her a fleet admiral too.

"Thank you for inviting me," Kitty said. Her mother glowered. Kitty said: "So interesting an appointment, Sir Palin-Marek. I would have expected someone more, er, forceful; or rather, should I say, someone less . . . less . . ." Kitty was foundering and I, who was surprised at her foray into diplomacy, chimed in like an idiot: "Arrogant," I said.

Both admirals' faces flexed. "Sir Anthony is by no means the dandy you might suppose," Admiral Belanger snapped. "He is famous around the Cloud as a hunter, and as an explorer of outlying worlds. His is an excellent appointment, in my opinion."

"And in mine," the fleet admiral added softly. "Though anyone sent to the Whole must have a touch of arrogance. Forty thousand worlds arrayed against us; it will take brazenness and more to hold them off."

"Nonsense," Admiral Belanger clipped. "We are more than their match; we are trained warriors, and they are passive, crushed too long under the mental heel of the Wholeth lords. *We* could take *them*; if the Admiralty would accept my recommendation of a punitive expedition, we could end this rumored war before it began."

The fleet admiral sighed; it was a theme she had heard before.

"I must see to Sir Anthony," she murmured to us. "So pleased to meet you both." And she faded away, every ounce the diplomat, while Palla Belanger glared at us and Kitty glared back, lips compressed sideways.

"I would speak with you, Kitty," the admiral said. She turned her cold eyes on me. "If you would excuse us . . ."

"And I would speak with you, mother," Kitty fairly hissed. "Test, my ass. If you want me gone, say so." Barely glancing at me, she said, "Go on home, Ryne; I'll see you later." She moved away with her mother, two tense figures in white, unlike, and yet alike.

Turning, then, I brought myself up short. There, facing me, were the two bodyguards from Glane, and their fiery faces didn't look happy.

Chapter 7

"Either we step outside and you take it here," one of them said, "or we track you down and you take it later."

Now I suppose that they were individuals, real people with mothers and fathers, friends and uncles, but to me they were cardboard cutout thugs. With their flaming red faces and elegant livery, there was little hint of what they could do, yet most of the men of the Polar Cloud held black belts in one discipline or another as a result of all the warfare, and bodyguards would be ninja-trained besides. I shouldered past them and they let me go, bemused expressions on their faces, and a trembling rose in me as I pressed through the crowd, and I swivelled my head behind and from side to side, expecting them to follow me, expecting them to rise up beside me like phantoms, holding shiv or garrote, or impaling me with stiffened fingers.

I looked all over for Kitty, circulating from one end of the hall to the other, peering in alcoves but not daring to leave the safety of the crowd. I found no trace of her, nor of her mother. Everywhere I expected to see those neon faces, but I didn't. Nor did I see the Honorable Contessa, who was doubtless in repair somewhere. The Vice-Regent too was missing, having graced us enough, and twice I had to deny to besotted partygoers that I was he; the resemblance was stronger than I had realized. That was the first time that it occurred to me that without the sword, his uniform was cut rather like mine, minus the trainee insignia.

At length I encountered the fleet admiral, and she broke off from a little group and took me aside.

"Have you found your two friends?" she said, concern in her soft voice. "The ones with the red faces? They asked after you only a few minutes ago, and even asked where you and Ms. Belanger lived."

"You didn't tell them," I gasped, horror-stricken.

"Of course not," she said, puzzled. "How would I know such a thing? I sent them to Information; I knew you two were in Experimental at least. Why, was it wrong of me? They seemed so anxious to find you."

It would be undiplomatic to scream at a fleet admiral that she was a kindhearted blabbermouth. Instead I muttered something polite and let her go back to her friends. She moved away, troubled, and I thought: it's bad enough she associates me with Palla Belanger; now this too. I weaved into the densest part of the crowd and found a table with an empty seat. "Do you mind?" I said to the surprised group around it, and sat down without waiting for a reply.

They were too gracious to throw me out, so I sat there shaking, and every time a waitress undulated past I grabbed anything she had, drinkwise. The liquor did little to still my thoughts, tumbling over one another. I took no comfort in the weaponry implanted in my fingertips and shoes; as bodyguards they would be festooned with invisible weapons too, making mine seem like toys. Imminent war had scared me already, but I was finding that the bully-boys from Glane had reached into my inner recesses and pulled out real, shaking, face-paling, blood-run-ning-cold, ice-sweated terror. What was I do? Where could I go?

To Kitty's? No, one of them would be waiting there, and the other outside of the cabin Jame and I shared. Where then? Some hotel? This was a mili-tary base, for G-d's sake; visitor quarters were regu-lated; I could never get in using a fictitious name, and probably not with my real one, and Glanians would have access to on-line guest registers like any-one else. Admiral Belanger's? That was a laugh: she would call the thugs herself if she knew about it, and stand by laughing.

So that is why, an hour later, I groped my way into the bistro where Celia D'Ame waited on tables and pined inexplicably for Jame Torrester. The groundcar ride through the darkened starbase had been a nightmare; every light behind me I had imag-ined to contain the bodyguards, and I had screamed at the automated vehicle to go faster, turn aside, etc., and it ignored me and lumbered steadily to the destination I had originally named.

I looked all about the interior of the place, trying to keep my eyes in focus, for I had taken in more than I knew at the fleet admiral's party. I didn't see Jame Torrester, but I did see an empty table, and a few minutes after I had sagged into a chair beside it, I looked up to discern in front of me the fair face of Celia herself.

" 'Lo," she said.

" 'Lo yourself," I hiccuped. "Where's Jame to-night?"

She shrugged with that graceful elegance she wore so naturally. "I don't know," she said. "At your cabin, I suppose. We had a fight over taking me for a ride on a fighter-ship."

"Sorry t'hear it," I said. Then I blurted: "Can I sleep at your place tonight, Lee?"

She frowned, then smiled: "Is that an immoral proposition?" she asked.

"Sure," I said. "I mean, no. If you want to, of course. . . . No, don't confuse me, Lee, dammit. I'm about potted, and two brahma bulls are after me, and I need a place to pass out. Please?"

She regarded me thoughtfully, then sat down across from me, her high forehead wrinkled. "I'm off duty in a few minutes anyway," she said. "Tell me about it."

So I babbled the whole thing, and as I dredged it all up, her face smoothed, and light seemed to come into her eyes. She was, as I have indicated earlier, a striking woman, and the force of her personality poured out on me that night, and enchantment eased into the air again. It was very gradual, and my judgement was gone anyway, though in retrospect I don't think I would have acted any differently had I been stone-cold sober.

"Have a drink on the house," she said as I wound down, and moments later I was raising a triple witslap rye to my lips, which had suddenly grown thirsty as I had described the war and how it worried me, and the thugs and how they terrified me.

"I'd be happy to let you stay at my place," she said, her changeable eyes green for the moment. "But if those guys know where you live, they may have ways of figuring out who all your friends are, and Jame's too. There has to be a safer place, Ryne. Let me think."

She had it all planned already, but she made the pretense. Then she finally said: "Why not one of those fighters you fly? You can get into one of them, Ryne, and they'd never think of looking for you there."

Yes, I thought. Why hadn't I thought of it? I could

hide out on OB IV herself, and no one would know
or care.

I moved as if to rise, and she placed a cool hand
on mine. "But you must bring me with you," she
said. "That is my price; I want to see one of those
magnificent fighter ships that Jame keeps telling me
about. He won't take me, so I rely now on you."

I looked soulfully into her wonderful eyes, and
said: "I would do anything for you, Lee. Anything."
And I meant it. She had given me my salvation, I
thought. And her eyes, her face, her slender body
. . . Thoughts of Kitty Belanger faded.

If you think I was fickle in those days, you are
right; and what's more, alcohol had clouded the
waters so, that I scarcely knew where I was, much
less able to cast off the habit of a post-puberty lifetime, that of seeing every woman I encounter as a
potential bedmate. That Lee had a hidden agenda I
had no idea, then. All I knew was that there was a
place of refuge from death or injury, and that a beautiful woman wanted to share it with me besides.

So at length we left her bistro, and I ordered the
groundcar to the outer tarmac of the starbase where
we had left the OB IV earlier that day. She was
carrying one of the largest shoulder bags I had ever
seen on a woman, but the significance of it escaped
me at the time.

Only one fellow appeared to be on duty as Lee
held me up and we maneuvered to the gate. "G'-
evening, Sanders," I said as we came near. " 'm
bringing my girl to Bonecrusher to show her
around." I might have winked and leered, I don't
remember. Sanders was one of those who are con-
temptuous of rules, and he winked back and said:
"Sure, hotshot." And off we went toward those
swept-back shapes, and Sanders was in ghastly
trouble.

I hoisted Lee up through the belly-hatch, and followed her unsteadily, ordering up the interior lights with the codes I knew so well. Lee stood up and looked around, tossing her bag into one corner; the interior was just high enough for both of us, and she noted the controls, the couchseats, the galley, the head. She noted everything. I felt my way to the pilot's seat and rolled into it.

"Made it," I muttered to myself. "Glane, go screw yourself. Screw the Contessa too." I giggled.

Lee said, "Ryme, is there some overall command that controls this ship? Some password or something?"

"Sure," I muttered, "but 'takes a wide-awake pilot to work her. She's a temperamental hussy, she is," I slurred. "Except for known destination coordinates, she's a bucker, is she. C'mere, you," I said, beckoning unsteadily to Lee. She came over and sat smoothly on the edge of the couch near my waist. I patted her where her bottom met the cushion, and said, "Here we are. Come to me, Celia D'Ame."

She shook her head. "Not yet," she said, trying to force coyness into her voice. I didn't know it, but she was under desperate control, the last part of her *ad-hoc* plan yet to fall into place. "Suppose those guys come up here, Ryne? Tell me how to run the ship; I don't think you'll be awake much longer, and I'd like to be able to death-ray those guys, or whatever weapons the ship has."

Well, death-raying them sounded like a capital idea to me. But: "I'll be awake, Lee. Really I will," I said. She bit her lip.

Suddenly she stood up and, with a wrench, slipped out of her dress. She took off her underclothes, and stood before my popping eyes.

"But what if you do sleep, Ryne?" she said hoarsely. "It's safer if we both can do it."

Gaping, I inventoried my own body, and to my horror, my raging lust seemed far more theoretical than manifest. I fumbled with my own clothes while she stood there, as magnificent a sight as I have ever seen. I was far gone, I thought, if I could not react to that. If I was that far gone, and the Glanians came . . .

I gave her the codes. And somewhere between struggling out of my clothes and reaching for her, I blacked out.

When I awoke, we were in interspace.

Part II:

The Whole

Interlude
Recorded Report
to: Celia D'Ame
from: Kel Kellem
(Remembering. . . .)

There came a time when the Polar Cloud, in its turn, made a determined effort to probe the scientific mysteries of the Roil. It was 189 years past, and the Cloud, though still without a central government, was flush with wealth and an economy constantly expanding as the outlying worlds were brought into the modern era. Governments were funding anything and everything. Scientific foundations flourished and grants were everywhere as men and women were, for a time, able to do what they enjoyed rather than what they had to. And while mysteries were falling like tenpins before analytical investigation, the Roil in its turn attracted attention and money.

The great Institute on the black planet was the

natural center of Roil investigation, for it was nearer
the anomaly than any other inhabited Cloud planet.
The black world had been settled early on by a com-
plex group to whom scientific investigation was a cul-
tural premise—would that such was the case in all
planetary cultures! The black planet was awash with
foundations and laboratories and research centers,
and there was that physical proximity. So it was natural that a proposal come from the Institute to inves-
tigate the Roil, and just as natural that it would be
accepted by the central research authority of the
minor federation to which the black planet then
belonged.

Alas, the Institute has lost some of its preemi-
nence in our day, having been given over mostly to
research connected with military science, but in its
heyday it was both respected and vigorous. A team
of four Institute ships brought themselves at length
near the Roil, probing with the most advanced techniques of the time the incomprehensible blast of cosmic particles and light and gravitation pouring out of
it. Probes were sent in and never came out, and
ceased transmitting almost as soon as they disappeared from physical view. Nothing was known then
of Crestor Falon and the Wholeth work over two
hundred years earlier. They never even detected
Wholeth holography, for the only Wholeth planets
within reception range were those in the Outer
Archipelago, and they were yet to be settled.

For two years the Institute scientists labored and
strove and came up with almost nothing, and finally
the grant ran out and the ships returned to the black
planet for the last time. They spent the last of the
grant money on a series of four robot probes, however, and these they placed in stationary orbit at
points equidistant around the perimeter of the Roil,
far away enough so that the entire surface was monitored, but within that restriction as close in as possi-

ble so that the greatest visual resolution available could be maintained.

Perhaps they were unlucky, or maybe some other force was at work, but they apparently managed to position the probes at points such that when an incident finally did arise, it lay on the edge of the visible fields of three of the probes and was barely seen at all.

But something was seen, indistinctly, inaccurately. The interspatial receivers at the Institute, linked to a repeater midway to the Roil, were having their usual trouble with clarity, the Roil being as it is a hurricane of electromagnetic turbulence; but the probes recorded the event, for every starship-type object keeps a continuous record of itself and its transmitted and monitored signals. Enough of a signal came through that day to make the Institute computers sit up and take notice, and in short order the scientists as well.

It was as if the Roil flickered, as if a part of its surface vanished and at length came back, or as if something from the outside punched through and was gone. The milky filtered rippling of the roiled surface was seen to pause. At the same time there was a wild distortion of the usually manic gravitational patterns of the Roil, wild and quick and gone at the same time as the momentary visual flicker.

At that instant the fourth probe was fried by an almost solid beacon of supercharged particles that roared out in several places around the Roil, places that had no apparent mathematical relation to one another and to the flicker that had been seen by the other probes.

Naturally the watching scientists of the black planet rushed one of the three remaining probes to the place where the flicker had been, but to no avail. There was nothing there. Just the surface itself, engaged placidly in that hot undulation that marked the Roil at all times and made the body so frustratingly and tantalizingly opaque.

Five years later the first of the three probes failed, due, the Institute was sure, to the irregular gravitational forces at work in the area, and the other two failed in two and three years respectively. The Roil research was shelved as a bad investment by a government inclining toward greater austerity.

Chapter 8

I ranted. I raved. I waved my arms and screamed. It was all to no effect; we were still in interspace, and I still had hijacked the most advanced fighter in the Polar Cloud's armed forces.

That my voice hadn't been the one to tell the OB to deplanet and hurl out of Sigma Rad space wouldn't be worth a quart of vacuum. I could see myself at the court martial: "It wasn't my fault, honorable sirs and madams. I was drunk and I let a waitress have the top secret codes and *she* did it, not me. Honest." That would change my sentence, I bet: they'd still stake me out on an anthill, but they'd cover me with maple syrup instead of honey.

I wondered what in fact the penalty was for hijacking. Death, to be sure, but what kind? No anthill; probably something quick and sure. The service wasn't sadistic, merely efficient. Whatever it was, I wanted to stay away from it. But now . . .

It had been bad, knowing that a war was coming and there was a chance I might be killed. It had been worse when I'd been nailed into pilot school. It was even worse hearing that a fleet was coming and action was imminent. But those fears had been hypothetical, though quite moving to a recreant like me. The immediacy of the goons had been gut-wrenching like nothing I had experienced before, and now this. My career was wrecked, my citizenship destroyed, there was no place I could go, and I was heading G-d knew where with a probably demented woman who was as likely to blow the hatches in deep space as to anything rational, so my thoughts went.

As I roared, the demented one was reclining languidly on the copilot's couch, regarding me calmly out of one half-hooded eye, the other covered by her fine auburn hair; she had switched the artificial gravity on, a blessing for my aching stomach. She was dressed again; somewhere in my caterwauling I did notice that. Truth to tell, she didn't look addled at all, but serious, sober, and even, a little concerned.

"And now what are we going to do?" I screamed at her for the tenth time. "We reenter Sigma Rad space and they'll take us out of the OB and kill us. We go to any inhabited system in the Cloud, and they'll catch up with us and kill us. You know the odds of finding an uninhabited one with a liveable planet? What would we do anyway, you be Eve and I be Adam? I wouldn't touch you with a ten foot pole." That shows how enraged I was, making asinine statements like that. "Want to go to the Whole, maybe? There's not enough food aboard to get there, and do you really think they'd reward you for bringing in this ship? They'll hang you by your eyeballs; they'll wash your mind clean and put it out to dry. You've left us with nowhere to go, Lee. We're finished; I want to hear it from you. I want to hear why you undertook this fool stunt. *Where are we going?*"

The shout didn't seem to faze her; she watched me, crinkles at the corners of her eyes, from worry

or amusement I didn't know, for her fine lips were
still in a straight line, still serious. And then she
opened that mouth and spoke: "The Roil," she said.

"WHAT?!!" I screamed.

Incredibly, it hadn't occurred to me until then.
Pieces clicked into place all of a sudden. I had heard
her talking with Jame about the Roil; her mother
and father had disappeared inside it, if I recalled. I
went over and threw myself on the pilot's couch,
and passed my hand over my forehead. The Roil? In
a fighter ship?

"We can't go to the Roil, Lee," I said, not looking
at her. "There's only a few days' emergency rations
on a ship like the OB. It takes weeks to get to the
Roil. We'd never . . ."

"Three weeks and two days," she said. Of course,
she would know. "That's why I brought that." And
she pointed to the big handbag she had been toting
around, and I understood.

"Concenfood?" I asked. She smiled.

"I kept a bag at the bar, and one at my place,"
she said. "There's enough for three months there.
When Jame finally decided to take me on a tour of
a plane, I wanted to be ready."

I groaned. The excesses of the previous night were
beginning to make themselves apparent. "Didn't you
ever think that it would be his ruin if he took you?"
I said then, "Just as you have ruined me?"

I could feel her stiffen, and dug further.

"He loves you, I think," I said. "You would have
destroyed him, maybe got him killed, if he took you
aboard and the admiralty found out. And you never
would have coaxed the codes out of him, just as you
never got him to take you in the first place."

She was silent for a moment, and then I heard her
voice, low and throaty, through tight-spaced lips.

"I . . . feel . . . for him. But only one thing rules
me, Ryne. As for the codes, with all the concenfood

in there there's also an atomizer filled with hyp-
noblab. I would have used it on *you*, except that it
interacts badly with alcohol and probably would have
fried your brain before I could get the codes. I used
another weapon, if you remember; I would have
pointed a gun at your head if I had had one, Ryne.
I would have done anything—*anything*—to reach the
Roil."

"It means that much to you?" I moaned. She
laughed, an edge of hysteria there.

"You're finally getting it, Ryne Sangre," she said.
"Let me tell you now who my parents were and what
they did; then perhaps you'll realize why I seduced
a scientist on the black planet, worked in a scumbag
bistro on Sigma Rad, wooed the kindest ear on the
starbase I could find, and then at last took my clothes
off in front of you."

"Just a moment," I muttered. "I have to vomit."

"What?" she said, startled.

"No, not that," I grunted as I jerked from the
couch and staggered toward the head. "It's last night
. . . I'll take some detox, but it's too late for . . ."
And that's all I was able to say.

When I emerged, pale and shaking, she had the
detox ready in its liver-colored packet. I wondered
how she had been able to find it among all the com-
pacted and virtually invisible storage places around
the cabin. But then, I had been unconscious for a
long time, and she had had the master codes for the
ship. All she would have had to do, and had undoubtedly done, was to sit down before the amorphous crystalline screen and call up any information she wanted.

The only panicky time for her must have been
just after lift-off, when half the starbase and all
the orbiting ships must have tried to intercept us.
But the Roil was a well-known object, its coordinates part of the locational memory of all ships,
public and private; so were the coordinates of

every star system ever visited by a Polarian ship. All Lee would have had to say to the ship, would have been, "The Roil, if you please," and it would have sought the closest jump point and headed into interspace. And the pursuers wouldn't have had a clue as to the OB's destination, once it flared out of sight.

"I suppose," I said wearily, stomach still in an uproar, "that we ought to turn around and go back to Sigma Rad and let what happens, happen. No ship has ever survived the Roil, Lee. I'm not taking this one in, not on your life."

"I'll drop you off somewhere," she said seriously. "But I want you to teach me all about the ship, Ryne. In three weeks I want to be able to pilot the OB."

You're doing pretty well already, I thought. "Forget it," I said. "I'm not taking her in there, and I'm not teaching you how to suicide. Perhaps Admiral Belanger will have mercy." Fat chance. "She mentioned you to me, you know. Said that you wanted to take a suicide mission into the Roil, and that I should warn Jame away from you. I never did; I wish to G-d I had. If we can persuade her that you're crazy. . ."

"Anyway," she said, softly, "I've put three security codes around the destination matrix. We're locked in; we can't turn around even if we wanted to."

"Of course we can," I snapped at her. My stomach was moving from a boogie to a waltz. "You put the codes in, so you can take them out."

"No," she said. "I let the shipcom pick them at random, and told it not to tell me; told it to erase them from active memory, in fact. We're locked in, Ryne. We're going to the Roil."

I drank the detox in a long, shuddering swallow while I considered. If she had done what she said, there was no way I could break through.

"Where would you drop me?" I gagged. The waltz suddenly slowed.

"I don't know, Ryne," she said, taking my hand, "and I would rather have you with me; you can't teach me everything you know, and Jame has told me of your quickness and skill with the OB. Let me remind you of something, and maybe it will make you see that entering the Roil is possible, especially in this ship. The OB IV is equipped now with one-way shielding, according to shipcom; I read up on it while you were, er, asleep. To me, that means that the hard radiation of the Roil can't get through even when the ship is using its inertialess drive. Kel's theory about the loss of the other ships was that they could not let their shields down even for an instant once they were sucked in, because then they'd be hit with a gigantic blast, way too much to survive. So even if their ships had enough power to do it— and they might have, for all we know—they couldn't have used it and stayed alive."

My head was clearing, the rage and nausea gone. The waltz had ended; everyone had gone home. "Lee, even if that were true, we just got this one-way thing; you would have hijacked any ship on the base, way before this, if you could have. And who's Kel?"

"Kel is someone I knew on the black planet," she said gently. She was trying to get me to meet her eyes; her hand was soft and warm around my cold, shaking one. I looked finally, and saw how deep they were, and drew back, as from an abyss.

"In another ship, I would have found them and maglinked the two ships together, and then used my ship to push theirs out."

"You would have died," I said hoarsely.

"I know," she said, "but I would have lasted a few days. It would have been enough."

Chapter 9

We were going to the Roil, and since I couldn't change it, I should have relaxed and enjoyed the trip. But my thoughts kept turning to our options once we got there, and my gorge kept rising, and I would begin to pace around the little cabin, driving Lee to distraction. She showed me Kel Kellem's research notes, some of which you have already read earlier in these memoirs; she had fifteen or so booksheets stuffed into that bag of hers, and each booksheet could hold a thousand pages, though they were not all full by any means. She had reams of data on the Roil, though, most of it known to the shipcom already, and a lot of historical stuff that the com didn't know.

But the research held my mind at bay only briefly, and then I was again filled with visions of execution by a vengeful Polarian admiralty, or descent into a fiery maelstrom. But Lee took action to soothe me, as you will see.

I spent the first day sobering up, trying to get used to the facts at hand. I kept my back to Lee as much as possible in that little cabin, and thought. None of my thoughts were worth much, in the end.

I could see no way out. Pleading that Lee was mentally unstable to the admiralty was fantasyland, reality told me now. Going to the Whole was out, seeking refuge on an inhabited Polarian planet suicide, and finding an uninhabited one impossible. Again and again those same three options revolved in my brain, and again and again they fell.

Lee busied herself with her booksheets, and once I heard her querying shipcom about some technical feature of the ship. We ate two meals in near silence, me brooding, she studying one of her booksheets with frowning concentration. She must have them nearly memorized by now, I remember thinking. I can still see her finely etched face bent over the sheets; it's one of the few images that stick with me from that first trip to the Roil, even though I knew her far more intimately as the days dragged by.

Despite my mental merry-go-round, I slept the sleep of exhaustion that night. My body was trying to reestablish order after the abuse I had put it through during the last night on Sigma Rad. I had thought about the narcotics in the ship's stores as I lay back on the couch, but the thought had barely crystallized when I was no longer thinking at all. If I dreamed, I don't remember it. If Lee stirred next to me in the copilot's couch, I never heard it.

On the afternoon of the second day, Lee once again asked me to teach her the details of piloting the ship, particularly the differences in command sequence when using inertialess drive versus interspatial.

"No," I said curtly. "I'm not teaching you how to vaporize yourself in the Roil. I haven't decided what to do once we get there, but going in . . . no. You've wasted your time, Lee; I'll tie you up if I have to, but I'm not teaching you how to fly this ship!"

Her eyes flashed, and I wondered just how easy it would be to tie her up. But then she did the one thing that was guaranteed to unnerve me. She began to cry.

Not all at once, and not faked. First a sob, then a shaking of her shoulders, and then silent tears coursing down her face. I didn't know what to do; I still don't when a woman cries, other than to hold her and let it come. I didn't know enough to do even that, then, though I reached out a tentative hand and placed it on her shoulder, and she reacted not at all, but shook under it as if it weren't there.

"You don't know enough to say that," she said brokenly at last. "You don't know what it is to be me; you don't even know what the stakes are for the Polar Cloud. My parents," she almost shouted, "were *scientists*. They were not spies, not saboteurs, not evil in any way! They did not deserve their treatment from the Whole, and they especially did not deserve the disregard of the Polar Cloud. Everything they did was in the interests of the Cloud, of peace and of everything you and all of them hold dear. *They* . . . were . . ." All at once her uncharacteristic emotion overtook her again, and her voice trailed off in an incoherent moan that shook her rigid body.

"Lee, please. . . ." I said feebly. I put out my other arm and drew her to me, and she shook with those dry, silent sobs, her control still there, still struggling for dominance over the rest of her. It was a new experience for me, holding a woman without anything carnal in it. It brought me a step closer to what I am today, and for that I am grateful.

At length it passed and she pulled away and sat, wiping ineffectually at eyes that were still leaking.

"You don't know why they came to the Roil, Ryne," she said levelly, suppressing the quaver.

"I know a little," I said gently, encouraging her to talk and let words distance herself from the past few moments. "They were on some kind of mission to the Wholeth Empire for the Polarian military, and they got sucked into the Roil on their way back."

She gave a short, barking laugh. "Look!" she cried, yanking a booksheet loose from the others, which scattered like chaff.

Words fairly leaped off the page as she keyed its heat sensitive strip to the page she wanted. She brushed angrily at her eyes and said: "This is a copy of the official record of their orders, Ryne Sangre. Don't ask me where I got them or how."

I had no intention of so doing; all I wanted was to get all this emotion out of the way. I moved over to the copilot's couch and sat next to her, bending over the sheet.

"Samel and Teelya D'Ame," I read. "Orders of the Military Research Bureau. Dateline . . ."

She fingered the sheet to scroll slowly down the document, and I lost the place.

"There's nothing so tedious as a document such as this," she said in a bitter voice. "The admiralty floridly points out that my parents were commissioned officers of the Intelligence and subject to all of the regulations and discipline thereto appertaining. Then the scientific area of their expertise is indicated, to whit, genetic biochemistry, and the mission is carefully described in language that covers the real intent and yet delivers the message that much more is expected of them than lay on the surface. In the document's words, they are to undertake a mission 'to penetrate the scientific establishment of the Wholeth Empire and determine, insofar as possible, the extent of the paranormal powers of the female rulers therein.' But the real intent is so obvious that I wonder why they bothered with such opaque language, as if the Whole would gain control of the document itself—it was left behind of course—or as if the Wholeth lords could somehow scan something that my parents had read months in the past. Maybe that was it, an excessive caution, as if my parents' thinking would be invisible to a psionic expert while an imprint of the document itself in the cerebral cortex would somehow be more accessible. Stupid. The only explanation that makes sense to me is that the military habitually obfuscates everything."

I said nothing, hoping to keep the flow coming. But she fell silent, and I felt forced to say, inanely, "Their mission was obvious, then?"

"Yes, it was obvious," she snapped, "when you juxtapose the superficial mission itself with their field of expertise. The extent of the power of the Wholeth Lord and minor lords held some interest for them, since it represented the crux of the security problem that the discovery of the Whole had presented to the Cloud. But the real aim was obvious from the beginning, to them and later to me."

She paused then, and I was afraid that another bout of emoting was about to come. But finally she spoke, just as I was casting about in my mind for a verbal prod.

"And that's what makes me so bitter, I suppose." Her voice had dropped to barely a whisper. "The mission was so difficult and dangerous that I believe that the Polarian authorities never expected them to come back. They were evidently expendable enough so that they were sent out alone in a utility starship and provided with no escort and no weapons and no power to speak of, other than their own brains and judgement and skill."

She was losing me. I gathered that her parents had been sent on a mission to the Whole nearly eleven years ago, but the rest was cloudy. She still hadn't gotten to the center of things, though she was talking and her emotional blast was falling further and further behind.

"And the amazing thing was that they got as far as they did," she said. "If only interspatial holography reached from the Empire to us, or if they had some kind of robot message drone, or if there were a Polarian message relay station in the Gulf. Then the Whole might have left them alone, once the secret was out, though I doubt it."

I was in the dark now, and felt compelled to speak, even at the risk of recalling to Lee the pain of the past half hour.

"And what was it they found, dammit?" I said irritably, in my usual suave fashion.

She looked at me as if she were looking at a half-witted eight year old.

"Their findings were . . ." she mimicked. "That the Wholeth lords were genetically superior beings, with great psionic powers, minds able to read other minds, minds able to move physical objects. Minds able to influence the decisions of lesser minds, to force human beings into any path they chose, to do anything they wished no matter what the consequences to the manipulatee. Minds with the potential of overcoming and swallowing the Polar Cloud, even as they had swallowed forty thousand planets along the galactic arm."

I said, "Big deal. Everyone knew that already."

She looked at me, her brown/green eyes at once beautiful and repellent, her etched face tightened subtly, caution struggling with distaste. I wondered at it even as she spoke, knowing in my insecurity that the distaste was directed at me, hoping instead that it was directed at the subject at hand.

"Ah, but they found even more than that," she said softly. "Intelligence has put all the information they have together, and there can be little doubt about what they accomplished. They found out exactly how the genetic manipulation is done. They found out how to reproduce a Lord."

I gaped. So there it was, the key to everything, the reason for her quest and her hatred and her pain.

I saw in blinding insight that she was not seeking her parents' lives alone, or their reputation alone, but that she sought also to make their mission whole, to bring knowledge to the Polar Cloud that might make the difference between defeat and victory. I realized then the many demons that haunted her, that she felt pain from a dozen directions, some of which I couldn't even guess at, and some of which I dared not probe.

"They found out?" I said stupidly. "How could they? Why would the Whole reveal such a thing to anyone, much less to a Polarian?"

"They revealed nothing," Lee said savagely. "My parents tricked it out of them.

"Feature the difficulty of it, Ryne. They made their way to the largest Wholeth university they could find and began to work on the Wholeth academics. They taught seminars on Polarian history of science, even as they ingratiated themselves to the scientists there, only to find that the academics knew nothing about the genetics of the lords, even that they feared to know anything, that it was an area of knowledge forbidden. Then they wangled an invitation to the capital city itself, for discussions with Wholeth foreign ministers about the Polarian 'problem,' acting all the time as dispassionate scientists uninterested in intragalactic relations. They allowed the Wholeth underlings to view them as tools, manipulated for Wholeth military intelligence, unwitting dupes."

She paused, lips pursed, then said, "That must have hurt; it would have hurt me, and I'm their daughter. In the meantime I stayed in the Cloud and didn't know anything about what was going on, and at first the admiralty told me nothing. Then they told me that my mother and father had both been killed in some unnamed accident about which they were so oh-so-close-mouthed because it was a security matter. I sensed some sort of vague shame, and it made me uneasy and was the reason, I suppose, that I went after it like I did and found out what I found."

The flood of words continued, and I let them come, for already a wild hope was rising in me. What if we could reach the spy ship? With a secret such as it carried, I might barter with the devil himself, or even with Palla Belanger.

"All the while my parents were probing, and," she waved at the other booksheets, "these records suggest that they finally made an opening by using a suggestion of sex. My mother was an attractive woman, and add to that the fact that she was an exotic dark-haired visitor to the Whole, and you can see that she must have drawn attention. And my father did too, among the Wholeth women, and while they fawned over him he evidently was able to find something out that gave them the clue that they needed. And remember that the Wholeth mores are highly Puritanical, Ryne. They didn't have to do anything overt, just suggest the possibility of something, to squeeze intelligence from the Wholeth moon-struck."

I wondered how much of what she said came from a need to believe.

"But one day they climbed into their ship," she went on, "and took off for somewhere that the other Polarian spies around the Empire could not specify. It was a planet, and I guess, and the records guess, that it was the original home of the lords, though the Whole does not admit to any of it and shrouds all aspects of it in as much mystery as they can. Someone must have invited them there, or they would have been blasted the moment they appeared in orbit around it. A minor lord, after my dad? Who knows?"

Her bitterness was palpable, and I held my breath, to give no excuse for any kind of hysterics.

"But they got it somehow." She passed a hand over her high brow and closed her eyes wearily, the booksheets forgotten.

"Something happened—the record doesn't say, and I don't think that the Polarian authorities know. But whatever it was caused my parents to take off out of there as if hell itself were after them. And maybe it was.

"Think of it Ryne. They knew a way to reproduce a lord! It would have put the Cloud on an even footing with the Whole. No, not an even footing, it would have put the Cloud way ahead, for the Cloud lacks the social structure that the Wholeth lords have built up over centuries of self-indulgent control. The Cloud could have had lords with the democratic ideal, if I can use such a phrase in a federation such as ours, lords with a conscience as it were. The Polarian lords could have been conditioned in such a way that a repetition of the Wholeth tyranny would have been impossible. Polarian lords could have been made so that their only mission would be to neutralize the psionic strength of the Wholeth Empire. It would have been the greatest coup that the Polarians could possibly have made, and the greatest danger conceivable for the Wholeth thrust towards domination of the Cloud."

I watched her, and now the lines of her face were getting to me again, my eyes just inches away. I could smell her scent, and it, and the idea she had brought to me of a bargaining chip to get me out of this mess, was going to my head. At the time, I could have cared less about the fate of the Cloud; it was my fate that occupied me.

"It was Crestor Falon all over again," she said savagely. I thought: *who?* I was yet to read his story in Kellem's notes. "From the moment they saw them arrive, the Wholeth police had hidden an interspatial transmitter on the skin of my parents' ship, and when my parents took off from the Wholeth home world, they knew that they were closely pursued even as they fled into interspace. The spies on the other Wholeth worlds spoke of a Wholeth fleet of incredible size, so large that its entry into Polarian space would have precipitated an interstellar war almost by default.

"Maybe my parents believed, like Falon, that the Roil would disrupt the hidden transmitter. In any event they did flee to the Roil, and they did sink in a mad cosmic ocean, swallowed alive like Jonah, and still alive inside, as I truly do believe. And they must be alive, Ryne; their ship would resist the radiation as long as the shields were up, and their ships artificial gravitation would preserve them even as the Roil's gravitational chaos drew them in and flung them around its mad insides. They'd have plenty of air; these ships will recycle air practically forever, and water too. And, unlike the OB here, their ship was large enough for a food reprocessor. I think they're alive, Ryne. I feel it. I know it.

"I'm going in there, Ryne. Come hell or heaven, I'm going in."

She held my hand, and looked into my eyes, and said: "And you have to decide, Ryne. There are issues here beyond my family's survival. We together, you and I, have it in our power to deliver the Cloud from the Wholeth lords. But I need you to do it, Ryne; I need you as I've never needed anyone."

I studied into her face, beautiful even when set in fanatical lines, and thought: *the admiralty won't kill someone who brings a secret such as that. Maybe I'm as demented as she, for she's getting me hooked.*

Ten minutes later, I began to teach her how to pilot a starship.

And that night, we made love.

Chapter 10

Did I seduce her? No. Up to that time I had never seduced anyone, though not for lack of trying. I might have undertaken it eventually with her, alone for three weeks on that ship as I was with a woman who filled the cabin with compulsion. But she was wiser than I, and she had analyzed me more thoroughly than any psychcom could have, and she, as she said, needed me.

Truth to tell, I was rather in awe of her. Many times I had cast an eye on uniquely desirable women such as, for example, Cassia Glane, but the track record being zero, I had long since believed myself incapable of attracting one of the ones who made my palms sweat and mouth dry up. I hadn't learned two lessons yet; one, that I was not so repulsive as I thought; and two, that sometimes I was useful. To this day I haven't met a woman whose motivation, no matter what she herself believes, is pure carnality, although there are sure to be some around, somewhere. Of those I have encountered in an active life, most are looking for permanence; some, like Kitty and Lee, seek other goals; and some are on a course of self-destruction, of which any man is only a part.

For the rest of the day, I taught Lee the details of the shipcom, showing her how to listen to it with half an ear, how to feed it commands, how to know when it cannot handle something. The routine was easy; anticipating the exception was the hard part. As it happened, drilling her on what to do in unexpected situations would occupy us for the next nineteen days. Contemplating the variety of death such situations could bring, I would have passed the time in a state of sweating fear, except for what she did.

We ate late in the relative evening; she used the ship's minuscule galley to wonderful advantage, and I was stuffed with artificial lasagna when finally I settled down in the pilot's couch for the night. I had no immediate thoughts of melding with Celia D'Ame; well, maybe one or two, but I dismissed them as unworthy and unlikely.

I dozed off, with visions of asteroids plunging at me, smashing me into a bloody pancake, Palla Belanger laughing hysterically and asking me to do it again.

It was after midnight, ship's time, when I awoke with a start, and there she was, crowding onto the pilot's couch. I put out a shaking hand in an instinctive warding-off gesture, and felt satiny skin, unencumbered by anything.

"I can't sleep with you mumbling so," she said silkily in my right ear. "Mumble something nice to me, Ryne Sangre. We both need the rest."

I couldn't believe it, and I told her so, and she laughed. "Why not?" she said. "Haven't you thought about it? Don't you look forward to it? I am coming to you, Ryne Sangre; you don't need innuendos and leers this time. *I* want *you*, Ryne Sangre. And you want me."

I did. But her needs had little to do with mine, and, though I, lost in a fog of infatuation, did not realize it then, she was putting a stamp on me that would hang over me all my life.

For here is the honest truth: there is such a thing as chemistry, that hackneyed line that seducers have used from time immemorial. And it can be one-way, like the shields; it does not have to be felt the same on both sides. Perhaps it is a form of self-delusion, but I don't think so. There's something innate in it, and by the time I had finished penetrating Celia D'Ame I was lost. I felt that something cosmic was happening to me, that I had found the reason for life itself. I was captivated, enchanted, and (I can't say it any other way) in love. Love; I knew what it could mean now, and for the moment I would have jumped into the Roil naked for Lee, to feel what I felt that night.

Hey, great for you, you might be thinking. Don't. Because it never lasts, not the way I had it. Oh, if you're lucky, you might be able to seal it with marriage, and then if you study how to continue it, and behave like an angel, you might be able to recapture it. But if you plunge inside every woman you can, eventually you'll run into one who will blow you away, and she won't want to stay with you because she'll see that you're the satyr that you are, and you'll lose her, and everything after will be stale and dead.

I had years to think about it later and, believe me, it was better in the old days when marriages were arranged based on a look at the social position and spirituality of each potential spouse. There was always the chance that the pair would feel the transcendent chemistry that I felt with Celia D'Ame; and if they didn't feel it, they would never miss it, and would concentrate on raising splendid children instead. No matter what, they were better off than I.

Find a woman and stick with her, my friend. Make

your ruling passion that you don't even glance at anyone else. Your life will be happier than most.

We spent three weeks in interspace, Celia D'Ame and I, and I taught her piloting during the starday, and jumped on her bones at night. She seemed to want me. She seemed to need me. She erased all the self-doubt that Kitty hadn't had time to.

And I cannot think of those days without feeling pain. I wish they had never been.

We flared out of interspace on the twenty-third day. We were both strapped in our seats, for I told her that I didn't trust shipcom when it came to an unsettled region of space like the Roil. I didn't want to dodge asteroid boulders unstrapped, for example. We saw the Roil dead ahead, and I looked at Lee, seeing the excitement in her eyes as she stared at the object she had sought so long. The readouts hammered at us, and I scarcely noticed them, for I could not take my eyes off the profile next to me, the high forehead, fair skin, brown/green eyes, auburn hair, half-opened lips.

"But there are a lot of ships, Ryne. What are they doing here?"

It took a moment for her words to sink in, and then I jerked around to the console and blinked at the screen. My heart disappeared. Ships? It could only be a squadron from Sigma Rad, come to fetch us, I thought illogically, since they could not have reached the Roil in advance of us, interspatial rules being what they are. Maybe Palla Belanger herself was there, waiting to take us, I thought. Perhaps . . .

I could see the round, twisting surface of the Roil, far ahead, the apparent diameter of a beach ball held at arm's length. And coming around its edges, filling space on all sides, was a fleet of ships, a larger fleet than I had ever seen.

"The Whole desires your reply," shipcom told me.

"What?" I shrieked. "Reply to what?" I looked at the rearward screens, and there were ships back there too, hemming us away from the jump point. None of them were Polarian, shipcom told me. It took a long moment for it to sink in: we had encountered the rumored Wholeth battle fleet. It was hanging around the Roil, no doubt waiting for orders to decimate the Polar Cloud. (They were there for another reason too, to back up Selah Maja, but that I did not discover until much, much later.)

There were 322 ships, the historical record shows. I saw battlewagons and dreadnoughts, ships five miles across, fighters by the hundred, every one except the fighters large enough to carry grav cannon, the only weapon certain against shielding. Of all the things I had expected at the Roil, this was the last, though now I know that it all made perfect sense, were I omniscient enough to see it.

Part of it was that the Roil was roughly midway between the Whole and the Cloud; why not rendezvous there? The Outer Archipelago of the Whole was close enough for interspatial holography, though static-ridden, and no rogue star or other wanderer outside of the galactic arm could say the same. We had blundered into the worst possible place for a Polarian fighter ship, and neither of us had prepared for this, despite all the contingency training we had accomplished. And there were other reasons.

Lee's face had gone ashen. I recognized it for what it was. She had finally reached the Roil, and no matter what happened in the next few months, there was no chance at all that a Wholeth battle fleet would let us through and into it. She had come so far, and now. . .

"The Wholeth flagship demands again to know who you are," shipcom said. "If you do not reply, you will be considered an enemy and dealt with. Please open holo channels and reply."

"Lee . . ." I said helplessly, beseeching her. She shot an irritated glance at me.

"You're the star pilot," she said. "Do something."

I faced the console, and stabbed at it with nerveless fingers. "I insist on speaking with the commander of your fleet," I shrilled. The thought was in me that I could bargain the secrets of one-way shielding for our lives. No thought of patriotism toward the Cloud passed me by, of course, only thoughts of saving my skin. Even Lee's skin, fine though it was, I forgot.

They will route me through layer upon layer of bureaucracy, I thought, but they did not. Almost immediately, a face appeared on my receiving screen.

"Her Lordship's Stead, Antil Lamonte, at your service," a cold voice spoke in passable Standard. I saw thin lips, a clean-shaven patrician face, tight curly blond hair, and eyes that would have frozen a nova.

And he saw me, in that two-way communication moment. And his eyes widened slightly, and he said then, "I am surprised. I had no word of your coming. Please accept the hospitality of the Whole, Mr. Ambassador. And do not be surprised that we know you; all the Whole knows of the imminent arrival of the Vice-Regent of the Polar Cloud."

I looked at Lee, and she looked at me. I switched off the audio/video link momentarily.

"Let's switch seats," I said, mouth hanging open. I tried to collect myself as we exchanged places, wondering what I could to, wondering were the advantage was. But a truism occurred to me, and I acted on it, and it was this: in most situations, it is better to be highly placed than not.

I switched on again, this time from the copilot's seat.

"Lead us in," I croaked. "My pilot and I will be happy to meet you."

Again I looked at Lee. She hadn't a thing to say.

Chapter 11

And that is how I became the Vice-Regent of the Polar Cloud, Sir Anthony Palin-Marek, newly appointed ambassador to the Wholeth Empire, roué, hunter, explorer, rake. The Wholeth Fleet had an on-line file, you see, but it was not detailed, for the appointment was too recent. They knew little about Palin-Marek other than various holos of him doing various things, filed among terabytes of spy-gathered information on the notables of the Polar Cloud. They had no voice prints and no retina scans and not even any fingerprints. And if Wholeth spies had gathered such since the appointment, they hadn't yet been able to ferry it across the Gulf between the Cloud and the Empire. Thank G-d.

Shipcom shook hands with the flagship shipcom and brought us together like a sparrow settling onto a tree. The Wholeth vessel must have been eight miles across, the type of ship that never saw landfall but spent all its life in space, ordering others around and making a nuisance of itself. As we approached I saw a large flat area pockmarked with the ring-like shapes of airlock shipjacks. The OB settled against the outer hull like a blister on the skin, and I felt grapples catch hold of us and seal us against the larger ship—the standard plug/jack configuration hadn't varied for all the centuries, I noted, for if it had, my ship wouldn't have fit and I would have had to suit up.

There were two or three other ships plugged against nearby rings, and one stood out from the fighters and shuttles like a diamond among stones. It was a golden ship, cone-shaped and starkly beautiful, twice as large as the OB. Its length was the same as its lowest width, as near as I could tell, and it looked as if it were made of antique bronze, though that metal that couldn't have lasted five minutes under the g forces of a starship, so it was some exotic alloy. I saw the Wholeth Lord's insignia near the tip of the cone, and memory stirred: the black planet, the strange ship's visit, a woman named Selah Maja.

Meanwhile I was ripping trainee insignia off of my clothes, pressing shut the thread holes, reading the shipcom knowledge base for everything it had on Palin-Marek, and swallowing a double dose of tranquilizers. Lee just sat there, as pale as paper.

"Lee," I told her as I scrambled around, "the only chance we have of getting out of this is for you to pretend you're a starship pilot, and for me to act the patrician. They won't dare mess with someone of Palin-Marek's stature, whereas Ryne Sangre and Lee D'Ame they'd jettison into space without a moment's thought. You insist on staying with the OB; they'd expect that of a pilot. I'll do what I can to confuse them, and feed them some story about the intrepid Palin-Marek exploring the Roil, that sort of thing. Maybe they'll let us through and on to the Roil. Maybe they'll let us go back to the Cloud. I'll come to you when I can. In the meantime, think about your life; it means something to me now, if not to you."

She looked grim-faced at me, and in her green/brown eyes was little that I wanted to see.

"You won't be able to pull it off," she said flatly. "You're no Palin-Marek; you're Ryne Sangre, who crawls into bushes when danger comes."

"Thanks for the pep talk," I said.

"I'm back on my own," she said, her melodic voice in discord, "as I've always been. If I have to, I'll blast my way out and go into the Roil alone."

"Don't do it, Lee," I urged. I came over to her and took her hand. Mine was warm this time, hers the temperature of ice. "You wouldn't get as far as a light second; a hundred ships would blast you out of space. Anyway, you don't know the OB well enough for the Roil; you would go down too deep, or hit something, or do something that would drop the shields. You need two more months of training at least, and can't get it feeling your way into a maelstrom. Wait for me. Wait for me, Lee. I love . . ."

"Did it ever occur to you," she said shrilly, jerking her hand away, "that no matter what, we have just delivered the secret of one-way shielding to the Wholeth Empire? Even now they're scanning this ship, and within an hour they'll know every molecule of it. You thought you would be branded a traitor for letting me take the OB off Sigma Rad, Ryne; what do you think the Cloud will do to you now?"

I smiled a thin smile. That I hadn't already melted into a heap of terror-ricketed jelly was surprising, and impressing, me. Perhaps my whole problem was one of imagination; when peril actually arrived I had to meet it, and I was discovering that if I had any chance of handling it, I would face it and try. I argued to myself that it was my usual realism; there was always the grim alternative, and avoiding that had always ruled me; why not in crisis too? The whole point was to maximize the chance of survival; if that took intrepid action, I'd do it; I'd have to. If it took flight, I'd do that too; I'd do it first, if it was an alternative.

It was not one here, and hadn't been from the moment we flared out of interspace. So . . .

"How long before they find out what's happening to the real Palin-Marek?" she threw at me. "They have spies in the Cloud, and must have some way to relay information across the Gulf."

"I'm not going to impersonate him forever," I told her. "If it lasts a day, it will be a miracle. I'm going to pay respects, explain that I was on a side trip to see the Roil, that my diplomatic pouch and codes and all that are back on Sigma Radidiani; now if you will excuse me, my pilot and I will go back there, and we'll meet you officially at the Outer Archipelago as had been originally planned, thank you very much and good-bye."

She snorted. I kissed her as shipcom opened the hatch, and her lips barely moved beneath mine. It was a startling contrast to the artificial fervor that I had felt in them the last three weeks. "Good-bye, Lee," I said. "Stiff upper lip. I'll do everything I can to help you. You took on the Polar Cloud and beat it, and now you've reached the Roil. I'm starting to think you can do anything you've a mind to. And G-d help me, some of it's rubbing off."

"G-d help you, Ryne Sangre," she said dully. Then I dropped down the hatch.

The bigger ship's artificial gravity was oriented at right angles to the fighter's, so that I popped through the hatch and found myself parallel to the floor, three feet up. I hit with a crash, and the escort of soldiery waiting for me, men and women, erupted into harsh giggles, until their commander silenced them. They walked me all of three paces to a little groundcar and installed me alone inside, and I barely had time to look around the gigantic hangar. A few of the ringjacks were gaping open, not into deep space obviously, but into the other ships I had seen outside.

The car hummed off on its way, and I saw long plasteel corridors, uniforms scurrying around, artificial grav on full, everybody looking self-important and grouchy—it was not much different from a big Polarian ship. I can't say I was all that interested in the ship itself; they wouldn't be parading me anywhere where military secrets were housed. I was more interested in the people. Though my belly was in a knot, I was eyeing them to see if they had diverged somehow from the Polarians in the twelve hundred years since we had fled them as they were still consolidating their Empire.

About the only thing that struck me was that they were all various shades of blond; the darkest among them had hair the color of Lee's. I wondered if that was the result of genetic manipulation too, like their abnormal female leaders. And, as the car sped through corridor after lift after corridor, I wondered if I would be meeting any of those women, to have my brain picked apart and my mind erased. It would play hob with my impersonation of Palin-Marek, I thought.

At length we disembarked and entered a fine stateroom of spartan furnishing and subtle silver, white, and black coloring. My escort faded away behind me. Somewhere during the trip I had been scanned from hair to sole, I guessed, and I wondered if they'd picked up on the crystals in my fingers.

Three persons, sitting in elegant cross-legged conversation on old fashioned overstuffed chairs, rose to meet me, and for the first time I met Antil Lamonte, Stead of the Lordship's battle fleet, Selah Maja, Governor of the Outer Archipelago, and Restor Kalil, Sub-Governor of same. It was a momentous meeting, though none of us knew it. That I got through it alive was momentous enough; but there were other things too.

The Stead was dressed in the starkest uniform I yet had seen, black and silver fabric so that he almost blended with the wall, and no insignia that I could discern. He was a tall man, and I have noted already his angular face, almost nonexistent lips, and curled blond hair. He moved like a panther, and his ice-blue eyes shot into mine as if he could control me by look alone. I wondered briefly if Wholeth men too were bred with hyperminds. If so, I was in for it.

Selah Maja—another stunning woman entered my life at that moment, and I wish now she had walked right out again. She was honey-haired, dressed in nearly the same outfit as the Stead, five inches shorter than he, and she moved with a fluid grace that made his catlike gestures seem those of a jerking puppet. I was not so far gone in heart-palpitating terror to be unaware of the impact of her perfectly formed face and body, but I was in no position to ogle as I strained to pretended refinement and tried not to trip over my feet. She could be one of the paranormal ones; I wondered if I'd feel her probing, if it would be like a feather tickling the brain, or fingers probing, or needles stabbing.

The third individual was Restor Kalil, and he was of another breed. He was as tall as Lamonte, but his shoulders were twice as wide, and he had one of those square-jawed faces one associates with beer and condom advertising. His eyes were as brown as mine, but his longish hair was the color of cream. His broad face was set in a perpetual petulant scowl. Unlike the Stead and Maja, he moved with little grace, suggesting a bulldozer with a broken tread.

"So pleased you could join us," Lamonte said coldly, stepping forward and extending his hand. "So unexpected, and so welcome. Please meet my colleagues. . . ." And he introduced us.

My hand had reverted to its usual clamminess, and he grimaced as he shook it. Then I held it out to Maja and she looked at it as if it had just been dipped in excrement.

Lamonte laughed without warmth, and Kalil reached over and grabbed my hand and clenched, and my bones ground together and yelled. He's going to set off the crystals, I remember thinking, but he let go at last, even as Lamonte was saying: "One does not shake a woman's hand among the Whole, Mr. Ambassador; doubtless it is a detail that your briefings have overlooked."

"Doubtless," I said, though I'd have bet a million credits that the real Palin-Marek would have made no such mistake. What other *faux pas* would I make, and which one would prove the fatal one?

Lamonte waved me over to a fourth chair and I sank into it gratefully; standing, I couldn't have concealed my trembling legs much longer. "One does not sit in advance of a woman in the room either," Kalil snapped, and I nearly sprang to my feet like a jack-in-the-box. *What would Palin-Marek have done?* I thought frantically. He was such an arrogant bastard that he'd probably have sat down in front of them for spite alone. I sat.

They settled themselves, and I said, trying to copy Palin-Marek's supercilious lisp, "I must apologize for this intrusion. I have desired an excursion to the Roil for many months, never anticipating that such an august delegation would be on hand to greet me."

"Your appointment was made known to us only two months ago," Maja said in lilting timbre. They spoke standard basic as well as anyone, with only a slight peculiarity of inflection to show that we had been separated for twelve hundred years; such is the influence of the mass media of both cultures.

"Um," I said. "You must be aware that exploration is one of my most favored activities." Lamonte nodded his head, barely; he had read up on the Vice-Regent, of course. "The Roil is of fascination to anyone; that I would be delayed on Sigma Radidiani, so close to it, was an opportunity I could not allow to go by."

"Yes, that delay," Lamonte said. "I must tell you that her Lordship does not understand why the Cloud felt itself moved to impose it. The excuse that there were rumors of aggressive action is absurd; this fleet, if that be the cause, is in training only, and the Roil is in open space."

"No one wishes to meet Her Lordship more than I," I lied. "However, I cannot elaborate on such matters, given that my presence here is fortuitous and outside of official intercourse." I was improvising like crazy, and now I gathered all the sternness I could muster and said, "Shortly I will return to my ship, so that I can come again under official auspices. We had planned to meet at the Archipelago, no? There I will renew our acquaintance."

I half rose, and Lamonte held out a hand. I eased back into the chair.

"A moment," he said. "I have prepared certain refreshments, and there are matters to discuss. Please. . . ." He gave some invisible signal, and in came a tray with a silver service, so help me, arrayed with dainty cakes and teacups and a samovar, of all things.

I cast about for something intelligent to say as I declined the cake and accepted the tea. The silver cup was hot, and I had to hold it between my thumb and two fingers; I wondered if I should stick my little finger out at right angles or something.

Meanwhile I was thinking, as much as I could think at all. Palin-Marek would have blustered and strutted, and I had to try to do the same. But I had little knowledge of the diplomatic history of the Cloud and the Whole; what could I say that wouldn't precipitate an interstellar war? I cast my mind about, and finally hit upon something; it had the effect of throwing gasoline on a fire. I should have known.

"It is glad I am to have discovered a man like yourself, my dear Stead," were the words that came forth, "who is willing to bring a mere three hundred ships to the close proximity of the Polar Cloud. Our people are, sad to say, rather bellicose after twelve hundred years of infighting; you, from your changeless Whole, cannot know what real fighting is all about."

I think that the words astonished them because they were the exact opposite of the impression that the Cloud had been trying to put across for thirty years. We had most definitely not wanted to antagonize the forty thousand planets down there in the arm, and had fawned and grovelled to avoid it. Our continuing attitude was the biggest source of inspiration for the militarily-inclined political factions of the Cloud, which declared itself ashamed of its spineless government, etc. Palla Belanger led those factions.

The Stead Lamonte opened his mouth to vent his anger; but Governor Maja forestalled him with a gesture of a well-shaped arm.

"Your words would suggest an underlying message," she said, "which belies recent protocols between our two governments. Are we to infer a change in the friendly attitude which we have been at such pains to cultivate, based as they are upon our sincerest desire for mutual understanding and cooperation?"

"In the face of the inhuman Onnish menace?" Kalil added, to a flicker of irritation from his governor.

I hesitated. I didn't know a thing about the alluded protocols, which I would have were I in fact Palin-Marek. I was not particularly interested either, except with regard to my own self-preservation; concern for Lee was foremost in the higher reaches of my mind, to my later astonishment. But with the tiny political consciousness that I did possess, I was determined that the Polar Cloud not bow before the Whole; as I have said earlier, grovelling almost never works.

So I chose my words carefully, turning upside-down the message that the real Palin-Marek, were he to follow his government and not his arrogance, might have delivered.

"It is merely," I said with a leisurely gesture of hand, "that the government of the Cloud sees no validity in recent rumors of Onnish invasion, especially given the distance of the Cloud from the Onnish Empire, and especially given," I said, allowing the hand to fall to the knee again, "the source of the rumors themselves."

Kalil sprang to his feet.

"Really, sir, the impudence of your words . . ." He was restrained by Maja, who drew him back into his seat and turned her eyes to Lamonte's in deliberate deference, waiting for him to show an official reaction.

The tall, blond envoy held a long silence while he strove against himself. I had guessed that he could not afford to offend Palin-Marek, at least not grossly. The early presence of the Polarian envoy was a heaven-sent opportunity to enhance his own prestige before his Lord, and he evidently had no intention of letting it go before he had squeezed every advantage.

So he smiled placatingly, a facial expression at variance with hardness around the eyes, and said in his smoothest manner, seizing upon Kalil's change of subject: "Rumors you may have heard, sir, yet they are based upon incontrovertible and well-documented facts. Consider the recent Onnish raid upon a human colony in the far border of the Whole, a raid from which, I might add, no living human being survived. We have conclusive satellite recordings of the event, which I will be happy to submit to your technicians for testing and verification."

I yawned with protracted deliberation, causing Lamonte's neck to redden despite his almost super-human effort at control. "I have seen similar alleged recordings," I said in a bored voice, "yet it is amply clear that the Onnish region is on the other side of the Wholeth Empire. That it impinges upon your borders I have no doubt; but that this fact has any inherent interest for the Cloud, you will permit me to harbor one."

The three Wholeth officials looked at one another as if doubting the evidence of ears which had hith-erto proven reliable.

Maja swivelled toward me slowly, so that the aspect of her face changed from one exquisite por-trait to another.

" 'Doubt?' " she said at last, looking directly at me as if to see through the facade into the center of my soul. "Are we to assume then that the Polar Cloud is taking a position . . . against . . . the Whole?"

For a moment my estimation of the power in the room shifted. There was something in her voice beyond the words that brought all my senses to their feet. I saw Kalil stir, to be withered by a glance from Lamonte.

"An unfortunate choice of words," I finally said.

And that was all I said.

For a long moment there was a test of wills, as the Governor's hypnotic gaze met and struggled with "Palin-Marek's" insolent, half-closed, wide-awake eyes—beneath which panic and terror were playing leapfrog.

It broke off abruptly, and I was never sure if I

had broken her, or if she had simply abandoned it as a bad effort, and switched to another line of attack.

"Surely the Cloud will see this as a danger to humanity, rather than to the Wholeth Lord alone," she said quietly, passing her hand over her face as if overcome by an immense weariness.

The Stead cut in, allowing his anger to vent just a little. "I also object to your use of the word 'Empire,' Ambassador," he said sharply. "The Whole is no more an empire than your own leadership on Tyghe, unless of course your autocracy has an imperial tendency?"

For an instant I was confused. Then I recalled a briefing at boot camp that I have not recorded here, when the lieutenant had drilled us on the history of the Cloud while I was trying to forget a humiliation of the night before. The Whole, he said, referred to themselves as, simply, the Whole. "Empire" carried too much negative connotation.

"But naturally it has," I, happy to depart from the line of thought that Maja had expressed. In a perverse way, I was enjoying myself, making Palin-Marek look like a warmonger. "There are over nine thousand inhabited planets in the globular cluster which forms the Polar Cloud," I said. "For most of our history, the Cloud consisted of widely-separated confederations and freeholds, as you probably well know. The gradual unification was largely diplomatic, but the arguments were the same that the Wholeth lords must have used when taking over your own side of the Galaxy. Perhaps the only difference is that no one planet dominates the Cloud. Whereas in your case, one is given to understand that the Wholeth world functions as what was called in crueller times, a dictatorship."

Again the three envoys exchanged expressions of common annoyance.

"Surely your language is needlessly direct," the

Stead suggested finally. "Our own realm functions around a common theme, loyalty to the Whole. Your culture is hardly dissimilar, I would argue, in your loyalty to the concept of a unified Polar Cloud. A somewhat more diffuse idea perhaps, but an idea that, like ours, compels respect and loyalty, even a large amount of devotion, as it were."

" 'Devotion' is not a word heard in the Cloud in connection with the government," I said dryly.

"Semantics," opined the Stead smoothly. "Naturally the great outward expansion of humankind could not have been accomplished in a unified fashion, by some central authority cohesive enough to compel obedience over trackless distances. Our own forty thousand worlds were inhabited by rebels and misfits and visionaries, by people who went outward precisely to get away from the constrictions of any and all authority. So were yours.

"But it was equally natural that a reunification would someday come. Yours and ours are separate movements, but the fact that they occurred at the same historical moment cannot be overlooked as mere coincidence. It was meant to be; it's one of those great natural cycles of history, and we are privileged to see it coming to fruition." The Stead leaned forward again, his blue eyes glinting and guileless, as if captured by a knowledge of great and wondrous things. I was disgusted. "You and I are but instruments of the last stage of that cycle," Lamonte went on. "In you the outermost reaches of humanity have been retrieved. It is all but providential; maybe it *is* providential. Just as the Onnish threat appears, mankind comes together once again for a moment of common defense."

Lamonte's eyes were now unfocused, looking into some marvelous kaleidoscope of visionary fulfillment. I shot a glance at Maja, and found her eyebrows knit in an irritated frown, which vanished as she felt my regard upon her.

"I do not think he realizes," I said to her softly, nodding at Lamonte, "that the Cloud will not necessarily take the Wholeth word."

The sardonic tone reawakened her frown. I found himself drinking her in, then remembered with a start that such regard would fit right in with Palin-Marek's reputation.

Lamonte's eyes cleared abruptly, and hardness poured into them once again.

"The Cloud may not always be in a position . . ." he began, and then stopped. Then: ". . . to face the Onnish forces with the Whole as a buffer," he finished carefully. "Who knows the end of this situation? Surely the Cloud must worry just a little about a time when the Whole has been overrun by a race a representative of which humankind has never seen."

"Really, sir, this smacks of treason!" Kalil butted in. "You suggest that the Wholeth Lord is easily taken, and the suggestion is . . . well, it's treasonous," he finished lamely, a little shakiness creeping into his muddy eyes.

This time Maja, sighing, made no move to restrain him.

"What will you do about it?" the Stead asked evilly. Obviously he was weary of the Sub-Governor's fatuity. Kalil paled. Having read Lamonte's character, I imagined that the Sub-Governor was recalling that the Stead's enemies had an unpleasant habit of surprise journeys down disposal tubes into deep space, or some such thing.

Maja cut in smoothly, turning the Stead's attention away from her perspiring lieutenant.

"My dear Ambassador," she said, "we have no wish to force ourselves upon the Polar Cloud. We do wish to point out our common bond, and the common threat that faces us—may face us, if you will."

"Yes, yes," I said dismissively, waving a hand again. "We've heard it all before, and no doubt we are fated to hear it all again from Her Lordship." They stiffened as if I had poked them with a dagger. "But all this is futile; we can continue the discussion at the proper time. Now . . ." Again I half rose. Again, Lamonte gestured me down.

"Quite frankly, Mr. Ambassador," Lamonte said, showing his teeth in a bared grin, "there is something in your visit here that puzzles us. Our latest information had you entering interspace after the fortnight delay, along with your escort, bound allegedly for the Archipelago; we were planning to leave Roilian space tomorrow in order to accompany Governor Maja there to greet you. You will understand that in matters such as these, uncertainty is unacceptable; we must check our information sources in order to make proper arrangements. Would you consent, perhaps, to remain our guest and let us bring you to the Archipelago? We have much to discuss; we can keep it as unofficial as you like."

"That, sir, is impossible," I said, trying to make my voice as cold as his. I was in a steel-belted panic. The moment they discovered that I was a fraud, it would be curtains not only for me, but for Lee as well.

They looked at one another. The strain of the impersonation was beginning to tell on me, and I could feel my knees trembling under my hands. I gripped them hard, but it didn't help. Dizzy with conflicting thoughts, I was finding that the idea of my own death was marginally less terrifying than the idea of Lee's.

"My dear Stead," I said then, astonishing myself once again, "there really is no point to all this. We have fenced enough, but we are men and women of reality. Of course I will accompany you to the Archipelago, if that would be enough to lead this fleet away from the Polar Cloud as early as possible. Truth to tell, I have some concern about my escort coming out of interspace and encountering the force you have arrayed here. I want no responsibility for an interstellar incident. Leave a ship behind to notify my escort of what I have done; I will code the message." In gibberish—I didn't know Palin-Marek's codes from a wart.

The Wholeths were conferring by eye contact. Something seemed to be puzzling them.

"We will leave your own ship here," the Stead said at last. I took a deep breath. "Your pilot will . . ."

"No!" I said. "That is out of the question. Things are being muddled enough without inflicting further uncertainty on my government. My pilot must return immediately to Sigma Radidiani. She must bear word of my agreement to accompany you; I cannot have such word reach the Cloud through any other channel, as it would not be believed. There will be confusion in any event: the twenty-three day transit time from Sigma Rad to the Roil ensures it. Being out of communication that long . . ."

Lamonte was barely listening to me. He had come to some decision, and was anxious to get on with it. "Perhaps," he said curtly. "We will not speak further of it now."

He signalled—I didn't see what method he used—and the door slid open and I saw my erstwhile escort of soldiery lined up outside.

Lamonte stood up, then Kalil, and then they waited for me. I took my time about it, and it seemed a full minute as I unfolded myself from the chair. Maja, scowling, was up the moment I was fully erect.

"Pray accompany the ambassador to his quarters," Lamonte told the escort.

I wondered: should I shake his hand and say "Pleased to meetcha" or something? Instead I turned my back on them without a word and strode through the door, not looking back.

Chapter 12

I could not believe it then, and even now I can scarcely credit it. I had sacrificed myself for someone else. Incredible. Assuming the Whole took me up on it, they would send Lee back home while they picked me apart at their leisure.

I might be able to maintain the imposture while in interspace, for no communication could reach them there. But when we emerged at the Archipelago . . .

My mind was wild as I stepped into the quarters they were providing. A subaltern must have been routed from it with little warning, for I could smell the greasy odor of cleaning robots. In the corner of the cabin was a shower with sonic cleansers; on the far side was a long couch which converted into an airbed. There were several screens and one holographic transceiver, no doubt disconnected now. The room was comfortable and functional, and I was as trapped as a mummy in a tomb.

The door slid shut behind me. I turned to reopen it. It was locked.

I had painted myself into a corner with strokes of fire, leaving a path of escape only for Lee. Perhaps she would be sent away, perhaps not. If not, then she would share my fate at the Archipelago; if so, then I had lost her forever, and that was a thought too painful to bear. I could feel her surrounding me even now, a cosmic life force in which I had imbedded myself, and from which I never wanted to leave. She had planned to ensnare me, but I wonder if she had any idea of the impact she actually caused. Reality itself had altered for me; I was another man.

I looked at the four walls of the cabin and screamed inside; not outside, though, for I was certain I was being watched. Outside, I strode over and began examining myself in a mirror that was imbedded in the wall by the sonic shower. Palin-Marek was fastidious, and so had I to be.

Through the tangle of despair, a thought arose from something I had sensed in Lamonte's cabin: there was some kind of tension between Maja and the Stead, with the Stead in ascendance. I wondered if I could put that tension to use somehow.

A hair or two were out of place, and as I diddled with one, I dislodged others. Palin-Marek probably spent a lot of time on his coiffure; I never had. I just poured grease on by the bucket. Now I didn't have any, and as I absentmindedly spat into my hands and worked at it, I wondered what would come next. It being late afternoon, starship time, I assumed that there would be at least one more negotiating session, perhaps disguised as a meal.

What did they make of it, Palin-Marek appearing from nowhere when they thought that no one of the Cloud knew they were there? Maja had operated in apparent independence at the black planet, and she was carrying the Lordship's insignia. Was she . . ? Naw; Lamonte would have been snivelling on the deck, his backside in the air, were she herself of royal blood. But if she were strong enough to erase minds from a distance, as she, or someone, had on the black planet, then I was in serious trouble. But why did she seem to defer to Lamonte?

I didn't think I could face them again. If Lee were to have a chance, though, I had to. My distaste for the Whole had grown exponentially with every moment among them. Lamonte was a first class fanatic; I had seen the fervent light in his eyes as he alluded to the Wholeth Lord. Kalil seemed to have the brain of a chimpanzee. Maja, on the other hand . . .

My mind wandered as I put one last ebony hair into place and stood back from the mirror. Ridiculous, I thought, grimacing at the image. How Palin-Marek could stand all the primping and preening I would never comprehend.

"You don't like it very much, do you?" a voice said.

Inside, I jumped. Outside, my body froze for a moment; then, sedately, I turned and looked at her.

Selah Maja stood just inside the door. Her clothes were different from the ones I had so recently seen. She was wearing something floor length and diaphanous now, and the light from the corridor poured through the garment and around her. Her blonde hair framed her round face in a deliberately unkempt halo.

"I beg your pardon," I said, face immobile.

"I saw your expression," she said, a half-smile on her lips. "You find making-up distasteful, don't you?"

With a suddenness that staggered me, the pressure of her beauty poured upon me in a wave of tremulous longing. Images of Lee faded faster than Kitty's had, and given my enchantment of the last three weeks, it didn't make sense. Dazedly I groped about in my mind for some way to cope with it. My experience with women was introductory, to be sure, but this was something odd. Almost instinctively, I reached for a trick that I had seen on a holo soap opera, one of the mannerisms of the rakish hero who had bedded everything in sight.

I kept my face quiet, without expression. Then I grinned, suddenly. And then I erased the grin as if it had never been.

She showed no visible reaction. But even as I fought for control, I felt a deepening of my desire, and I took a step forward, hunger in my face.

Somewhere my rational mind wondered frantically, what was happening to me? What was she doing there, and whence the intensity of this craving for an unknown, alien woman? This was something beyond my usual panting lust. This was . . .

I shuddered as I focused on her again. And then another shudder as it hit me again. I didn't care what it was anymore—she drew me like a magnet; her eyes were female essence, forcing me toward her with a compulsion to gaze into them long, to melt into them and the rest of her.

Lee, I thought. *Lee!*

"Your . . ." I almost choked. I tore my eyes away from hers. "Your Wholeth doors are quieter than ours," I finished weakly. And then inspiration struck. "I am not accustomed to a prison in which a ravishing woman can appear like a ghost, without any decent warning."

She flushed. I had hoped for it. If I couldn't shake her hand under Wholeth custom, it stood to reason that calling someone "ravishing" was tantamount to an immoral proposition, especially in contrast with the word "decent."

For the shard of my mind still rational was telling me that this intense craving for her, though delightful, was not natural. It was coming, I thought confusedly, from somewhere else. But she would not be able to go beyond her super-religious sensibilities—if she were using some Wholeth mind trick on me,

I would not be compromised, and would get at the root of what was going on.

You may wonder at this, given my traditional willingness to be seduced by any woman, reinforced by the rarity of the event. But it was sinking in to me that seduction had consequences. I had been dragged into the turmoil of Kitty and her mother's relationship because of it, and almost killed, and Lee had me so captivated that I was ready to die for her (I still couldn't believe that). And now here I was, ready to fall into a Wholeth woman's arms. No. Self-preservation still worked, and there was something wrong here. I would insult her mortally if I had to; I had to take control.

But beyond the flush, Maja showed no reaction. Whatever her plan, such a minor verbal slur was not about to deter her. The foreigner was, after all, from a more decadent culture than her own.

"I regret the sealing of your door," she said, taking a slow, languorous step toward me. "Not all Wholeth are as overbearing as my associate, the Stead Lamonte."

I steeled myself. I was Sir Anthony Palin-Marek, I told myself. I was.

I put on a mask of superciliousness.

"Yet you yourself march in as if my own desires have no consequence. Really, madame, it is the action of a backport whore."

This time the flush that leaped into her skin radiated heat like a furnace; I could feel it from across the room. Abruptly, I felt a lessening of attraction for her.

"I apologize, dear sir," she said angrily. "But your own behavior is not what we of the Whole would call gentlemanly. For example, dear sir, you call me 'madame'; I am neither married nor the curator of a house of questionable repute. Nor, most assuredly, am I its inhabitant."

I felt the blast of her anger in my head, and I was certain then that she was one of the paranormals. But how strong? Her seduction routine suggested that she had to weaken me in advance of picking my brain. I had heard that real Wholeth lords could move entire ships. One thing I knew: if I were to survive intact, I would have to keep her off balance.

"You would prefer then not to be referred to as 'madame'?" I inquired gravely.

"Indeed, the gentleman is more perceptive than I ever did think," quoth she sarcastically.

A silence. I was torn between my actor's role as the meat-headed Palin-Marek, my need to control her, residuals of the attraction toward her, and a natural gallantry; I had always wanted to remain on the good side of women, ham-handed though I was. Also, I was wondering what an enraged psionic woman of unknown power might do to me.

"My dear lady," I said courteously, deciding that Palin-Marek would not necessarily be a complete boor. Control had shifted to me, I thought.

I queried the room, and an armchair folded silently out of the floor.

"Thank you," she said coldly, taking her seat. I raised another chair and settled myself into it. She had given up for the moment. We regarded one another with cautious hostility.

"Madam . . . er, Governor Maja," I said at length, as if nothing had gone before, "my view of the present situation is simply this. I am not in a position to properly negotiate with you and your Lordship's Stead. I lack many tools which were aboard my ship; in particular I lack a method of transmitting coded information and receiving coded instructions from my government. I would therefore renew my request to be permitted to return with my ship to the Polar Cloud."

She regarded me levelly. Evidently she was willing to operate on the plane of rationality—for now.

"You have already agreed to accompany us to the Archipelago," she said. "You pilot may be on her way already if the Stead has given the order. I look forward to your company, Sir Anthony—may I call you that? There are so many things about the Cloud that I do not know."

I groaned, then concealed it with a cough. Lee already on her way? It was what I had wanted, but how could *I* get out of here without the OB? Maja's pale eyes seemed to bore into me like a hot iron. I found the Palin-Marek pose more and more difficult.

She spoke. Her voice took on an unusual cadence which my mind followed with a growing fascination.

"Your presence at the Roil at the same moment as my mission to it concerns me. Should you freely accompany me to the Archipelago and permit me to dispatch you into the Whole proper, then my concerns will be dissipated. If not, if you persist in this desire to remain near the Roil . . . do I have to finish, Sir Anthony?"

"Pray do," I said, "because I have no idea what you are talking about. I have no interest in remaining for any length of time at the Roil; it was an excursion, a way to pass the time while the admiralty made up its mind." What was that all about, I wondered? The Roil—weren't we talking about the Whole and the Polar Cloud?

Was she testing me in some subtle way? Had she or some other Wholeth woman scanned Lee in the OB and discovered her obsession? Did she already know that I was not the Vice-Regent Sir Anthony Palin-Marek?

But my mind was somehow divided into two. The dominant portion held my body lax, staring vacantly into Selah Maja's eyes. *She's at it again*, I thought fleetingly. My mouth opened, and to my inner horror I spoke: "One-way shielding will be on every Polarian fighter within the month. Kitty's mom wants to mount a preemptive strike against the galactic arm," was what I said. My mind gaped at itself. A sort of helpless horror began to seep through me.

"A preemptive strike?" Maja said, sitting suddenly erect. "And who is this Kitty and who is her mom?"

Her surprise seemed to give me an opening, weakening the pall that she had extended over me. With a tremendous effort I brought my mind into integration again.

I found my body bathed in a sweat. My consciousness instinctively inventoried the weapons in my fingers and shoes. I felt an enormous animosity behind Selah Maja's serene facade.

"I refer to the pro-war faction only," I said hoarsely. I tore my eyes away and fixed them in the vicinity of her navel. "Kitty is someone I fornicate with every chance I get," I said, offhand.

I risked a glance at her face. Outrage. She tried to recover, moving to rise. "You will be with us for ten days," she stammered. "I look forward to further conversation. Peace between our peoples is my desire; nothing more." Her fair skin had a waxy sheen now, in stark contrast to its recent scarlet.

"One moment, if you please," I said. My mind continued to repair itself. I kept my eyes deliberately away from hers. My confidence grew. I had her on the run. She had squeezed two bits of information from me, but it meant nothing. *The real Palin-Marek would have been babbling like a baby by now*, I thought.

"You speak of peace," I grated. "Is that why you erased a dozen minds on the black planet? Do go away; desireable though you are, you disgust me. And take that sexy body with you."

It might be possible to push too hard, I thought then, too late.

"And one more thing," I said. "Hypnotic coercion is not appreciated by the government of the Polar Cloud, even from one as . . ." I considered, and then thought, why not? ". . . even from one as promiscuous as you."

She flushed so deep a crimson that I feared for her heart.

"You pompous prig," she shouted at me. "Do you not realize your position here? We will use you until we are done, and then throw you out like the infidel that you are."

"I suspected as much," I said, needling. "The Whole does not want an alliance; it wants conversion."

"Yes," she shouted, on her feet now. "Yes! We will face the Onnish threat together, in humble obedience to the luminous and omniscient Whole!"

For a moment she faced me, her lower lip trembling. Then, realizing that she could not continue, she ran stumbling to the door. She turned and regarded me with cold fury. I say an unnatural glimmer in her pale blue eyes.

"You have come closer to death today than you can possibly know," she said, hissing. "I could have made it easy for you, you inflated idiot."

In a flash of insanity, I saw myself coupled with her on yon airbed. It wasn't mental probing from her, this time; it was my own nature reasserting itself. I drove the image out of my mind, but perversely it came back to me in words calculated to goad beyond endurance.

"Would you care to remain here for the night?" I asked.

She gave me a look that was so tangible that I

swore that I could feel it physically, like the hot breath of a carnivorous beast. Fear passed through me, as if it hadn't been there already.

I dominated her, I exulted, and fear fled. I was Anthony Palin-Marek, ravisher of women and men. If seduction had been her plan, then . . .

In a single long stride I was across the room. She barely had time to show surprise. With a convulsive movement I grabbed the insubstantial fabric at its shoulder and ripped it away. It shredded down the front of her body as she twisted, whirling toward the door.

"You wanted me to desire you," I growled. "And now I . . ."

Agony shot through me in a roar of sound so loud that I heard it with my bones. I screamed and clutched at my ears. But the sound was not abated; it was not there. It was all around. It was inside. I sank to my knees, mouth opening in a soundless scream.

Clutching her ruined clothes, she almost fell against the door as it sensed her and sank into the floor. Her eyes erupted in tears, and she hissed at me: "You are a cesspool. Inside your mind, I see . . ." She stopped suddenly, drawing back as if I had touched her. "You are in fact . . . *Who are you?*" She swayed, not able to take any more. She sdtaggered out into the corridor, bent forward blindly as if holding in her intestines. She swayed again, half in and half out of the door.

I felt the roaring pass and at the same moment thought: my G-d, the cat got out. She knows I'm not you-know-who; it's death for me now, without any interspatial interlude to the Outer Archipelago. Through a haze of pain, I saw her twisting in on herself before me. I closed my mouth and opened it again, drawing in a huge gasp of air, at the same time knowing that action was called for and praying for the power to perform it.

Maja reeled fully into the corridor and groped forward, seeming to be blind, finding her way by touch and instinct. Dizzily, I jerked on my knees through the doorway just as it shot upward behind me like an inverse guillotine. I felt it scrape my shoes as I tried to plaster against the wall, to keep out of her sight.

But she was not looking toward me. She was looking at nothing. She staggered forward, bent over like an old woman, moving down the curved corridor, shamed and opened and naked.

I huddled in the doorway until she was out of sight. I wondered what she had done to me. My body ached as if I been forced to run thirty miles with someone always behind me, jabbing with a forked stick. My brain was dazed; I knew that she had twisted me, first subtly and then, as her plan backfired, savagely, in a sort of mad terror.

I wondered then if she could have killed me, merely with the power of her mind.

Although it was probably for only a few minutes, I pressed against that wall for what seemed to me a long time, allowing my body and brain to recover as best they could. I knew that I must move, knew that what I had done was about to bear fruit in some unpleasant way, knew that if I had a prayer of seeing Lee again, of seeing the Cloud and tasting open air, I would have to rouse myself and act. And I hated to act; I preferred the serenity of letting things happen and taking no responsibility, as had always been my way.

I thought of Kitty; I thought of Lee. At last I reached upward, clawing my way up the locked door. I stood there for a moment until the dizziness passed.

It may be the only chance I would have, I

thought. If I could reach Lee before they sent her away, then perhaps . . .

It was a forlorn hope, but it was all I had. Unless I escaped, one way or the other, I was dead.

I staggered forward.

Chapter 13

Reaching the ringjack bay was so absurdly easy that I wonder at it even today. Were they so unused to warfare that they had no scanners about the ship able to spot unknown personnel? Had they counted me as an accepted face when I first came aboard, and their computers now stupidly continued it?

What I did, was to stride out of the apparently restricted residential area into a crowded corridor. Those I passed looked curiously at me, but seemed afraid to raise any challenge. If I was there, I was supposed to be there. I wondered what kind of life they lived on their home worlds. If anyone raised any questions, did a Wholeth paranormal erase his mind? Probably something like that.

The first little groundcar I saw parked, I climbed in and said, "Fighter bay, please, where the Polarian ambassador's ship docked, and Selah Maja's golden one." Obediently the car raced away, and onward I sped through the ship, wondering what Maja was doing. Revealing all to Lamonte? Not likely, not what I had called her and done to her. But telling him I wasn't Palin-Marek—my life hung on how long it would take her to pull herself together and do that.

At length the little car rounded a corner and zipped right into the middle of the fighter bay, and there was the gigantic plasteel wall covered with shipjacks, a few gaping open, most sealed. A squad of soldiery was just breaking rank, having lined up for some reason, but I was not looking at them as I leaped out of the car. I was looking for the OB's hatch.

It wasn't there.

I ran toward where it had been, oblivious of the soldiers around me, trying not to believe my eyes. There was the ring through which I had dropped through only a few hours ago, sealed now with an inverted saucer of white plasteel. Not far another jack yawned at floor level, probably the golden ship.

And it was the only opening in that part of the bay; there could be no doubt, Lee had gone. I was on my own.

"Hey!" I heard behind me. The voice was familiar; I whirled on my heel, and Restor Kalil, Sub-Governor of the Outer Archipelago, was shouldering his way through his soldiers. "What are you doing here?" he demanded. Then he recollected himself; I was, after all, the ambassador of the Cloud, and perhaps Lamonte or Maja were right behind.

"I had certain last-minute instructions for my pilot," I said feebly. I remembered the sonic device in my shoe and turned it on full blast, an inaudible tone of relaxation and peace. I wanted Kalil to be calm and to avoid excitement.

"Well, she's gone; we saw her off not a minute ago," he said. Then his heavy face deepened. "But why was I not informed of your coming?"

"Beats me," I said honestly. Then, as if taking a grip upon myself and my image as a Polarian representative, I drew myself up with a visible effort.

"One moment, my dear Sub-Governor," I said, an audible tremor in my voice. I toed the sonic device frantically. "I urge you to consider both my diplomatic mission, and the fact that I face you now on the direct instructions of your own superior." I almost added the words "Selah Maja," but something rang in my mind and I left it out. "I was told that you would be here, and that you would monitor my interaction with my pilot in the interests of . . ." I smiled patronizingly, ". . . intelligence."

There was no change in the vacantly suspicious face of Kalil. But around him, the soldiers' expressions were softening as the soothing sub-audible sound from the shoe had partial effect.

Kalil raised his wrist, exposing his wristcom. "I know nothing of this; I will check it with the Stead," he growled. "You stay right there, Mr. Ambassador. My boys here will shoot if you try anything funny." Undiplomatic words, but Kalil was a line soldier, and diplomats to him were a pestilence upon the universe. I never found out why the Wholeth Lord had chosen him as Sub-Governor; she owed him something, but I never knew what.

The "boys" were looking less and less alert. Kalil shot a glance of irritation at them and shouted, "Snap to!" They jerked, and I was afraid that they would blast me into atoms purely by reflex.

They did not.

After a second during which I realized that I was still alive, I again raised my voice in the direction of Kalil.

"Bear with me a moment, if you please," I said, sounding as confident as a girl on her first date. "I assure you that if you do not step aside and listen to what I have to say, that things will become very difficult with your superior who, as I have already said, instructed me to find you. Which I have already done, as you can see. Now it is your turn to hear the orders which we did not dare to broadcast over shipcom or indeed by any mode that could conceivably be intercepted." I was conscious as I babbled of a drop of perspiration heading down my cheek. Daintily I dabbed at it to the amusement of the soldiers, who again were entering a period of advanced relaxation.

Intelligence struggled against insurmountable odds on Kalil's face.

"Orders, you say," he said finally.

"Aye. Orders," I said. A plan was beginning to form in my mind, a plan that would leave me dead, stunned, or free. "In any event, your soldiers have me at your mercy, for as you can see I carry no weapons."

"Yes, that is true," Kalil said, confusion uppermost in his mind.

I waited impatiently. At length, Kalil's puffy face settled into the peace of decision, and for Kalil a decision, once made, was carved in granite for all time.

"Over here," he said, stepping away from the soldiers and away from the ringjack wall. I stayed where I was and, in fact, took a sidelong step toward the nearest open shipjack; he was forced to follow. "No tricks," he said, balling his fists.

I sighed. I beckoned to him while looking apprehensively at the soldiers, who appeared at peace with the universe.

Finally I looked up, into Kalil's bloodshot eyes. I considered a moment, and then lightly touched Kalil's arm.

"My friend . . ." I began.

Kalil brushed the arm aside. "Forget that," he said angrily. "Get on with it."

At the movement the soldiers took a renewed interest, but relaxed again when nothing further happened.

So much for buttering him up, I thought. My subsonics were having no effect on him again, except perhaps to make him more irritable. Luckily I had already come up with something which I hoped would sound plausible in the face of Kalil's stolid lack of imagination.

"As you know," I said in a conspiratorial undertone, "there is some tension between your honored Stead and your revered superior Selah Maja."

"Aye," Kalil said harshly. "I would rule the Outer Archipelago myself if Maja had not wormed in. The Stead himself . . . but this is none of your affair!"

I nearly choked. My plan took a complete flip-flop. I had intended to use Maja as my authority against the Stead, but evidently I had underestimated the complexity of Wholeth politics. The male-female tension among them was operating. I could not know the depth of emotion in a typical Wholeth man such as Kalil. He had been in forced proximity with the highly desireable Selah Maja for many weeks, and never once could he contemplate touching her. She had treated him, no doubt, as a mere pilot, a mere servant, a mere *man*. She had also concealed the essence of the golden ship from him. He was in a constant agony of self-induced thought-suppression, except when he was certain that no paranormal mind could observe him; no wonder, at such times, he raved inside.

"Exactly the point," I said enthusiastically. "You should have been Governor already. The Stead himself introduced me to some of the court machinations of this woman Maja, or I would never have seen it. She is a smooth one, is she not?"

"Is she ever," Kalil said fervently. He towered over me, a head taller and twice as wide. I gulped.

"Anyway, it is fortunate for both you and me that the Stead outranks her and has perceived the injustice of her appointment here. But did you know," I

said, my voice dropping still further, "that the Stead
has discovered that her appointment emanates not
from the Lord herself, as she led you to believe, but
from some court underling very probably bribed?
And that she was appointed without the Lord's permission at all?"

Kalil's eyes widened. Hope thrust itself onto his
bovine countenance.

"The Stead is greatly annoyed, as you can imagine," I proceeded. "But you know the closeness of
communication which he enjoys with the Wholeth
Lord. Since she is omniscient, she of course knew
of the intrigue, but did not consider it of sufficient
importance for immediate rectification, given her
many other divine obligations, if I may express
myself in this way."

"It is nothing," Kalil waved it away abstractedly.
"How could you know our words for the resplendent
majesty of the Lord of the Whole?"

*A real Polarian ambassador would have been well-
schooled in such things*, I thought, but did not say
so.

"Yes," I said. "Anyway, the Stead Lamonte has
even today engaged in revelatory communication
with the Lord Herself, which is the rare and gener-
ous privilege of all of the Lord's Steads, as again you
well know."

Actually Kalil had not known, but he knew it now.
His eyes shone with the profound reverence that he
felt. My estimation of him plummeted even further.

"In his revelation today, the Stead emphasized the
vital importance of the Outer Archipelago governorship and the injustice of your position. The Lord was
incensed, and she gave the Stead leave to correct
the situation. Even now he is confronting the scheming Maja with the Lord's unquestionable command:
step down from the falsely-acquired governorship
and allow Restor Kalil to assume his rightful place!"

Kalil's eyes glowed. This was more than he had hoped for, come more quickly than he had ever dreamed.

The shoes sang softly. The soldiers sagged. But suspicion still lurked in the muddy depths of the Sub-Governor's mind.

"This does not explain why I had no instructions about your coming here!" he said with sudden severity.

I sighed again, heavily. The hard part was still to come. I looked around ostentatiously, and took a step closer to the open mouth of the golden ship. A ripple stirred the group, and I felt my stomach tighten. Then an instant of dizziness hit me, and I quailed. I had felt it many times before, but hadn't expected it now, so soon.

The flagship had entered interspace.

"Interspace!" I yelled. The soldiers' eyes leaped awake, and I could have bitten my tongue off. Lamonte had not wasted a moment; after sending my pilot off, we were already on our way to the Outer Archipelago.

Panic seized hold of me, and I almost collapsed at Kalil's feet. Interspace had never occurred to me. Now I was well and truly lost and . . . Wait a minute. Wait a minute! Is this providence after all?

"Let me put it this way, my friend," I said soothingly, trying to lure him closer to the golden ship, choking on the word "friend." "Let us assume for a moment that the Lord is annoyed by the Governor's . . . I should say now ex-Governor's . . ." Kalil grunted. ". . . outrageous conduct toward myself as a bona fide representative of a foreign power. She did something to me with her mind; I won't go into it now, but it was not by the command of the Lord." This hit him where he lived; I'd have bet the Roil itself that every man in the Wholeth Empire felt the same way about the lords stirring around in their minds, though they daren't say it. To live like that? Not me. "But the Stead strongly suspects that Maja's traitorous spies are scattered even among his own crew, perhaps among these soldiers here." Kalil shot the squad, which was yawning again, a baleful glance. "What would you do in such a case, my friend, knowing that the only people aboard that you could fully trust were myself, an unbiased emissary, and you, the only individual aside from the Stead himself of unquestioned loyalty to the Wholeth Lord?"

"Well. . . ." Kalil began, again in confusion.

"You could not use electronic communication," I ran on, giving me as little meditative time as possible, "for fear of interception by Maja's cohorts. What would you do then were you the Stead? I'll tell you what you'd do," I said hastily as Kalil seemed about to speak. "You would send me, the foreigner, the only man you could trust besides yourself, to Restor Kalil with the orders for resolving the ambassadorial mess that Maja has caused, while as Stead you personally brought Maja to task for her betrayal, face-to-face. That way, should Maja somehow attempt to thwart the will of the Lord, it would be too late, for you as the new Governor would already have carried out that will to its final conclusion!"

Kalil frowned heavily as he tried to cope with my barrage of muddled ideation. I risked a glance behind me; we were directly in front of the opening to Maja's ship.

"Shake my hand," I said suddenly to Kalil. Automatically he reached out his right hand and I seized it, and then I whipped my left hand around his right wrist and, pivoting, I yanked him with all my strength toward the open mouth of the waiting ship. And then, as he barrelled past me off balance, I activated the stunner crystal in the little finger of my right hand and shot him.

Pain exploded up my arm. I turned, left arm pointing rigidly, index finger out, and activated a blaster crystal. Fire roared out of my finger, catching some of the poor devils just as they were becoming aware, struggling out of their sonic sleep, that something abnormal was going on. The force of the blast threw me backwards, and my head collided ringingly with the top edge of the open hatch. I fell to my knees and there was Restor Kalil, half in and half out of the golden ship. Whimpering, blood from my fingers streaking the floor, I wrapped my arms around his dead weight and pulled him backward. A stunner bolt thudded over us, and then his body jerked convulsively as another one hit him. I dropped down further, using him as a shield as much as I could, and dragged.

"Put down that blaster, you fool!" I heard someone shout. Yes, put it down, I yelled in my mind. A blaster can wreak ghastly havoc anywhere, and pointing it toward the skin of a ship is against everything a space soldier is taught. If they ruptured the hull, we would all die in ghastly decompression, the vacuum of space turning our bodies inside out. I blessed their fear, and another stunner bolt hit Kalil. He and I were almost inside.

Alarms sliced the air in the shipbay. But the golden ship was not security shielded or, if it was, it was coded to allow Restor Kalil and guest to pass through. More footsteps sounded in the bay, dozens of them.

The golden ship's gravitational orientation was the same as the flagship; I blessed that even as I found Kalil's blaster and yanked it from the holster. In a single motion I raised it and fired at the battleship's portion of the shipjack that connected the two vessels. A pencil-thin stream of terrible energy poured into the doorway. Microcircuits fused and failed. The gravitational seal was disrupted.

The ship trembled. A gap appeared into which air rushed with a scream. Both ships reacted instantly with clanging seals that covered the openings, closing off the air loss.

A wave of dizziness poured over me. I embraced it, welcomed it. For it meant that the golden ship had left the battleship and had fallen out of interspace.

Chapter 14

From what transpired later, this is what Maja must have been doing while I was flummoxing Restor Kalil:

In her cabin, she still felt dirty. She let a blast of warm air pour over her and blow away mists and sonics of the shower. She saw in a wall mirror that the tear streaks were gone. Inside, numbness; the encounter with me had drained something out of her, leaving her emptier than she had ever been. Thank heaven, she thought, that the Little Lord had not been there to see what had happened. In her amateur's attempt at weakening me, she had discovered a barbarian, and had not been prepared. She had triggered something atavistic while stumbling around in my mind. Having spent most of her life at the largely female court of the Wholeth Lord, she had never seen the dark side of men, for only the Lord Herself indulged, preferring her ladies to remain uncompromised. No man near Maja had dared, and when younger she had felt deprived. As the years had gone by, she had grown to prefer it that way.

It was what was in his mind as he tore at me, she thought, sickened.

But she was soon to learn more about man.

The shredded, filmy garment had already been consigned to a chute. Now she eased into a costly tunic with embroidery around the hem. Dinner wear. Halfway into the gown she saw that her hands were trembling. She stood a moment, taking control. Then she tried again, but now one foot was standing on the hem. She gasped, the embryo of a sob.

Finally she was able to squirm into the tunic and, with gritty effort, to close the clasp that tightened the cleavage between her breasts, without which the slick-fabricked gown would slide off. That done, she stepped over to one of the pastel wall panels and called up something alcoholic, dry and smooth. Her hand, she noticed, was almost steady.

He is not Palin-Marek, she thought over and over. But it did not occur to her to reveal me to Lamonte, not yet. She was an independent agent of the Lord, and she needed guidance. From the Archipelago, she could tachholo the Lord Herself. It would satisfy her, she decided, to delude Lamonte. Let Her Lordship then know of his gullibility.

She was just easing into a chair when her door abruptly opened. Stiffening, she found herself looking at the saturnine features of he whom she would deceive, the Stead himself, Antil Lamonte. He took one step inside, and the force of his long, steel-edged body struck her, and not in a pleasant way.

He was arrayed rather more formally than she, his tunic embroidered liberally, a belt of many-faceted woven gemstones tight around the waist. In his face she beheld self-confidence, arrogance, and conceit. For a moment she hated him, when before she had merely dismissed his maleness out of mind; already she had him categorized with me, you see.

"Ah, you are in," he said with a voice like ice. "May I join you?" Irony.

"You already have," she said, reaching for indifference, crossing her legs and leaning back. "The ship is yours."

"Yes," said he, striding languidly toward her and taking a seat just in front of her, a little to the right. He put a powerful hand on her knee, and she started despite herself. His cold eyes probed into hers, dominating.

"Something to drink?" she quavered, and then bit her lip in frustration. The emotional wreckage of the past half hour had ruined her equilibrium.

"No," he said shortly. "I want to tell you what our attitude is to be at the coming meal with that Polarian dandy Palin-Marek. And then, I want you."

The two thoughts were placed together, side by side, with no stress one upon the other. Maja's face drained as the meaning sank in. She became acutely conscious of her body, straining at the tunic, no weapons inside the fabric or out.

Lamonte proceeded as if the matter were routine.

"The Vice-Regent will be . . . annoyed, let us say, by his enforced confinement. He may complain publicly, despite the lack of propriety. We will ignore it." His fingers moved, rippling on her knee. She shuddered. He didn't appear to notice.

"What about Kalil?" she managed to say, trying to prolong the discussion. I am going to kill Lamonte this day, she thought; what will the Lord do when she finds I have scrambled like an egg, the brain of this favorite of hers?

His fingers paused and grew rigid.

"You will have to control him," he almost hissed. "I will not be exposed to that . . ." Then he contained himself, and his fingers began again. "Send him on an errand,' his voice came, more smoothly. "Get him out; he's not fit for this kind of thing."

Maja tried to bring some heat into her voice.

"It seems that we go too far by needling this Polarian." *Sangre*, she thought. A name that means blood. "We risk the Lord's wrath by interfering needlessly in the flow of diplomacy."

No doubt, she thought, Lamonte was taking her rising color, as she remembered me, for something else.

His hand moved slightly forward, above the knee.

"I," he said frigidly, "am the lord here. My word is absolute. I am Stead!"

Stead! *Yes*, she thought, terror rising now. Her own status was anomalous; the Little Lord was not available, and in that absence Maja was no more than Prelate of the Outer Archipelago, while this man was serving inStead of the Lord herself. But he had blasphemed, using the word "lord" to refer to a man.

If she took no action, the Lord would most likely not know or, knowing, care what he did to her, as long as she lived to help the Little Lord. But if she acted and killed, the potential consequences were . . .

His hand slid down and insinuated itself between her crossed legs, still close to the knees.

With a single movement she tossed down the drink in her hand as if it were water, and dropped the glass onto the floor, where it bounced once on the hard nap and then rolled aside. She tried to smile, and it must have been a ghastly thing. She uncrossed her legs, dislodging his hand, and leaned forward, taking the hand into hers.

"Time is short," she said, the quaver almost gone. "Dinner is upon us . . ."

His laugh was short and sharp. He flung her hands aside and took hold of both shoulders, eyes probing into hers so that she felt his quick breath on her cheeks.

"My lovely Maja," he said, his voice almost sneering. "You do not seem to grasp the situation. I don't know what you did to offend the Lord, to cause you to be sent out here, but here on the fringes of the empire, in this battle fleet, *I am lord.* You will obey *me.* The choice is . . ."

Again the blasphemy. She reached out her mind.

For an instant she thought that her technique was somehow gone, blasted away by her encounter with "Palin-Marek." In her mindsend to him she was carrying queasiness, even nausea. She was intending for him to see her as ugly, to feel a roughness in her skin, and to make her scent unpleasant to his brain.

But the message seemed to shiver past him, as if glancing off some closed-off opacity and flying out into the endless starlit night.

And the smile on his angular face broadened toward triumph. She felt his fingers moving now on her shoulders, saw his eyes bore into hers.

"You see," he hissed softly, "I have learned to hide from the minds of you lordly women. You cannot penetrate me; but I can, and will, penetrate you." He dragged her forward and kissed her then, and his lips were hard and cruel, and ground into her like stone.

He thought she had been sent here as punishment! Surely he must have wondered at the Lord's insistence that he meet her golden ship, and give it every assistance, at the Roil. But of the truth of her mission, he could not know; no one must know, save herself, the Little Lord, and the Lordship Herself. It was imperative that no one know, for if even the possibility that males could be bred to the Power were to emerge and inflame the men of the Whole . . .

The kiss meant nothing to her, and she brought her mind's probing fingers back again and touched the shield around his lusterless mind.

In an instant she saw that it could be broached. She was easily strong enough. A true lord would not have noticed the attempt at shielding at all; she, relatively weak in these matters as "Palin-Marek" had so recently shown, even she could ram through this self-constructed shield. The effort would be great for her, however, and she knew with that once through, the forward thrust that broke the shield would damage him before she could draw it back. How badly, she could not guess. It might kill him; and without the permission, expressed or implied, of the Little Lord or the Lordship herself, it would be likely death for her to kill a Lord-appointed Stead.

He drew back from the kiss, eyes as hard as ever. His breath was coming more quickly. He drew his right hand down from her shoulder, almost caressing across the top of her breast, until he had reached the clasp.

He clicked it open, and the tunic sagged.

And then the alarm went off.

Lamonte cursed and, turning quickly, a shaken Selah Maja forgotten for the moment, he called to the intercom for an explanation.

An officer appeared as if by magic in a holographic image in the center of the cabin. He evidently caught sight of Maja behind the Stead clutching frantically at her frictionless robe; the officer turned scarlet and looked hurriedly away.

"Obeisance to the Stead," the officer said, then: "The Polarian Ambassador has escaped in Governor Maja's golden ship, sir."

"What!" Lamonte screamed. As if propelled by a spring, he leaped off his chair and through the image to the door and then, as an afterthought, for the briefest instant faced Maja, who already had the tunic closed again, her hands shaking wildly.

"Later," he said simply, savagely. And then he was gone.

And Maja looked at her shaking hands. But this time, her terror was caused in no way by the Stead Lamonte. The ship, gone? Oh no, G-d no!

Defying Lamonte was possible death. But if she did not get the four-seater back, and the one who was in it . . .

"My Lord, what shall I do?" she wailed. No answer, no answer, no answer. Nothing but echoes in her mind.

Chapter 15

Reaction set in. While Maja was palpitating in her silent cabin, I was undulating too, shaking like a leaf, my arms trembling so badly that I couldn't trust myself with the blaster and had to holster it. I leaned against a bulkhead, eyes streaming tears, legs as solid as pillars of water. The pain in my belly was there again. My right foot had apparently caught a piece of a stunner bolt; it felt as if I had hit it with a hammer. My two ruined fingers throbbed and bled.

I couldn't believe what I had done. My first thought when the Cloud had drafted me had been how to get out, and I had spent three years of training working at it. Any other time I could have wangled it, but the Cloud was in such a fever of military preparation that flatfooted anemic asthmatics were being called up and no one was being released. Perhaps I had been too cautious; I had wanted nothing too drastic, nothing to harm my civilian career. I was drunk a lot of the time too, and that had impeded a lot of the scheming.

And in the light of that, I had just taken on a Wholeth fleet? If it had been anything but my neck—the honor of the Cloud, for example—I would have stayed in the sealed cabin and treated Maja like a nun.

The tremors subsided, and I found myself looking at the recumbent figure of Restor Kalil with distaste. I had no desire to keep company with the Sub-Governor, a one dimensional character of pronounced intellectual insufficiency. On the other hand I needed him, and now I went over the powerful body and discovered few ill effects from the stunner bombardment.

I knew that the chance was vanishingly small that Lamonte could find the golden ship; we had been in interspace, and no matter how fast he had fallen out after me, I was half a light year away at least, floating in a space so vast that it was the nearest thing to intergalactic. But I had to revive the Sub-Governor, I thought, when I would have preferred respite.

For I knew not the first thing about the inner workings of a Wholeth starship. I dared not probe its computer without the proper protocols, knowing that if I did so, I would likely end up speeding involuntarily toward the nearest Wholeth military base.

I shook Kalil violently. He turned over and snored. I slapped the Sub-Governor across the face, three times. Kalil coughed and muttered and did not wake up.

I shook my own head. With all that had happened to me, I seemed no closer to resolving this incredible mess than I had when I had originally awakened in my fightership with Lee. Sometimes the whole thing seemed like a juvenile grail quest, led by a fanatical woman whose every pore captivated me. That was the bottom line, of course, that I believed myself a part of Celia D'Ame now, and no matter how fantastic her intentions, I was prepared to follow her into the heart of a blue-white sun if I had to. Suicidal? Perhaps. Remember that I was twenty-three.

Kalil snored dreamily. Sighing, I placed one foot

on Kalil's mouth and manipulated a control with my little toe. A blast of the most terrible odor Polarian scientists could devise roared up Kalil's nostrils and back out into the air. I reeled away, coughing and retching. Kalil sat up with a roar of olfactory agony.

Really a peculiar weapon with which to equip a fighter pilot, I thought. I suppose they had done deep psychological studies on Wholeth hang-ups. But how many pilots are taken alive?

When the air cleared Kalil was still sitting on the deck, eyes streaming tears, shoulders heaving with convulsive coughing. I had the control chair swivelled away from the starship's screens, and was sitting in it with a blaster pointed loosely at the Sub-Governor. Thoughtfully I twisted the damper control on the weapon, wincing as I jarred the oozing index finger; no point in blowing the ship into splinters.

"Make yourself a chair," I said hoarsely. I had held my breath, but some of the scent had reached me nonetheless.

Kalil cried silent tears.

"Makes no difference to me," I observed, leaning back. I could feel the tremors beginning again in muscles all over my body. Kalil was big. He radiated ignorant danger, like a bull.

"I'll kill you," Kalil said. His voice was an echo of the power that it had normally had. It shook me nonetheless. The thought it expressed brought my teeth to the edges.

"Now is that nice?" I inquired in a croak. "What's to stop me from putting a blaster bolt through your fat body besides your eager and willing attitude of cooperation?"

"No cooperation from me, damn your pagan hide." Kalil wiped his eyes feebly, hands shaking.

"Well, now, I disagree," I said, watching him. "But first get your backside into a side chair."

Kalil cursed and struggled to his feet. Under the muzzle of a suddenly rigid blaster he staggered to a side wall and slammed his hand against a small square pastel panel. A chair folded up out of the floor. Kalil fell into it, hands groping for his eyes again.

"Now before we begin,' I said quietly. "I want our respective positions made as vividly clear as possible in your flea-sized brain." The trembling was getting better. I had always savored the upper hand, and I had it here. Trickery had always been more my style, but I think, now that I look back on it, that I could have come to enjoy brute force. I had never figured that I had any, is all.

Kalil cursed some more. His eyes kept filling up on him, and he gouged at them ineffectually with his fists.

"First of all, I have the blaster," I said relentlessly, confidence growing. "You have nothing except your arms and legs."

Kalil shook his head, drops of tears and sweat flying in all directions.

"Second of all I will blast you if you make the slightest motion I don't like. Don't ever doubt it, my friend. I've never hesitated before." That was true too, in a way; I'd never been in a position to point a blaster at anyone at all, except that hapless deserter a few years before.

"Who the hell *are* you," Kalil grated, peering at me through flaming red eyes.

I laughed. "Sir Anthony Palin-Marek to you, my friend. Do you doubt it?" I stiff-armed the blaster, pointing it at Kalil's head. I would make the Sub-Governor believe that "Palin-Marek" was desperate, maybe slightly mad. "Tell me, who am I? WHO AM I?"

The yell rang in Kalil's ears and his lower lip

curled downward. I made the blaster as still as a corpse's heart. Realism struggled in the old soldier.

"Palin-Marek!" he gasped at last.

"Very good!" I said, the blaster not even quivering—even I was impressed. "Now I'm going to tell you what you're going to do for me. And then you're going to do it. And if you hesitate for even a second, I'll press this firing stud and you'll be hurting. Or maybe dead. And I don't care one way or another."

Yes, I could get into this, I thought. It was hard to say how deeply my threats were sinking in, though. I did not trust Kalil for an instant. Of all the things I had figured out about him, it was the religious fanaticism that I distrusted the most. But I had to forge ahead. I needed Restor Kalil.

"Now, I know that you know exactly how to operate this vessel. You also know about the private screens and other security devices, the hidden weapons, the holographic transmitters and all the rest. I've thought about putting this blaster to your head and ordering you to fly us to the black planet, but I don't believe that I could trust you to get me there. You'd fly us to the Archipelago, you'd trigger some screen or weapon against me, but I don't believe that I would wind up at the black planet even if it meant your death. Maybe not at first, but you would bring yourself to it. Maybe I'd relax for a moment, who knows?"

Kalil watched me, a baleful hatred in his eyes.

"What difference does it make to me?" the big man asked finally, his voice breaking into pieces. Maudlin? Restor Kalil? "Whoever you are, I'll be court-martialled the moment I reach a Wholeth world. And then shot. You've seen to that. Palin-Marek!" The bitterness in his voice was something I could touch. But I was feeling cocky now, and the old devils were playing in my head.

"Maybe not," I said happily. "In any event we're

going now to the black planet; there you can stay if you wish. There is always something on any planet for a good military man.

"Or you can go back. I assume all of this is being recorded. You'll have no end of extenuating circumstances on your side." I waved the blaster.

Some of the despair filtered out of Kalil's bloodshot eyes. I gave him a moment to dredge up a little hope.

"And then again maybe you'll take me," I said softly, grinning.

Kalil shot a glance of analytical fury at me. I smiled, and a chill settled over the room. *I* caused the chill. This guy was afraid of me!

"The first thing I want from you," I said, "is access to the technical data banks. Now that's simple enough, isn't it, my friend?" The blaster sat loosely on my knee, pointed in his general direction.

Kalil said nothing. His eyes flickered around him. A mulish craftiness rippled over his face and was gone again.

I let the silence lengthen, but not too long.

"Remember what I said, my friend?" I said at last, in a voice as soft as down. "About hesitation?"

The dampened blaster spat. It was not apparent that I had aimed at all. Kalil's body jerked. In openmouthed surprise, Kalil looked at the cauterized hole where the center of his left hand had been.

Then the pain hit him and Kalil screamed. I leaped over to him and wound my right hand in the thick blond hair. I knew he was helpless now. I forced the contorted face up to the light, and thrust the blaster against the bridge of the nose.

"Access to the data banks," I breathed. "Just that one thing right now. You can fight . . . some other time."

In agony, Kalil pointed at the control panel, good arm shaking like a leaf in the wind.

"There, is it?" I hissed. I dragged the sub-Governor by the hair to the controls. "So do it, and then we'll kill your pain."

Whimpering, Kalil slapped at part of the control panel, a blue pastel part. He missed it the first time, then hit. Gasping, crying, he said: "Security screen was keyed to me or Maja. Now off." He gasped with a sound that was like a sob, a long drawn out convulsion of pain. "Priority four five ought ought ought two six," he choked at last. "That's the code that opens it up."

I considered a moment, hand wrapped in oily hair and blaster still bent against the trembling Wholeth nose. Then I flung Kalil away, and the Sub-Governor sprawled across the deck in the direction of the side chair.

"Fine," I said, still with that eerie, cold softness in my voice. I was acting, but the cockiness was bolstering me. I wondered: if you act courageous long enough, would you eventually become it?

"Now use the medical module," I told Kalil. "Remember this blaster and what else it can do."

Kalil clawed upward for a wall panel with eyes looking backwards toward me and seeing only the level, casual weapon.

The medical panel opened. Babbling, Kalil thrust his enholed arm into it. A pain-killer of some kind coursed into him.

"Go ahead," I said, almost kindly. Kalil stared at me through eyes in which hatred struggled through the anaesthetic's haze.

Kalil touched another part of the module. A packet about the size of a softball came forth. He thrust the hand into it; it molded around it like something alive.

"Tissue regeneration," I observed, dead voice cracking with the elation I was feeling. "Now you see, that wasn't so bad. You'll be as good as new in a few days."

"I'll never be as good," Kalil cried groggily.

"Aye," said I. "You'll remember the pain."

I had guessed that that same pain would drive calculation and resistance from the Sub-Governor's mind. Otherwise I would never have let Kalil near the controls.

"Back to the chair," I said, waving the blaster negligently. And then, a clause that surprised me: "I regret your pain," I said.

"You must be a madman," Kalil babbled, "firing a blaster inside a starship. You're lucky you didn't hole it."

I expressed mock surprise.

"Gosh, that's right," I exclaimed. "By golly, I never do think of that!"

Kalil was evidently struck by the stark idiocy of the words. He offered a lurid, disjointed description of my ancestry as he scrabbled drunkenly into the chair. I never took my eyes off of him.

Actually, the blaster fire had been fairly safe, for behind Kalil was the length of the ship, and it would only have taken a bulkhead or two to dissipate the dampened blast. Kalil was wrong; when it came to my skin, I calculated most carefully, all the time.

"Priority four five ought ought ought two six," I said suddenly. "Ship condition." Kalil's head swivelled toward me. In the same moment, I dropped the blaster into my lap and drew Kalil's stunner with a single fluid motion.

"Normal," the ship's computer said.

I lifted the stunner. Kalil raised his good hand in an uncertain gesture of defense. "No," he said, his voice slurred. "Wait." A kind of slow panic came into his eyes.

"Why wait?" I asked conversationally. "With the data banks I can figure out the ship with no help from you. You've waited too long, my friend. The data banks weren't the first thing I wanted. They were the last."

Kalil suddenly flung his good hand outward toward a pale crimson wall panel. The arm froze in mid-air as the stunner bolt hit. He crumbled over the arm of the chair, his head lolling from side to side.

I went over and arranged the Sub-Governor's body more comfortably. Why was I doing that? I thought. The whole interview had been most satisfying, in all kinds of ways. Why, then, did I lift his weight off his arm, and lean his head against the backrest?

I turned my attention to the ship.

It took me five hours of studying before I mastered the ship enough to fly it. During that time I found out how to shackle the Sub-Governor in his chair, and had done so. I had also discovered such amenities as interspatial holography, inertialess and interspatial drive, life-support mechanisms, and gravitational engineering modules—everything a pilot needed to have at hand, to operate a modern-day starship. And I began the repair of my two ruined fingers.

The first thing that I did when I had the golden ship under my will was to leap into interspace and out again at random, the whole process taking no more than a few seconds. The end was that I was now several parsecs away from the original location, making a trace by the Stead's battleship impossible in the remote chance that it somehow blundered near my first original interspatial exit point.

I inventoried the golden ship's facilities. The design, being based upon rigid principles of elementary interspatial mechanics, was not that much divergent from Polarian designs once certain peculiarities were mastered. I spent the bulk of the five hours

learning the precise meanings of the specific short-
hand commands that the ship's computer recognized,
as opposed to normal conversational interchange. In a
crisis, such knowledge could be crucial.

Then at long length I relaxed. I allowed myself
the luxury of a look at the region of space in which
the ship now rested. I turned the holographic projector on for a 360-degree spherical view, so that the
room disappeared and I seemed to float naked in the
eternal vastness of interstellar space.

The scene struck me hard; I had not expected a
reaction like it. Like milk into a sponge, the starfield
sank into me. I felt my ego fade into insignificance
in the penultimate blackness. No nearby sun broke
the irregular symmetry of the millions of bright cold
stars around me, arranged in all the kaleidoscopic
colors of the prism and more. The globular cluster
that was the Cloud hung overhead in an enormous
panorama of individual pinpoints whose identities
were lost only in the blazing center. The dust arm
of the outflung galaxy puffed out below me, opposed
to the cluster by a wide black emptiness—the Gulf—
dotted here and there with rogue stars and weak
and scattered nebulae. Somewhere in the dust of the
galaxy's arm was the Outer Archipelago, which the
ship's microcircuits could have pointed out for me if
I so chose.

But I did not so choose. I sat and gazed at it and
felt a microscopic identity with the wholeness of
it. I sought for and for a brief moment found the
peace of timelessness, the serenity of oneness and
nothingness, the end of my identity in a universe
where consciousness was a freak and asymmetrical
irritation.

When I at last drew a deep breath and turned
away from the screen, I did not know how much
time had passed, and did not particularly care. In

fact it had been only minutes, but I remember them still, hours in my soul.

As I switched off the holographic projector, a moan announced that Kalil was coming around. Time for beddie-bye, I thought, wrenching my mind from infinity.

So I asked the data files to outline the Wholeth procedures for cryogenic stasis. They were so simple that I executed them at once. I unlocked the shackles to the chair, dragged the quivering mountain of loyal Wholeth flesh to a certain spot on the deck, and stepped back.

A thick haze began to rise slowly from the perforated deck around the rotund figure of the Sub-Governor. It crept like a thousand inch-worms, rolling like tiny clouds which the faint circulating air of the golden ship did not in any way disturb.

As it reached halfway up and more, the Sub-Governor's movements began to still. A sort of frigid peace began to descend over the room, especially at home in the tired reaches of my over-extended mind.

The milky haze had almost covered Kalil's ears when the Sub-Governor's eyes opened, startling me out of the reverie. Awareness flooded into Kalil's eyes, lighting them with more intelligence than I had ever expected to see there. They rolled around the cabin, clearly conscious of the cold that was on the brink of rolling over them.

I watched in a sort of horror-stricken fascination. The Sub-Governor's lips trembled, but no sound came out. A horrible fear poured into the eyes, an evident fear of the possibility that they would never see anything again.

My spirits dashed like crystal. Pity, for G-d sake! In Polarian mechanisms the slow onslaught of cryogenic cold is performed out of sight, with a built-in drugging mechanism. The hard visibility of Wholeth body-freezing was unnerving. I did not like the Sub-Governor, but I suddenly realized that I also did not like to see the fear that was haunting the dim sentience there. It was so at variance with my self-image that I tried to shake it off. But it wouldn't come.

With the fog trembling at the edge of their sockets, the eyes suddenly turned upon me, and into them there came so painful a hatred that I winced before it and shrank back into my seat. Like baleful embers the eyes struggled against the insistent cold and held my face to them.

Then the cloud rolled over them, easing them shut with frigid gentility. The fog eased upward and at last covered the broad belly in a grip that was unutterably soft, unquestionably hard.

For an uncounted time the fog rested there, and to my eyes it took on a greater and greater solidity, until it looked like a mass of knobbed and dented clay.

At last, with an audible hum, the mini-mountain sank into the deck, to be covered by a panel which slid silently into place.

I found myself staring at the empty floor, and wondering if I would ever dare to revive Restor Kalil again.

Chapter 16

I knew where Lee would be heading: the black planet, where (I thought) her friend Kel Kellem was piecing together random information on the Roil, as he pined for her. Kel Kellem: not much more than a name to me, and I couldn't bring myself to examine what their relationship had been; every time I tried, a vision of her throaty voice, high sweat-sheened forehead, eyes closed in ecstasy, auburn eyelids quivering, hungry lips gasping, elegant body intertwined with mine, hit me like a knee in the groin. I couldn't bear it. It hurt too much, and it was not jealousy for Kellem, but a consuming memory of her, that ate me alive.

The black planet: the one world in the Polar Cloud whose coordinates, I know for a fact, were imbedded in the memory of the golden cone. What a lucky coincidence, I thought, when the black planet/Celia D'Ame was what I hungered for the most. It never occurred to me, as I ordered the Wholeth ship into interspace, that it was no coincidence at all.

The black planet, Kel Kellem, the Roil, Lee's parents, the Wholeth fleet, Crestor Falon, the golden ship, all were linked like the lines of a mosaic. The

war's outcome would be determined by the obses-
sions of two women, one of the Whole, long dead,
and one of the Cloud, still vitally alive. I and my
lust were mere blobs of grout surrounding the main
players.

I tried to anticipate Lee's thinking as my stolen ship
poured through interspace. The anomaly was not due
for another eight weeks or so; enough time for her to
collect Kellem and whatever new information he'd
doped out. Also, she would think, enough time to
study the OB to the point where she'd be able to take
it into the Roil. Oh, Lee, my mind cried; it might not
be enough. And even if you mastered it, the ship
might not have the power, one-way shield or no.

I want you, Lee; I want to keep you from foolish-
ness and feel you all around me. I would be willing,
with you, to take the OB near, to move closer and
closer to the Roil while the ship extrapolated and
told me if it would survive. But I want to do at least
that before I would be willing to risk you to the
anomaly itself, if it were riskable at all; I want to be
aboard with you so that you would have my experience and speed on your side, Lee. I want you, and
I want to save your life, and if I have to, I will stun
you with one of those crystals in my fingers and take
you away from the deathtrap, away from the maelstrom and back to the Polar Cloud, and scuttle your
dream once and for all. For I will not let you go into
the Roil to probable death; only if survival were
likely, would I let you go in, and go in with you.

Pretty far gone? Yes, indeed I was. A month ago,
it would have been more in character for me to take
the golden ship to Sigma Radidiani (if it knew its
coordinates) and try to bargain for my life with it, to
trade it and whatever secrets it might contain for the
erasure of my alleged hijacking of the OB IV, and
Lee be damned. It was exactly that that Selah Maja
feared, though I did not know it. But I was no longer

the same man; Lee had seen to it, G-d help me, and though I thought about Sigma Rad, thought about it very hard during those long days to the black planet, my hunger for Lee consumed all things. Anyway, I thought, after we diddled with the Roil, *then* I'll take the golden ship to Sigma Rad and see what I could do. I could have it both ways. What a young idiot I was!

As for the Wholeth fleet, I remember thinking, it would have no reason for returning to the Roil, and there would be no chance that it would be waiting for us when we came. They might be slavering for their golden ship, but they'd have had no idea where I would take it. You must remember that at that time, I knew nothing of Selah Maja's plans vis-a-vis the Roil. No one did, save herself, the Wholeth Lord, and the Little Lord (about whom later).

And that golden ship! As Lee was no doubt studying the OB while in interspace, I was studying the golden ship, and as I did so I became more and more impressed, and more and more puzzled. The OB IV was the most advanced fighter-sized ship of the Polar Cloud, and this ship seemed to have all of its features and more. It had one-way shielding, for example; had the Whole been able to implement so quickly the secret stolen by Maja during her raid on the Institute, or had they had it all along? If they'd had it all along, as seemed likely given the time factor, then what had been the point of the raid?

The ship had all the familiar weaponry, and appeared, too, to house a kind of miniature grav cannon set-up; that shook me, for grav cannon had been the province of the largest ships hitherto; if fighters had them, then the advantages of one-way shielding were erased. For, as I indicated earlier, shielding was effective against everything except the violent twist in space-time that grav cannon caused.

For a moment patriotism seized me, and I wavered;

perhaps I should go to Sigma Rad after all, for this was important. But then selfishness kicked patriotism in the backside. I could always reach Sigma Rad via tachyonic holography from the black planet, and that would be enough.

And I also found, during my studies of the golden ship, that there were layers of operation inaccessible to me; apparently I didn't have the proper passwords; the ones Kalil had so graciously provided were not complete. But, comparing the OB and this ship, I could not imagine what those layers housed, for I had as much control of this ship with Kalil's codes as I had had of the OB. *Whatever the hidden layers were, they could hold no danger for me*, I thought. I contemplated reviving Kalil for another quiz, but it was far too risky.

And so on I sped, my thoughts filled with reunion scenarios. Lee would be delirious with joy that I had escaped the Whole, and vastly impressed that I had done it so quickly, and in one of their own ships yet. It would be obvious that I would be far more valuable to her than Kellem. I'd dump the golden ship and we'd honeymoon back to the Roil; no point in taking Kellem; the thought was insupportable. He wouldn't fit in the OB anyway. No, I thought smugly, the conjugal scene flashing again; she loved me as I did her; we were one. Kellem would be an ancient memory.

I dreamed the light years away, and as I did so, Selah Maja told the Stead a terrible secret, and they turned their fleet and headed for Sigma Radidiani. And Lamonte took her, brutally. If I save the golden ship, he told her, then Her Lordship's gratitude will know no bounds; and if I don't, then the blame for its loss will be on you and Kalil, and She won't care what I've done to you. Perhaps Maja should have killed him then; but she needed his fleet, she thought, and had no way of asserting control over it other than through him.

The eighteenth day: the black planet. The golden ship flared out of interspace and there was the soft puffy globe of the Polar Cloud, a dandelion gone to seed, one of its stars a brilliant thing that dazzled the eyes: the black planet's sun. The tachyonic channels came alive. Signals from near space and from all over the Polar Cloud poured into the little ship, and shipcom scanned and correlated and reported and scanned again. I had told it to look for the OB's ID above all, and it found it. Lee had landed already, but not long ago; I ordered the golden ship in, my heart beating faster, and tried to reach her via tachholo, but she had left the ship. The OB had recorded my message automatically, as all ships recorded every signal that reached them, remembering as much as the gigantic amorphous molecular storage capacity of the particular ship's skin would allow.

There were no warships in black planet space, I saw with relief, and some surprise. Shipcom informed me then that the interdiction of the black planet had been lifted four weeks ago; the admiralty had shifted the secret operations elsewhere, not risking another Wholeth incursion. There were various governmental ships about, civilian bureaucrats, who observed my arrival and reported it to Sigma Radidiani, but by the time anyone could reach here, I fully intended to be gone, Lee with me. I knew how to security shield the golden ship now, and they would not be able to touch it until I returned to it someday to bargain for my life.

As I schemed, something touched my mind.

I shook my head but it did not go away. It probed gently but decisively, like a hundred prying fingers digging into my brain.

Seriously alarmed, I tried to close my mind to it while I frantically called up readouts from detectors all over the ship. But there was nothing there; no alien presence of any kind either inside or outside the skin of the ship. There were no Wholeth ships in near space. Certainly nothing to account for a mind touch. Nothing . . .

A sound behind me brought me whirling to my feet. To my openmouthed surprise, a mottled grey glob was rising out of the deck, a sort of cold mist whirling off of it into the air.

"Priority three five eight," I shouted. "Any resurrection order countermanded."

The grey glob shuddered and halted. Then, with a sigh of compressed air, it began to sink slowly into the floor again.

And the mind touch was gone.

I stared for a moment, confusion chasing itself. The blob reached the level of the floor and slid quietly out of sight. The panel slid over it soundlessly, and all was as it had been.

Looking fixedly at the blank floor, I said: "Analyze source of resurrect command."

The soulless voice of the shipcom answered.

"Audio circuits," it said.

"Impossible," I breathed. "I gave no such command."

I turned back to the console and called out a screen readout. I recalled the mind touch. Had it somehow brought a lapse of memory, caused me to order Kalil's resurrection hypnotically? But I remembered no blankness, no lapse of time. And the automatic log, keyed to the chronometer, showed that no extra time had passed.

For the next hour I studied the readouts, straining for some hint of abnormal activity on the ship. I found nothing at all; I didn't even find the memory of what my own eyes had seen. Those hidden layers—I had obviously encountered them, but a mind touch? How could a ship engineer a mind touch? There was no one on the ship except Restor Kalil and me.

I double-checked on Kalil, but he was safely frozen in his cryogenic pod. The readouts showed six such pods, numbered one through six, and only number one was occupied. The rest were empty. I even took temperature readings of the other five—what if the ship were lying to me?—but the pods were too warm for stasis. A shipcom could not lie in the first place; it was one of the three laws of AI.

Grimly, I decided to take the vessel into orbit so that I could check further. Could these preternatural Wholeth women have built into the ship some kind of mechanical mind control? It seemed unlikely, but I had to find out. Or was it a residual effect caused by the past proximity of some powerful psychic presence? I doubted that Maja had that much power, but who else had been aboard the ship?

I altered the trajectory so that the Wholeth ship skipped on top of the planet's atmospheric shield like a rock on water, and then flung itself outward in a low arc. Restlessly I moved around the control cabin, casting around for some way to explain the mind touch.

And then shipcom broke in. I had instructed it to report any news from the interspatial channels regarding myself, or Wholeth or Polarian military action. And now the computer was catching something.

I listened with growing foreboding. A military alert was in effect throughout the Polar Cloud. Admiral Belanger and her war party were in the ascendancy, and rumor had it that the admiralty was about to move her into the fleet admiral's position on Sigma Rad, retiring Shela Rankin as an ineffectual and overly-cautious hamlet. The Wholeth fleet had disappeared; not even the spies at the Wholeth

Lord's court could discover where it was; the Lord herself apparently didn't know. Speculation of an attack on a Polarian target was rife.

I shook my head with disbelief. The warmongers knew almost nothing about Wholeth capabilities. I knew more than they, merely from three weeks in the golden ship. If they knew of its capabilities, its one-way shields and minigrav cannon, they would not be in such a hurry to throw the nine thousand Polarian worlds against the forty thousand worlds of the Whole.

"Shipcom," I said hoarsely. "I want a file dump: every specification, schematic, and design fact about this ship. I want broadcast on tachholo channels. Make it a general call; let the on-line files pick it up. Send it continuously until I tell you otherwise."

I thought a moment, then added: "Add the following message: 'This is in exchange for the cancellation of all charges against the loyal trainee and secret agent Ryne Sangre.'" The admiralty wouldn't buy it. But the news organizations would, and if a court martial were ever to ensue, I would have (I thought) significant public opinion on my side. Unless the admiralty executed me out of hand . . . the thought brought a fandango into my belly, for I was playing with a supernova, and I knew it.

I was meddling in intragalactic politics again, you see, and I told myself harshly that I didn't care. I was feeling patriotic, dammit. The Cloud and my skin both meant something to me, not just the one. Lee's influence, no doubt.

But I was not going to let it keep me away from Celia D'Ame, nor separate me from OB and/or the golden ship. There were limits.

The effect of my broadcast was almost immediate. Tach channels were virtually without number, and were also completely lacking in privacy without the use of a scrambler. The lack of privacy had never disturbed the general Cloud populace; mankind (as opposed to its governments) had always rather preferred an interplanetary communication free-for-all.

Now, as Polarian news sources scanned and selected from the bewildering array of channels ranging from information services to private tachholo calls, my unusual signal was heard, and as the huge computer minds correlated and culled according to their preset criteria, my broadcast rose in rank until it reached enough importance to be reported by the advertised news channels.

The uproar was inconceivable. The Polarian military asserted that none of it was new, and that I was a craven traitor, spy, and leaker of top secrets. News commentators leaped forward to suggest caution in dealing with the Whole, and to express puzzlement at the official denial of the success of a brilliant Polarian spy. The Wholeth embassy on Tyghe demanded the immediate return of their ship and delivery of the pirate to them. Instant polling revealed that public opinion on me, whom they had never heard of before, was adulating; the admiralty raved. Regarding the coming war, the public began to waver; no one wants to die because of the idiocy of warlovers. The militants found themselves on the defensive for the first time in years.

A task force was ordered from Sigma Rad to the black planet to bring me in. Black planet native police were ordered to capture me if they could.

I snorted. I was in one of the most powerful ships in the galaxy.

I spent three hours enjoying the emerging chaos; I could imagine the look on Palla Belanger's face. What would Kitty think, I wondered? I had forgotten the mind touch for the moment. I had cast my first defensive move against the admiralty. Maybe I could save my skin yet.

"Now, shipcom," I said at last. "Take her down. Land next to the OB IV. And broadcast this message to the planetary police: if they do not bring Celia D'Ame to me, I will destroy the Institute with grav cannon fire."

Madness? Yes, but I was in love.

Chapter 17

I instructed shipcom to find the OB and land as close to it as possible. The ship entered the daylight side, and I saw why the globe below me was called the black planet.

The vegetation stretched endlessly, as deep a purple as a living thing could get before entering a total ray-absorbing black. The landscape became confused as shadows disappeared in dullish darkness. Heights did not reveal themselves. Only water showed another cast, and then only when the sunlight bounced off of it into the observer's eyes. Even the algae therein were purple-black.

Presently the ship announced that it had reached its requested location, and I let it take me in. The stolen ship spiralled downward, toward no evident sign of human habitation.

It was only at twenty thousand feet that buildings finally came into view. I saw what looked like a series of sugar cubes dotted along the landscape, here and there a dish antenna, and then finally, directly below me, the incongruent greyness of a landing field, a few one and two seaters scattered about. Presently I could see the OB, sitting handsomely near an outbuilding along one edge of the field, directly below now. The golden ship settled without a jar or sound, and I knew we were fully down only when shipcom told me so.

I sat back from the controls, barely relaxing. People were running toward the ship from the buildings. And I was still deeply troubled by the mind touch.

I consulted the databanks carefully and then said, "I want a personal shield around the ship. Execute priority delta eighty-nine." I pondered a moment.

"Also I require the following on override priority seven six eight oh three, self-destruct provision. Preconditions. Any successful breach of the personal shield from outside, without my express instructions. Any uncoded instructions from inside, whatever they may be, unless the source exits the ship within five standard minutes following your klaxon and verbal warning; in that case, ignore the uncoded instructions and seal the ship until you detect my brain pattern attempting to enter. Also, any cryogenic resurrection without my prior physical presence for one standard hour; suppress all such."

"Executed," the ship said.

I considered. I arranged a radio link with my wristcom so that I could control the golden ship from the outside, were I close enough so that it could detect my brainwaves. But there was nothing else that I could think of, that would protect the ship any better than I had already arranged.

I looked outside. Squads of Institute security personnel had already taken positions around the two ships, weapons aimed. I saw heavy blasters and impact weapons, but nothing like a grav cannon, which in Polarian technology would have required a casing the size of a house, at least.

"Tell them to withdraw," I told shipcom, "or I'll blast their landing field to powder."

They did withdraw. It took awhile, and I think

they did it only because a canny chief of security at the Institute had formulated a plan, and wanted to lull me to carelessness.

I directed shipcom's attention to one of the little ships nearby, a two-seater sitting in squat loneliness toward the center of the landing field, and said, "Shipcom, is anyone in that ship?"

"No," shipcom said.

"Minigrav it," I said.

The bolt went out, twisting space-time like a hammered balloon, rupturing, putting molecule against molecule, sending them along different gravitational troughs. . . .

The two-seater blew apart as if every molecule had lost its cohesion with every other one, which was not far from what had happened.

As the debris rained down, I said: "Bring Celia D'Ame to me, or an Institute building is next. Then another. Then another. Then . . ."

The amorphous crystalline screen in front of me cleared, and I beheld a beefy face in it, a man with the weight of muscle gone to fat, but not entirely.

"I am Chief of Institute security, Anselm Dooty," the man said, his voice ruined by too many whiskeys and cigars. "I have Ms. D'Ame in my custody. I will release her under the following conditions . . ."

"No conditions,' I snapped. "You have seen what this Wholeth ship can do. Where is she, with Kel Kellem? Bring her here."

The florid face frowned. "Aye," it said reluctantly, "she is with Kellem. If you would . . ."

"No conditions!" I shouted. "Shipcom," I said loudly, "blast that big white building over there. . . ."

"Wait," Dooty said. He seemed to think, the foxy bastard. Then he said: "I'll bring her to you; it will take a half hour. Wait."

"I'll wait," I said. I told shipcom to cool it, and waited.

I was biting my fingernails to the knuckle twenty-eight minutes later, when a groundcar appear in a cloud of dust on the edge of the field. It roared up to the two ships, and a hatch opened and two figures emerged.

Lee! My heart leaped in my chest, and other things leaped as well. The long, straight auburn hair. The graceful carriage, the . . .

The other was Dooty himself, a potbellied tall man wearing a uniform with which I was unacquainted. The Institute's, of course. He held back, urging the woman forward.

She hesitated, looking at him. "Come on, Lee," I breathed. "Come on, get in here. Shipcom, let that woman in."

Finally she strode forward, and the ship enveloped her in its shield, and the hatch opened.

"Lee!" I cried, turning. Eighteen days . . . eternity! I was starving, and . . .

The woman who came at me was not Lee. She had been made to look like Lee; her face, her hair, her height . . .

She had a fingerstunner in her hand.

I came to groggily and found myself regarding the weaving tentacles of a cockroach about four inches from my nose. I held my body still and groaned inside. Jail, I thought. Palla Belanger had won after all.

The cockroach scuttled away, alarmed by my movement. I surveyed my surroundings as best I could from the floor of a cell. I saw the low dusty bases of three or four steel cages. My ears heard nothing but the irritating hum of a faulty ventilating fan. My nose smelled . . . but I decided to forget about that for now.

I waited about five minutes, but nothing stirred and I realized at last that I had to get up, if only to relieve the cramping that was making itself felt. So I rolled over in a smooth movement and came to my feet ready for anything.

The whole world reeled and WAUMMM! a headache descended like a steel curtain. I must have looked as if I belonged exactly where I was, in a drunk tank, as I swayed, clutching my head, waiting for my eyes to adjust.

There was no one there. Just a forest of steel bars—six cells worth, three in a row on either side of a narrow aisle.

The Institute's brig, or perhaps the jail of the nearest town.

I looked for my wristcom and found, naturally, that it was gone. So were my shoes, stunner, and everything that the police had thought might conceal weaponry. The clothes on my back were all that I had.

Without the wristcom, I could not contact the golden ship. Ruefully I held up my hands with their two bandaged fingers, one on each, and regarded them. Carefully I flexed. I felt a stinging around my eyes. My head pounded.

Wherever Lee was, I had failed her. Now someone from Sigma Rad would come and take the OB, and the golden ship as well if they could figure a way to penetrate the screens I had set up. Perhaps the substitute Lee had already done it. Or someone from the Whole would turn up and collect the ship. Whatever. Lee's mission was ended, and I would die at court martial. And I would never touch her again, never hold her, never . . .

The stinging grew worse, and I tried to distract myself. I studied the cell; the cell doors belied the primitive arrangement of the cell block. They employed no locks; instead they used gravitationally-induced molecular bonding within their door frames.

The doors and frame were melded together and there was no seam, no crack, no opening at all.

That there were monitors watching me, I had no doubt. But I guessed that the facilities were not very elaborate. Nothing fancy would normally be needed here. The Institute population was more likely to tend to its own affairs than to engage in jail-inducing activities, and any local town would be the same.

Where, I wondered, was Lee?

I flexed my right hand again. Perhaps it was time to blast my way out, if I could. But I would need the wrist computer, and I didn't know where it was. If the false Lee had dragged me out and the golden ship had closed up behind, then the only way back in was if I myself gave the override, priority seven six eight oh three. It would resist any other attempt to breach it, and if the attempt seemed about to succeed, would blow itself up with such violence that there wouldn't be much of the Institute left.

I sensed that someone had entered the room. I looked toward the door.

From years of habit I noticed her body first, trim and strong, well rounded, moving with practiced power in the combat uniform of the Polar Cloud. Nice. And then I saw the speckled granite eyes, the salt and pepper hair, bones like a bent shovel.

Admiral Palla Belanger. Or was it Fleet Admiral Belanger now?

She strode over and stood a little way off, analyzing me as a cat analyzes a bug. I was vividly conscious of my lower intestine as memory flooded back, and I said nothing. No grovelling. I'd use one of the blaster crystals on her first.

The silence stretched uncannily as we watched one other. But finally she spoke, her voice the low rumble of an idling chain saw.

"For two days, Chief Dooty has kept you drugged and out of the picture, waiting for me to come."

That's why my head felt like an elephant dancing. "And then, this morning, only hours before I arrived, a Wholeth fleet erupted into Sigma Radidiani space and attacked. The Sigma Rad base is useless to us now, a pile of twisted metal, eighty thousand people dead, the entire planet affected by dust and radiation. Those ships we were able to raise encountered one-way shielding and grav cannon and they died. Do you know what the Whole said as they withdrew? They said: unless you bring us the golden ship that you stole, bring it to the Roil by one month from today, the same fate will befall every planet of the Cloud. *And I was not there; I was on my way here to deal with the likes of you."* She hissed the last words, and I saw in her eyes the fury of a thousand devils.

"Kitty. . . ." I said feebly. Her face broke into fragments, and she growled: "She lives; I brought her along to see you die. And let me be the first to tell you something, you bastard," she spat. "She is *pregnant,"* Palla Belanger screamed. "And she won't give it up. She is going to have the child of a coward and a fornicator and a traitor. You *bastard."*

Pregnant? My brain, numbed by the news of Sigma Rad, couldn't take it in. Pregnant . . . how? Well I knew how, but why? I mean, why did she allow it, and why did the fates decree that my seed would do its natural work? And how did I feel about it when most of my thoughts were on ravishing Celia D'Ame? And what would I do when there was a little Ryne or Ryna running around wondering where Daddy was?

I forgot, for the moment, that I would not be alive by then, almost certainly. My legacy to the Polar Cloud: eighty thousand dead because I stole a Wholeth ship, a war begun, and an admiral's daughter with my child.

You women reading this are saying: why didn't

you think about responsibility when you were busy impregnating Kitty Belanger? All I can say is, *now* I know the type of man I should have been. Then I just wasn't it.

"Well you should go pale," the admiral hissed. "Well you should die inside. The last man in the universe I would want for the father of my grandchild is you. Kitty says that you gave her more love and more understanding than I. Does she remember when she was a baby, the nights I stayed up with her, the diapers, the vomit, the fights? No, and she had no father either. She has opened tragedy for herself because of you, and when I kill you, I want you to think about it, and think how worthless your life has been."

"Why don't you kill her outright, as you tried to do once already?" I croaked. And incredibly, hit a nerve. Her face, under its disciplined shock of salt and pepper, inflamed.

"You think I tried to kill you both, that day when I threw you against the meteoroid?" she said through clenched teeth. "No. All reports I had about you, said that you were quick enough to survive, and they were right. No, what I intended was for Kitty to see your character, and she saw it, as half the admiralty did when they viewed the holoed record. Your cowardice was written in your words and actions; you nearly clawed your way through the cowling. I could smell your fear when I watched you, and I hoped Kitty could too, despite her disgusting suggestion of low-gravity carnal acrobatics. But no; do you know what she said? She said that anyone would be afraid, knowing as you both did that I, her mother, was trying to kill her. *Can you believe it?* As if I would throw away my career, and very likely the Cloud itself, to kill two fighter pilots worth less to me than the meteoroid they managed to avoid?"

Palla Belanger—she truly believed that her military skill and ruthlessness were critical to the future of the Cloud. It was eye-opening, to have it so starkly revealed, and for the first time I began to think that Kitty was wrong. This was before the height of her power, you must remember.

"Of course, you pile of feces," she said, always the diplomat, "you might have fooled me and played Dick Danger for her; at least you could have given her that."

Not in a month of Sundays, I thought; it wasn't in me, though I had to admit that after what had happened to me since, my acting ability was improving.

"But now we are at war with the Whole, thanks to you. And what I mostly want to know now, Ryne Sangre, is this: why? Why did the Whole react the way they did to your absurd imposture and theft of that particular ship? They have been trying to talk us into alliance against the ravening Onn; if they had been looking for an excuse, why this particular one?"

"They think 'Palin-Marek' made a monkey of them," I suggested lamely. She laughed, and it would have sheared a steel bulkhead.

"No, though we had considered it. But even then the reaction is extreme. Why stage an international incident at precisely the time when the Whole is lobbying hard for a military alliance against this alleged alien threat?"

"Maybe to recapture a Vice-Regent and Eleventh in Succession to the Leadership Itself," I suggested.

She snorted. "You must be joking," she said. "Even the Whole cannot be so obtuse as to think that someone so fatuous as Palin-Marek holds any real importance to the Polar Cloud. They know that you aren't Palin-Marek; they revealed such at Sigma Rad." So Maja had blabbed to Lamonte; well, I had expected it. I would have been surprised to learn, at that point, that she had delayed it as long as she did. The admiral went on: "It's going to be very interesting for the real Vice-Regent when he finally emerges from interspace at the Archipelago; we won't see him again, I think. No loss." And I had thought she liked him, from what she had said at Palin-Marek's reception.

"Now you will give us the golden ship," the admiral said finally, getting to the main point. "The codes, if you please."

"In a pig's eye," I said, guts churning. It wasn't easy for a recreant like me to go eye to eye with someone with the force of a Palla Belanger. But giving away the store wasn't the way out and I knew it.

Her granite eyes narrowed. "We will drug them out of you," she said.

"Shipcom won't let me back in if it detects that," I said, "and it will detect it. The Whole can do remarkable things with mental detection; they are experts on the mind."

"We're scanning the ship," she said. "Some electromagnetic force can penetrate the shielding, else it could never respond to anything, much less a holo command from you."

"I already gave the Cloud more detail on the ship than your scanning can reveal," I said. My mind was beginning to recover as I held my own against her; the hammering in my head had subsided, and I was thinking about death and life. "I'll give you the ship," I said, "if you clear all the charges against me, and Celia D'Ame too."

She snorted again, a gobbet of mucus hitting the floor with a snap. "I would rather jump into the Roil bare-ass naked," she said. "What I will do, for your information, is land a cargo freighter around the gold ship and pick up her and a chunk of dirt beneath her, just outside the shielding, and carry the whole thing to the Roil myself."

She could do it, too, I thought; the shielding wouldn't react to that.

"But then," she said, "part of the Wholeth fleet is on its way here. It, too, can scan tachyonic holography, and it read your damnable message and knows where its golden ship is."

Great, I thought, as if things hadn't been bad enough. We glared at one another, me searching frantically for some bit of information to offer her, she gloating, no doubt, over the web in which I was enmeshed.

"And now," she said with savage sweetness, "I will leave you to your girlfriend." She made the last word sound like "pig." And with her preternatural grace, and without another word, she turned to the door and walked out.

Almost immediately two soldiers marched in, and my heart leaped as I saw Lee walking somberly between them, the real Lee. They pointed a grav key at the cell across from me, and the door separated from its frame and fell open with a clang. They pushed her inside and locked the door and, without glance or word, strode out.

I have thought about it many times, and only one conclusion makes any sense. Admiral Palla Belanger wanted the golden ship gone, since she knew everything there was to know about it already, there was little advantage in keeping the ship itself. She would never be able to bring up a heavy freighter before the Wholeth forces arrived, and once on the scene, they would never allow it to raise planet with the golden ship inside. Celia D'Ame had been badgering the admiralty for years to send an expedition into the Roil, so the admiral knew where Lee would go, had she the chance.

And I . . . let the traitor be taken by the Whole. If the Polarian populace insisted on making me out

to be hero, she could stomach it, if barely, as long
as I were dead. And maybe if I broke cover and ran,
I would be a hero no more.

None of that occurred to me then. I wondered
fleetingly why she hadn't excised the crystals that
remained in my fingers, but that was as close as I
came to guessing her scheme. All I could think about
was Lee, Lee, Lee at last.

And there Lee was, across from me, her high forehead tight, eyes brown today, wonderful lips compressed. I drank her in, devouring her with my eyes,
with a kind of hopeful joy, while she looked back
with no perceptible emotion.

"Captain Sangre, looks like to me," she said at
last.

"So they took you too," I said.

"Evidently," she said.

Then to my astonishment she began to sing. For
a moment my mind followed her lilting voice with
delight; and then the meaning of the words sank in:

"Oh an arrogant blustering fop of a man,
A pompous ass was he;
He fooled the Whole for just so long,
Then exited clumsily.

"He bragged like a goose for the network news,
Made the Whole crawl, you see.
So what if they grind the Cloud to bits?
He's got their gold ship, does he!

"So now he sits in a jail cell,
A downer for him you might say.
But since he'll be back in the news again,
He can't wait 'til they take him away!"

I felt as if my jaw were in the vicinity of my knees,
and snapped it shut angrily. Something between

rage and outrage raced through me and came out in a choked gasp. Across the cell she watched, and smiled enigmatically.

"I have more," she said softly. Still she showed that strange, Mona Lisa smile.

"No," I said. But the hard thing was, there was some justice in what she sang. I did enjoy the public attention . . . to some extent, I amended.

Where, I thought, *was my reunion scenario?*

"They tricked you out of the OB with Kel Kellem, I suppose," I said gruffly.

"Never say his name to me again, Ryne Sangre," she said softly. "In a manner of speaking, they did what you say. He could not come to me, so they brought me to him."

She paused, then with nearly inaudible emotion: "I found a babbling infant, Ryne; his was one of the minds that that Wholeth woman erased."

I looked at her, trying to divine what words she might want me to say.

"I . . . I'm sorry," I said at last. She acknowledged it with a lift of her exquisite eyebrows.

"At least," she said, "that wasn't your doing."

G-d, I thought, have I lost her? She has that fierce patriotic streak in her, and she, like Palla Belanger and half the Cloud, thinks I blundered into war.

"You shouldn't have left the ship," I said, an unnatural harshness coming into my voice.

"I know that now, naturally," she said, and I could see that she was forcing calm over herself. "But I had no choice, in the end. The admiral's flagship took control, and I couldn't fight it."

Of course, I thought. The OB IV was built to serve a flagship with dozens of other fighters. Pilot control was the exception rather than the rule.

I began to pace back and forth, indignation at her song in me still but with part of me, the survival part, taking note of the surroundings, probing. Lee seemed disinclined to add to her lyrical output, watching me with half-lidded inscrutability.

"We'll get out of this yet," I told her. "The golden ship is out there, and if we can't take the OB, we'll take it instead."

"Right," she said coldly. "Escape. Open your mouth and eat the bars."

"Eh?" I said.

"Escape," she repeated. She was as languid as ever now.

"Perhaps," I said.

"And then, perhaps not," a new voice interjected. It was masculine, and belonged to a man striding through the door through which Palla Belanger so recently had gone. With him was a single police guard, wheeling a cart. The door closed silently behind them.

In a few steps they were opposite my cell, and I observed with interest that the cart held my shoes, wrist-computer, Lee's oversized bag, and the Wholeth stunner and blaster that I had taken from Kalil. Lee was on her feet now, and I could see her eyes shining hungrily on the weapons.

"Just a few questions," the man in charge said in a sort of authoritative baritone. I looked up and saw the face of Anselm Dooty for the second time, this time in the flesh. I guessed that he was an athlete gone to seed, a small town boy turned rent-a-cop. But his left hand hung easily in the neighborhood of his stunner holster.

Small town, and competent, I thought.

The cop turned and bowed briefly to Lee.

"Missy, I'll come to you in a moment. The Admiral figures maybe I can get somewhere with you where they haven't." I wondered what they had been doing with Lee. "And I don't mind telling you that those booksheets in that big bag of yours are classified Institute property; if Kellem were still with us, he'd be in big, big trouble. Now the Admiral, she realizes the value of cooperating with local authority." *I'll just bet*, I thought. And she would be listening in somewhere, and no doubt this local cop knew it too. "So Missy, I'll be getting to you in a second, just you don't go away."

Smiling at this uproarious improvisation, he turned to me.

"Boy," he said, "my name is Chief Anselm J. Dooty, and I've got something to ask you about these shoes." He gestured with a fist barely smaller than a basketball. "Now Simpson here is our nearest thing to a lab man, and he began digging into those shoes when he received a big surprise, he did indeed."

Simpson, a wiry weasel-faced man, was looking rather green around the gills, and also scowling dangerously at me. Slightly, I smiled.

"Oh, it's funny, no doubt about it," Chief Dooty said. "You never heard a yell so loud since Taylor— that's the local undertaker—went and got drunk and smashed some of our windows and ended up in here for three days when the widow Morgenthraler was a-ripening over to the parlor, and Taylor had forgot plumb all about it, and by the time he got back there I'll tell you he was emptied out and there was nothing wrong with his nose. 'Course no one thought about it 'afore he got there, the widow having no kin and all, but you could'a heard that shout clear to the other side of the Cloud, and it was the middle of the summer too."

Dooty's puffy face held that little pointed smile of the regaling politician, the salesman forcing himself to be one of the guys, but he had obviously been in the role so long that he was in fact one of the guys, and probably he was used to everyone laughing besides.

I didn't laugh, however, and this seemed to irritate the Chief. Meanwhile Simpson drew his stunner with an angry jerk and said; "I'd better just cover him, Chief. No telling what he's got up his sleeve. Can't be too careful." The setting, I saw, was way up to maximum, ready for a good jolt, one that would likely kill someone with a bad heart, and leave the previously healthy not so much so.

Simpson, I thought, was seriously annoyed at having dug into the scent pods in that shoe.

"Point that somewhere else," Dooty said irritably, taking his glance away from me. Simpson let the weapon drop, his hand white with strain.

"Now," the Chief said, pinpoint eyes firing darts at me again, "I want to know just what you're doing with those secret agent weapons. Didn't help you much, did they, boy? You fell for that copy of missy here like a ton of concrete. 'Course, now that I've had a peek at the real thing," he said, flicking his chin in Lee's direction, "I can see why you let her in without taking care. I'da let her in too, if I thought that that was what I was going to get."

Lee snarled at him, and he threw back his head and laughed, never taking his eyes away from me. Simpson had the stunner up again, aimed at the pit of my stomach.

"Is she still in the ship?" I said.

"Why should I tell you boo?" he asked cheerfully. Then: "Hell, why not. No, that ship of yours wouldn't let her back in once she dragged you out. You know, boy, you owe Carlton Mery 400,000 credits for blowing up his two-seater? He is one unhappy man, is Carlton; how you going to pay that back, boy? Not to mention how long you'll rot on a jail world for blowing it up in the first place."

I laughed, and the Chief's face stilled, another politician's trick. The admiral hadn't told him how quickly I was going to die. Money was something I had no interest in anymore.

Simpson's finger tightened on the firing stud.

"I told you to point that thing away," the Chief snapped at him, his attention glancing again.

I pointed my right middle finger and shot Simpson with the stunner crystal imbedded there. Simpson stiffened and his hand-held stunner went off. It clipped Chief Dooty's arm and ruined his aim, for the moment I had moved, Dooty's left arm had flashed upward, stunner in hand in a motion so fast that later I couldn't believe it had happened. The stunner bolt speared past my right shoulder and into the ceiling, while I jerked my right thumb at the Chief as if hitching a ride and shot him with my third stunner crystal.

Competent, I thought. Dooty was as competent as they come.

Lee, openmouthed, looked at the two bodies sprawled on the floor. Then she looked at me; I was on my knees, holding my shattered fingertips to my shirt and trying to reach with my left arm the two bodies.

"How did you do that?" Lee asked, still trying to preserve her air of languid amusement. "Even more, why did you do that? Listen . . ." I could hear alarms, muffled by the walls. "They were watching all the time. And you knew it too. They . . ."

I couldn't reach the bodies. Dooty had been competent, all right. Too competent to stand right up against a cell, where a prisoner might reach out and grab.

I rose wearily and looked up at the cell/ceiling intersection. I sighed, and pointed my left middle finger at the joint

"That's the solution all right," Lee said with mock sagacity, nodding her head vigorously. "Give the cell the finger. We're in here, and they're out there, coming on fast. Or are you going to stun the cell? If you . . ."

Gritting my teeth, I fired the blaster crystal and

the words stopped pouring out of Lee's open mouth. The pain was much worse than the stunners had been . . . hotter, longer. The one second blast tore away my flesh and burned what was left around it. I would need tissue regeneration eventually to bring the finger back.

There was a loud WHOOM, and I was thrown backward to the cell floor as the ceiling erupted. The blast tore into the circuitry that held the gravitational bonds together, and with a subdued clang the forces let go and all the cell doors relaxed, no longer contiguous with the rest of the cell block. It also blew a hole the size of a garbage can into the floor above.

I staggered to my feet, threw open my door and stepped out, appropriating the Chief's stunner, as well as the Wholeth weapons and the wrist computer. I left the shoes. They had never fit right anyway.

"You're bleeding," Lee said. I looked up. She was out of her cell and already was clutching the bag. I looked down, and saw that there was a trail of drops from my cell to the bodies, and a a tiny red pool below me catching the dripping fluid from my ruined finger and thumb. The look in her eyes had altered from the irony a moment ago. Now something had revived—love for me, or for her mission?

"Just follow me," I said sourly, "and hope that the Roil is worth all this." But I allowed myself a moment to peer into her enigmatic eyes, and doubt became a fugitive.

Rapidly I spoke into the wrist computer as I eased open the door through which Dooty and Simpson had come. Shipcom answered, and I felt a burst of relief; we were close enough to it for it to detect my brainwaves, wherever we were. I peered out. As I had hoped, the jail was conventionally laid out, with a corridor straight ahead and doored stairways on either side. A stunner bolt ripped through the air near me, and I almost absently answered it with a couple of my own from the Wholeth weapon.

From the paucity of the attack I guessed that there were only one or two men at the end of the corridor. Probably Palla's soldiers were somewhere outside, and maybe had a narrow door and a flight or two of stairs in front of them. I shook my head in bewilderment. Why weren't we buried already in a platoon of marines?

Which stairway, the right or left? It was an important question. But I couldn't tell by looking at the closed steel doors. I sent a blaster bolt down the corridor, hoping it wouldn't kill anybody, and heard a satisfying KABOOM in return as it blew out a couple of walls. I stepped out of the cell block and to the right; Lee a shadow behind me. The small T-shaped dust-filled corridor shielded us for a moment as I wrenched at the stairway door. It held fast.

"Damn!" I spat. Without any further word, I stepped back and pointed the blaster at the latch and blasted.

The door blew inward, pieces of it hurling down the stairway. Down the stairway; there was nothing going up.

"Aargh!" I shouted incoherently. I whirled and jumped back toward the corridor intersection, and collided full-bodied with Lee. In a tangle of arms and legs we fell across the center of the T. Stunner bolts hissed through the air over us, where we would have been except for my clumsiness. From the floor I spotted and fired. Only at the last instant did I remember that the hand I was pointing held a blaster, not a stunner. I wrenched it upward and the bolt ripsawed the ceiling.

There were two men halfway down, one on either side. They had been creeping cautiously forward, and our floor-level appearance had taken them by surprise. One got a shot off, but the ceiling was com-

ing down on top of him, and they both screamed
and threw up their arms. Broken bones they would
have, no doubt, but they would live. I hoped.

Then Lee and I had rolled to the other side of the
T, and I again gritted my teeth and blasted a latch
away. Even as the echo died, I heard scrambling in
the ruined corridor and from the other stairway.

Lee had thoughtfully snagged Simpson's stunner,
and she poured a few bolts into the wall at random,
the sound harsh in the dim light. The scrambling
paused.

"Why up?" Lee panted. "We'll end up on the
roof!"

I did not answer. I was preoccupied with the gathering pain in my fingers and trying not to trip on
the stairs as we scrambled. Footsteps sounded now
in the stairwell down below.

We burst upon a black-tarred roof upon which the
sun was shining cheerily down, through a doorway
whose steel closure was propped open with a two-
by-four which I kicked aside. We pushed the door
shut with an effort, but it would not latch. It didn't
fit correctly into its opening; the door frame was
warped.

Faint, confused sounds drifted up from below. I
sent several stunner bolts into the stairway for effect,
and then tried something that I had no idea would
work. I pointed the Wholeth blaster at the door and
tried to spot-weld it shut.

With a gigantic sound the door exploded inward,
raining fragments into the chasm below. The little
building around it shuddered and collapsed, sending
concrete blocks and masonry tumbling inward. I
heard a scream, and hoped again that I hadn't killed
anyone.

All that was left of the stair housing now was a
pile of rubble, choking the opening below.

"Well, if that doesn't take it," Lee said in an awed

voice. She turned and saw the agony in my eyes as I clutched my seared fingers to my body.

"I never seem to remember how violent a blaster is," I said weakly. She held me then, as gently as a cat holds a kitten, trying to cradle me standing up, my head bowed and hands held tightly against my body. I was aware, dimly through the pain, of the scent of her, of her touch. Not the reunion setting I had hoped for, but the comfort was there.

"It was a noble effort, Ryne," she whispered into my ear. "Someday you'll have to tell me about your magic fingers. Perhaps we'll die up here together, and at least I won't see the Cloud fall. Now pull the rest of the rabbit out of the hat."

My blurring eyes informed me that we were on one of the buildings at the edge of the landing field, and nowhere could I see the OB or the golden ship. But there were military ships aplenty, where before there had been none.

To the east, a series of dark hills shimmered in the morning sun. Behind them, somewhere, Kel Kellem drooled and soiled himself, and Celia D'Ame was hugging me as she had once hugged him.

And something flashed in the sky like a golden arrow. It arced from high above through the clean air and then swelled toward us like a falling train. Lee looked upward and gasped, sobbing suddenly at a resurgence of hope.

And the hulking, almost perfect cone of the golden ship settled quietly on the black tar of the roof. The hatch sagged with a dull thump onto the surface of the tar roof, which boiled and smoked at its touch.

And we were inside.

Soldiers and police fired blasters at us from the ground as the golden ship rose. The energy poured around and off of the shields like water from a fire hose. One-way shielding; I was in love with it.

And then the ship dwindled straight upwards into nothing, in the bat of an eye, the flick of a finger. Soldiers and police were left gazing openmouthed at an empty and frustrating blue.

Chapter 18

Tensely, I watched the digital readouts and listened to the staccato coded reports from the ship. I could see no sign that the ship had been disturbed during my two day absence; no doubt it had been surrounded first by Institute police, then by Polarian soldiers under Palla Belanger's command, and scanned relentlessly with low-level electromagnetics. But nothing had been damaged, I saw with a cursory glance.

Now, as we leaped off the black planet, the ship was studying real space for anything that might offer a threat before interspace. Once in interspace, of course, detection and pursuit were not possible.

It was essential that we reach the Feldschacht limit of the black planet's star system before attempting interspace, for prior to that distance from the star, the solar system's gravitational trough would disrupt the interspatial drive. Many ships had been lost in the past, before Feldschacht had undertaken her classic series of studies. In every case there had been debris, but not enough to make up the mass of the lost ship. Where the rest of the ship had gone, was still anybody's guess.

I had expected a Polarian task force orbiting the black planet, but while the readouts indicated an unusual number of trading vessels, only Palla Belanger's flagship, five mini-dreadnoughts, and a few fighters were detected. This puzzled me, and then I guessed that Palla had come in a hurry with minimal support.

I knew how fast the golden ship could go. Of Belanger's eleven ships, three alone were in position to intercept us; the flagship was on the other side of the planet and out of the game. We had escaped much faster than she had anticipated.

But the situation could hardly have been worse. The three were all dreadnought class, small ones, but with more than enough firepower to take on the OB IV, for example, or from what I knew of it, the Wholeth golden ship.

The Feldschacht limit lay almost two standard hours away, even at the inertialess speed that the tiny ship could travel. One of the dreadnoughts was the main problem; it had been in optimum position and now was fleeing ahead of us, clearly planning to force us backwards into a minigrav barrage from the other two ships when they were in range. The ship-coms of all four ships could calculate equally, and all of them could see that we could not make it, that we would have to heave to, or be blown out of space.

Lee. . . . The light had been in her eyes again. I couldn't bring myself to put it out so soon. I'd tell her when I had to. Meanwhile, we would hurtle toward the limit as if we could make it through. I owed her that.

"Well, aren't you the cute one!" I heard Lee's voice proclaim. The remark struck me as grotesquely inappropriate. Without looking around, I said; "Thanks, you're not bad yourself," with heavy irony.

"Oh yes, that do feel good, don't it?" her voice drifted back after a moment.

Given that I was in considerable pain from my shattered, bleeding fingers, a kind of confused outrage tore into my mind. The baby-voiced comment was so bizarre that I turned to vent my lack of appreciation.

"Lee, that's the damnfoolest thing that you've ever. . ." All at once, my jaw dropped—it had been doing that lately—as my eyes focused upon Celia D'ame.

Or rather, Celia and the other personality that coexisted in the cabin.

For she crouched before a furry sinuous creature which rubbed back and forth across her shins and graciously permitted her fingers to scratch back and head and ears.

"A cat!" I shouted foolishly.

Lee looked at me. "Very perceptive," she said.

I reeled my jaw in and stepped over to her. I reached down and touched the animal's fur with an undamaged finger. It was only barely softer than a down mattress, as warm as a feverish child.

"A cat," I said again.

"You've already said that," she said. "And Ryne, your fingers—you've got to go to the med module, please."

I looked at her with wide-open eyes.

"But don't you get it?" I said. "This cat wasn't here before. The golden ship was empty. *How did it get in?*"

Trouble came into her eyes.

"You mean that it wasn't with you all along? That it's not a Wholeth cat?" Her hand's cadence altered subtly, and the cat purred restlessly.

"Maybe it's a Wholeth cat, but I was in this ship alone for eighteen standard days, and no cat."

She frowned. "Perhaps it came from the Institute. Ryne, your fingers . . ."

"I don't see how." My voice trailed away. We

looked at the cat with a sort of awe. The animal's fur was a deep brown, bordering on black, a black that the beast now began to preen languorously with its rough-coated tongue.

"And it couldn't get through the screen?" Lee asked, evidently just to break the silence.

"Hardly," I said. "It would have been thrust away, just like a human being."

"The rooftop?" Lee inquired.

I stood shakily up. "No," I said. "We didn't see it, and anyway a cat would have fled all the violence long before the ship came."

"If you don't get to that med module, Ryne," said Lee severely, "point it out to me and I'll do it myself."

Wordlessly I pointed a bleeding digit at the same panel that Restor Kalil had used so recently, or was it so long ago? Lee moved over and opened it.

"Come to think of it," she said, "I've never seen a black cat on the black planet, odd though that sounds. There are orange striped and grey striped cats all over the place, but no black cats at all."

"Maybe the original settlers were tired of black," I said. "No black cats at all. But here, without a doubt, is a black cat."

We fell silent. I gazed at the beast as Lee moved over to me and began applying the tissue regenerating dressing that would heal me, given time.

The animal appeared absolutely at ease, as cats had for the twenty thousand years that they had lived as empathetic companions of humankind. I felt the usual things that I sensed around cats: understanding, mystery, and a self-sufficiency uncomplicated by philosophical meanderings about one's place in the scheme of things. And beauty. The cat was undoubtedly something beautiful to look upon.

"Well, at least we don't have to worry about varmints on the ship," Lee said lightly, standing back and surveying my hands. But there was nervousness there too. I held up my hands, and they appeared to me about as supple as crowbars. But the pain had already stopped.

Suddenly the audio background of the ship, still delivering coded reports, came up with something that made me forget the cat altogether. I whirled and jumped at the console.

"What is it?" Lee demanded.

"The ship in front of us," I said tersely. "It has turned to attack."

I monitored the readouts and studied the screen, which was magnified to its maximum limit. The black planet hung behind us, receding. Already it was scarcely the size of a baseball, with a shimmering corona which, in its central darkness, was the only way that the orb was visible at all. Its sun swam silently behind it, off to one side. The halo of the globular cluster pressed in, shining coldly in its multiplicity.

"I didn't want to tell you before," I muttered. "Perhaps we can evade them." I didn't believe it, but I would try.

The leading dreadnought swung in an inexorable arc toward us, and I could see the trailing ships, spaced equally behind. The trap was closing, and I wondered if Palla Belanger had planned this all along: jail escape, guilty flight, and destruction. The golden ship atomized—sorry, Wholeth friends, we had no choice, she would say. She wouldn't care how they would react. She wanted war.

"Can we make it?" I breathed to the ears of the ship. "Can we take evasive action, and reach the limit?"

The ship calculated and recalculated, listing the calculations and permutations and conclusions.

"What is it?" Lee asked suddenly. Like a shadow,

like a sinking heart, something had passed over my face.

"The ship says no," I said quietly, searching for her eyes, sadness and empathy in me. "They will come within grav cannon range before we reach Feldschacht. Not much before. But before nonetheless."

I paced around the tiny cabin, avoiding the cat on the floor. The beast glanced at me once.

"Is there a way?" my voice grated aloud. I flung my mind down corridors of experience and knowledge, looking for a shred or a memory to latch onto, a shred that would tell me how to give Celia D'Ame the quest that she had spent her adult life pursuing. How, also, to save our lives.

Ten minutes passed, fifteen. The little golden ship was fleeing now directly away from the oncoming warships, but directly into the teeth of the lead ship. I described it all to Lee, and she found some comfort in it, for it meant that the Polarian forces were at least the equal of the Whole in speed, if nothing else. But the comfort was mostly buried under the burden of the personal, crushing the theoretical.

The ship reported demands from the task force, demands broadcast over holographic channels.

"Ignore them," I growled.

Shipcom asked me if Polarian weaponry were any different than Wholeth.

"Not to my knowledge," I told it. "Grav cannon, laser guns, particle beams, projectiles of one kind or another. Nothing much has changed for a thousand years."

The ship was silent. We sped through the void, and the warships gained.

Then the ship spoke again. I stopped dead, as if a wall had run into me. I stepped hesitantly to the controls, then stood there dumbly, unable to respond to what they told me.

"What. . . ?" Lee barely breathed. I motioned her silent, and checked the readouts over and over again.

Finally I straightened. I uttered a short, sharp command. The image on the screen disappeared, and suddenly the entire cabin vanished into a holographic space scene. The cat mewed and fled into a corner somewhere.

Lee stood beside me, our disembodied figures illuminated by the lights of the control console. I had to show her how hopeless it was. I had to make her understand what I was going to have to do. I pointed out for her the highlights of the scene, an enhanced miniature of what was going on outside of the golden hull.

"There's the black planet," I said, pointing to a tiny sphere well to the door of the cabin. "The sun itself is off the field of vision. And here we are." I pointed to a tiny golden cone. "Magnified, of course."

Lee grabbed my arm. "Then those must be the dreadnoughts," she said, indicating the two ships behind us. Both they and our ship were moving at a sharp tangent away from the orbit of the black planet.

"Aye," I said. "But that's not the point. Remember the lead ship? Here," I said, pointing rigidly, "it is."

She gasped. Directly ahead of our golden cone, exactly in the direction in which we were headed, was the dreadnought, a tiny silver ball driving straight at us.

"Lee, I'm afraid they've got us," I told her gently. "There's no way out. We don't dare go into interspace at this distance from the sun. We can't outrun them. Our choices have gone to nothing."

"But how can that be?" she asked me frantically, clutching hard at my arm with both hands so that the pain in my fingers reawakened at the blood pressure change. "We could not have come this far, and then fail. No, it cannot be."

"But it is," I said, as gently as I could. "They're good soldiers. The only choice we have is to heave to, or die."

"Go into interspace, right now," she cried.

I saw the agony on her face, and said; "You wouldn't feel it. You would be dead in an instant, and after that . . ."

"Fire on them!" she shrilled. "You said this thing has minigrav cannon; use it!"

"Perhaps," I said, wincing at the vision of a hundred people blasted into space. "But there are three of them, and one of us. The shipcoms know all the possibilities, all the trajectories, everything we and they can do. They would evade the bolts and destroy us, Lee. Our choice is, and I am deeply sorry to have to say it, is to heave to and throw ourselves at the mercy of Palla Belanger."

"No!" Lee's voice cried, an unshuttered wail of some primal agony that forced its way into my soul and echoed there like a demon laughing. Her self-possession fell away like a cloak from a statue. "I need this ship!" she shouted shrilly, hysteria in her eyes. "I can't lose it now. I must have it. I *must!*" She flung away from me and beat upon the control panel before I could stop her. I uttered a code word and disabled it before she could do damage. She beat frantically, fists raising and lowering in the starlit darkness, adding a strobe effect to the strange scene.

I stood rooted to the floor. It was out of character, this outburst, varying insanely from the intensely controlled woman that I was used to seeing. Then I stepped forward and reached, and she spun around and swung a fist at my face so suddenly that only my lightning reactions enabled me to block with an upthrust elbow.

She gasped as her arm hit, and the pain seemed to drive some of the madness out of her. Her other fist, coming up at me, wavered and my parry was scarcely needed. Then she gave a great sob and collapsed into the console chair, shoulders wracking with heaving gasps of frustration.

Amazement kept me standing there. I could not believe that any sort of physical danger could shake her. It was something more, more than the setback in her plans for reaching the Roil, for on that she had been working for ten years and could, I knew, work for many more. It was something deeper, I guessed, as if some horrendous guilt were forcing its way upward.

And she had swung at me. Why? Could hysteria be enough to explain it?

I stood there, watching the lone warship bear down upon us at twice the apparent speed of the trailing vessels.

Lee's agony was lessening as I told my ship to take any evasive or defensive method at its disposal. But I had no hope at all. I would have to heave to. I was only delaying, trying to make her see.

Contact was now imminent. The gold and the silver were converging rapidly, and the conclusion would come at any time. I opened my mouth to speak, the fatal words of surrender.

Then a yellow streak blasted forth from the warship. It flashed across space and disappeared into the distance. It seemed to graze the figure of our ship. But I felt nothing, heard nothing.

They had shot prematurely, but the accuracy was precise. Had Palla Belanger guessed it? Had her analysis of this ship shown her what must, what would happen? Is that why she allowed her dreadnoughts to come at us, to make our escape realistic to the watching population of the Polar Cloud, to whom our escape was breathtaking news?

Another bolt came forth, and then another. The second missed us completely as our ship wobbled and evaded. The third, like the first, hit dead on. Involuntarily I braced myself.

But nothing happened. The yellow bolt bounced as if it had hit something hard. I frowned. Theoretically, nothing was solid to a gravity bolt.

The trailing ships came into range and unleashed more bolts, each of which danced off the golden ship like light off a mirror. And then suddenly our ship flashed past the silver warship and continued on toward the Feldschacht limit.

At the moment of proximity, something leaped out of our ship and transfixed the dreadnought in a golden lightning flash. The warship shattered like a piece of glass, fragments spinning wildly off in all directions.

I gaped. My mind tried to reject the message of my eyes, and failed.

Loudly, so that my voice made Lee jump in the stillness of the space scene, I demanded to know what my ship had done. The reply left me stunned. Lee looked up confusedly.

"It's impossible," I shouted at her. "The ship says, as if it's something it says every day, that it simply shielded itself from the grav cannon, and then put its opponent away with its own minigrav."

Lee's tear-streaked face came up at me.

"You mean we're getting away?" she cried, grabbing me by the shoulders.

"Yes," I said horribly. "But we have just killed a hundred odd Polarian soldiers, Lee; do you understand? We have killed them, twisted them into atoms. . . ."

Her composure was rapidly returning. She looked at me as if I were a drooling four-month-old child.

"But it's wonderful!" She shuddered prettily, de-

liberately. "Are you crazy, Ryne? We're getting
away. The ship is ours!"

I screamed. It was a cross between a cry of agony
and a wail of despair. "She set us up die, and if that
didn't work, to kill." I wept, banging my fists against
my forehead. "And now we can't come back; a hundred families would hound us, and a trillion people
hate us already. Lee, Lee, don't you understand?
We have shattered a dreadnought full of people."

"Ryne, *you* don't understand," Lee said, grabbing
me. "A hundred people don't matter at all; we are
going to the Roil, Ryne, and that's all that counts,
that's all that matters."

"You're crazy!" I had to say it. I pushed her away
and watched the golden ship approach Feldschacht.
"A hundred people, and I killed them. . . ."

And then I turned on her and screamed. "And
there's another thing you don't see." I raised a bandaged fist at the console. "The confounded ship never
told me that it had these capabilities. Now it says that
they were classified, though no longer so now that
they have been used. I can't believe it! I knew this
ship inside out."

My fist held for a second and then dropped weakly
to my side. Behind me the other two ships were
veering away. They had seen what had happened to
the first ship. They were looking for survivors now,
not confrontation.

Lee took hold of me and shook me violently.

"Stop jabbering and tell me what it is that makes
you so stupid," she cried. "We've got the ship! That's
what matters now!"

A grav bolt shot out of their ships from long range;
the golden ship didn't even bother to evade.

"Incredible," I murmured, shaking free of Lee.
The dreadnoughts continued gathering up the wreckage. The golden ship sped on.

"Now we're home free," Lee exulted. "Nothing

stands between us and Feldschacht. Say something, Ryne! We've made it!"

I turned to her sharply.

"You don't see what this means, Lee?" I said. "Even beyond a hundred people dead. You don't see at all? Let me spell it out for you."

She waited almost contemptuously. My voice came again, so soft that she had to lean toward me to catch the words.

"This is something we Polarians do not have, Lee. Some sort of defense against gravitational cannon. No one has ever seen such a thing before, at least in the Cloud. Grav cannon were our one invincible weapon. But now . . ." I paused. She only half sensed the pain in my mind.

"But now the Cloud has no real defenses," I said, my voice cracking. "It was not enough that the Whole were forty thousand planets to our nine. But now they have something which makes their ships invincible to our technology. No wonder they're moving on us now. They can take us. They know it."

I searched for some spark of interest in her eyes, and found nothing there. I tried one last time.

"Don't you see, Lee? Without some kind of miracle, the Cloud is finished. You, of all people, superpatriot Celia D'Ame, should see it. We're all about to become devotees of the one and glorious Whole!"

Cunning and ruthlessness flicked into her face and out again.

"It doesn't matter, Ryne Sangre," she said silkily, coming toward me. "Now that we're together again."

I buried my face in my hands and cried.

Part III:

A Roil of Stars

Chapter 19

It wasn't the same, not at first. It couldn't have been, I suppose. I had dreamed of three weeks alone with Celia D'Ame, of her writhing body and palpitating heart and love poured all over me like whiskey. Instead, for awhile, there was heartache and recrimination and guilt.

She tried. She seduced me the first night, and let me devour her eyes and enter her body and cry on her breasts. But a change was in me, a change of self-knowledge, a change of awareness. I wanted her and yearned for her and despised her. She had used me and given herself to me, and I was hated by two civilizations because of it. Eighty thousand Polarians on Sigma Rad and a hundred more around the black planet were dead; a Wholeth ship was stolen, a war begun, and all she cared about was keeping me trimmed and relaxed for a descent into the Roil of stars.

Perhaps Jame Torrester was dead, and Pascal Tortelli, and Cassia Glane, and Fleet Admiral Rankin; I didn't know, and wouldn't know for many months. And that wasn't all, for beyond death was life: Kitty Belanger was pregnant with my child. That was still sinking in, for the dead were dead and beyond my succor, though guilt wracked me for it; but with Kitty my own seed was growing, and I might never see it.

And on top of it all, less personal but more immediate, there was the cat.

The fourth day out: Lee stirred on the other side of the cabin. She was engaged in a slow perusal of Kellem's booksheets for about the tenth time since our entry into interspace; she alternated that, with studying the piloting of the ship.

I swivelled my chair away from the console. I still couldn't penetrate the hidden levels of the shipcom, and somewhere in there was the explanation of the presence of the cat.

"They'll be after us, Lee, the Whole and the Cloud both," I said, trying to pierce the gloom in the cabin corner where the backlit booksheet illuminated the outline of her angular and beautiful face. "Where we're headed will be obvious to the admiralty, once they realize that the only reason for my landfall was to pick you up. And from what you've done in the past, they'll know what you're after and where you're likely to go for it. And as for the Whole, they expect delivery at the Roil anyway, and will be waiting for us, or at best will be close behind us."

"No doubt," Lee said absently, letting the pages flicker by.

"The admiral said that half the Wholeth fleet was on its way to the black planet; where is the other half? Back to the Roil, I'll bet; if they're not waiting for us there, I'll be plenty surprised."

"No surprise," Lee agreed, bending forward to peer at the text.

"And furthermore, there's something in all this that we're missing," I fussed. "I just don't see why the Whole got so hot about this ship in the first place."

"Me either," Lee said without interest, muttering some note to herself onto the sheet's memory.

I got up and began to pace the cabin.

"And that cat!" I said. "That's the thing that bothers me the most. Where did it come from? Whose is it? What's it doing here?" The animal was stretched out at Lee's feet, preening a paw and then delicately wiping the whiskers on the side of his face, eyes closed in contentment.

"What's it doing here," Lee repeated, leaving out the question mark.

"And the mind touch!" I said. "Did I tell you about that, Lee?"

"Humph," said Lee.

"Where did that come from? Lee, I've been a lot of places and done a lot of things, but never have I been in a mess like this; it has got me worried!"

"Worried," she said.

I looked at her.

"Lee, are you paying attention to me?"

She grunted. I looked annoyed.

"Lee, did I mention that the cat is Onnish and that I am the Wholeth Lord?"

"Pooh," she said, not even looking up. I threw up my hands and paced.

And the golden ship fled, and I fretted and constructed paranoid scenarios, and at night ravaged Celia D'Ame with uncontrolled fury. She responded relentlessly, and neither in mind nor in flesh could I conquer her, try though I did. "It's all legs and softness and release to you, isn't it, Ryne Sangre?" she cooed into my ear one time. "There isn't anyone here at all. I could be an animated mannikin, and you would respond to me all the same." I denied it hotly. You are every woman in one, I argued; Venus and Aphrodite and Vera and Diana and Helen of Troy combined, I said with gross lack of mythological consistency. Also Cassandra and Mata Hari. In my mind I reached for my earlier obsession with her, Celia D'Ame as the universal feminine principle, Celia D'Ame as the essence of woman. It escaped me, and I thrust at her more savagely for it, and she played me like a violin.

She got to me again, eventually. Enmeshed in her as I was, I hadn't the experience to know what was real and what was not. Between bouts of cynicism, she gave every sign of admiration for me, preferring, as she said, to express it with her lips and tongue and hips rather than with words. And there were responses that could not be faked, I thought, that I saw in the throes of lovemaking, trembling around the lips and eyes, gasps of satiation, moans of delight. As my confidence in the sexual part of me grew, so did stamina and technique, and she came to me in the night as often as I came to her, sought me and pressed against me and—I have to say it—loved me. I think now that her physical need was as great as mine, that it was powered by fear and determination and the need for momentary escape from the mission that had devoured her for nearly eleven years. She was a fully functional woman, and delighted in it.

I owe her the end of my neurotic obsession with sex. She gave me the chance to see myself without an overlay of unreleased need. If nothing else, I never again would be terrified that I could not do it adequately, a terror that haunts man after man, usually without foundation other than the ridiculous excesses of superhuman pornography.

But I'll also tell you, if you ask, that what happened to me is not the way to attain what I attained. Because it hurts, even today. It hurt then so much that I nearly burned into ash. You can see what I went through, from sexually contracted disease in my school days to the contempt of everyone around me to a vengeful parent to surprise impregnation to, eventually, disillusion. The self-esteem of most people would not have survived it; I still don't know why mine did.

No, my advice is this: stick with one woman, the first one if at all possible, and work from there. You can perfect yourself, and her, no matter who it is. As I said once before, the old ways were better: arranged marriage, dowries, the works. More people survived. More people prospered.

And you know a funny thing? I never told Lee about Kitty and the child. She knew about Kitty and me, but whenever I thought about the baby, I could not bring myself to tell her. It was, in the last analysis, none of her business. I was learning that, no matter how close you are to someone, there is a part of you that you must keep to yourself if you are to survive.

Around my self-analysis, reeling in mental orbit during those long/short days in the golden ship, was, of course, the Roil. I had told Lee I was worried, and I was. Even with Sigma Radidiani and the black planet and the OB hijacking and the golden ship theft and Cassia's thugs and the mind touch and the cat, the Roil represented something beyond my experience, beyond the experience of any reputable spaceman. I reviewed again and again how we would skim the surface and study it and calculate if we could survive it, nagging Lee and screaming at her and telling her what I would do and what I would not. And she sat there and smiled at me, and pulled me to her when she thought it would work, and argued good-humoredly or sharply with me when she saw it would not.

It looked like a ball from far away, shipcom said. But close up it seemed to be something more amorphous, twisting in on itself and yet blowing outward like slow-motion nuclear fire. Stirring like something alive, a great roiling boil of light and rock and starstuff and . . . what?

According to everything that I could discover in the ship's encyclopedic memory, no astronomer really understood it. Probes sent in from either civilization never came back. Some suspected a series of neutron stars, singularities, antimatter, or a weird melange of all three, causing its inexplicable violent opacity and seemingly random gravitational uprisings. Most astronomers back and turned their instruments elsewhere. There was no point studying something that didn't fit any theory, they said.

It was clear from those who had gone before that electromagnetic and tachholo transmission from any ship or probe trapped inside could not escape the Roil. It was not a question of an event horizon, such as would surround a massive black hole, but rather of chaotic interference from whatever gravitational anomaly was stirring in its depths, triggering explosions of particles and waves, erasing in randomness any attempt of communication from within, had there been any. Lee firmly believed that her parents had attempted tach transmission, indeed were still attempting it, and that Crestor Falon and the others before them had done the same. But there was no eternal evidence.

Could a modern starship with modern inertialess power and one-way shielding survive? The irregular rippling of space was something like grav cannon, though it couldn't pull a ship apart except possibly close to the Roil's center. But the sudden release and imposition of forces would put vast strain on inertialess engines. Whether any ship could survive and reemerge was an open question, and there was only Lee's hope to say it could be so.

During those eighteen days, I reread Kellem's

booksheets with fearful fascination about *The Defiant*
and the astronomer's son, of the fugitive Wholeth
lover Crestor Falon, and of the futile efforts of the
Institute to divine the mystery of the Roil. But the
more I pondered, the more frustrated I became.
There was simply not enough information.

Two days before emergence. One last time I
reached the end of the official records from both
human cultures. Irritated, I sat back in the pilot's
chair, mulling the whole thing over in my mind and
coming up, as usual, with nothing.

"Lee," I said, not looking at her. "I'm not at all
sure that we can do anything once we get to the
Roil." My voice trailed off. I looked blankly down,
the usual worries bedeviling me.

Across the cabin Lee looked up from her work and
frowned. If similar thoughts were on her mind, she
gave no sign. Instead, after a slight hesitation, she
gathered up her booksheets and placed them again
into the leather bag. Leaving it on her chair, she
rose languidly and moved over to me, so deliberately
that I felt the approach by a tightening in my chest
and heightening of my pulse.

She settled on the arm of my chair, her own arm
lying behind my neck, leaning slightly toward me so
that I caught her scent and felt the gentle wisp of
her breath in my hair.

Almost afraid, I looked up at her eyes, very close,
and then reached up with a bandaged hand and
brought her head down and kissed her carefully,
with a controlled passion that remained controlled
only for a moment. As my fingers tightened, she
broke away and laughed, and rummaged her fingers
in my hair and then bent down and kissed me again,
not letting it last long enough to bring forth the
devil.

"Ryne," she said, her throaty voice sounding like

a chorus of angels. "I thought it once too, that we could do nothing, and in the beginning I only wanted to go there, to be near the place where they lay spinning somewhere close by."

I was confused; it didn't fit in with the hard-headed woman I knew. I thought about it, and didn't believe. She would have gone into the Roil in a rowboat.

"But now I wonder," she went on heedlessly, her gaze moving away from me and into the distance. "This ship is something I didn't count on, because I never thought that there was hope for anything like it. The OB IV was a revelation, and this one is bigger and more powerful, has one-way shielding and capabilities beyond that. It's surprised you and it surprises me, and makes me wonder if the wild dream I've had all these years could actually be, that I could go into the Roil after them and bring them out. And Ryne, the secret they carry can win the war; it can wipe away the guilt, Ryne, that I feel in you every night as you make love to me."

I let it pass. "The Roil eats ships for breakfast, Lee," I said instead.

She stood up as if she hadn't heard and wandered around the little cabin while the cat regarded her with half-lidded eyes, and then settled back down into a cat-dream-filled sleep.

"I'm sure they're in there," she said, her body turned away from me in quarter profile. "And they might be alive, that's what has tormented me all these years. They might still be alive and looking outward, feeling trapped and feeling as good as dead already."

"Lee . . ." I began, but she went on speaking as if I were not there.

"The Roil isn't some living thing, Ryne. There's nothing mysterious about it. It's just a bizarre pulsing object with a bunch of stars and debris abnormally close around it, and the strangeness is due to the irregularity of the pulsations and nothing more. It has no will, no feeling, no life. It can't insult or attack or bear a grudge. It's not an enemy nor a friend. And most of all," she said, her steadily rising voice smoothing out as she turned to face me, "it can be understood and manipulated just like any natural thing."

I faced her, somberness in my eyes.

"Some natural things are best left alone," I said.

Again she seemed not to have heard. She came over to me.

"We have only two more days, Ryne," she said softly. "Let's make the most of them."

We did.

Chapter 20

"There it is," I said.

Midafternoon, standard time. As we flared out of interspace it appeared in front of us, exploding into a brilliance which the ship's sensors turned into a much attenuated, but still dazzling flood of light.

The Roil. It blazed at us like a golf ball battered out of shape, cut and dented in a hundred places, with streams of fiber spilling out here and there and looking like a badlands of excited light. We felt that we could almost see it move, see the boiling and churning of the infernal surface as it twisted under a gravitation so unsettled that it was almost malevolent, so capricious that it was as if it were the product of a conscious mind.

We each thought of many things then, Lee of her father and mother and how near she now was to them again. And I thought of my fascination with her angular face and green/brown eyes and supple body, and with her swings between bitterness and joy. And I realized that for me she was, among many other things, an archetype. She was, I saw in an instant of self clarity, a maiden that I might save like a knight against an evil Duke, but the Duke was her inner darkness, and my weapon not sex alone, but all of the interpersonal skill at my command. I had never thought there was such idealism in me.

And, as usual, I questioned himself, and challenged the arrogance that had brought me to interfere in this other person's life, knowing at the same time that everyone everywhere was interfering in some way in someone else's life. It couldn't be helped; it was set up that way. And I had not so much interfered, as been swept along. I had taken control too late.

"Orbit now, at a safe distance if you please, to pass over the coordinates that we specified yesterday," I told the ship. Yesterday we had fed in the conclusions from Lee's Kellem notes, and now we watched as the ship settled calmly into a stationary orbit over the place where Lee's parents and Crestor Falon and the astronomer's son may have gone, to their destiny and, probably, death.

There were, I saw with relief, no ships of any sort in the Roil's near space. But if the missing Wholeth half-fleet had headed directly toward the Roil from Sigma Radidiani, they could be here at any moment.

I petted the cat on my lap absently and looked at the holographic image of the surface below us, knowing that its apparent solidity was nothing more than the hotness of incandescent gas, lit by the dozens of fires within. . . .

The cat dug all eighteen claws into my leg and howled. I yelled and grabbed at it, but with incredible speed it clawed its way up my torso as if climbing a tree and slipped in a sleek blur over my shoulder, leaving torn flesh behind. I leaped up from the console chair and whirled angrily to face the cat. And . . .

Something touched my mind.

I looked wildly about, feeling the mind touch and frantic to know the source. The cat? It couldn't be. I saw its last jump as it tore across the cabin and huddled in the furthest corner, yelling in that nerve-throbbing feline yell, like a siren rising and falling. Lee was on in the study console, her arms braced against the chair as if she had been about to rise. But her face was rigid, fixed in an expression that she would never have consciously worn. And her arms were shaking and seemed to have no strength, and she did not rise.

I took a step toward her, and then the mind touch seemed to dig in and squeeze. My step faltered and failed to complete. I felt my body stiffen and my balance go. Wildly I threw out my arms to break the fall, or at least tried to. The arms twitched upward, and then lost their momentum and stiffened in place.

I fell sideways, heavily, striking the wall to my right with a shoulder and rolling over, pivoting on a head that felt as stiff as an iron poker. For a moment I hung as a hypotenuse to a right triangle whose other two sides were the wall and floor, and then my legs slid out from under me and my roll forward continued, and I hit the floor solidly, my head landing on one ear and sending a ringing throughout my brain. The roll brought me over one more time.

In a moment the ringing had stopped, and I found myself on one side, facing across the cabin at Lee, who was still frozen in her chair, that horrible grimace twisting her face. and still, there continued that unearthly howling from the cat.

Then something happened that truly frightened me.

I felt it even before the action began, felt my brain awaken in a certain region and send a command to my lips, felt them open and felt the air drawn in and then expelled over my vocal cords, and my mouth shaping words that had no connection with my own will.

"Cancel . . . override . . . orders . . . for . . . resurrection," the voice grated, scarcely my own and yet identifiable enough to the ship's computer. "And . . ." I said, horror mounting sharply, "resurrect!"

A panel on the floor began to slide slowly aside. A thin haze of cold drifted unhurriedly from the opening.

"Pod number?" the shipboard computer inquired cordially.

"Zero," my voice croaked. Zero?!

Into the slot in the floor, now fully open, there appeared the knobby top of cryogenic stasis.

"No," I ordered my vocal cords to say, but nothing came. I remembered Restor Kalil's eyes as he had slid beneath the frigid clay. Kalil, I knew, would kill me out of hand.

The mind touch kept squeezing, and I felt as if a hand were wrapped around my head and chest, blanking out coherence and making breathing itself difficult. Across the cabin, Lee had not moved at all, still sitting in that unnatural position, her face gone leaden grey, her breathing coming in forced gasps that scarcely moved her chest.

The cat continued to howl, its tail rigid in the air, back arched at the rising knobby mass on the floor.

Suddenly something struck me as odd, and I forced my constricted mind upon it. There was something about the mass. . . .

I got it. It was too small. It was smaller than the last one I had seen, sucking upon the heat of Restor Kalil.

The mass was fully out of the floor now, mist streaming off it like hair off a beaten head. Smaller! I thought. But there had been nobody in stasis when

I had put in Kalil; I had checked. The computer had assured me. . . .

Of course, that damnable computer had deceived me about the ship's weaponry too.

The knobs themselves were dissolving into muddy haze, which poured off into the round holes around the slot in the floor. I could still blink my eyes, but only with difficulty. They watered as a consequence, when I could not summon the will to blink.

What was going on? I thought desperately. This had to be Kalil! But it was too small, I could swear it was. Could Lee somehow be doing all this; did that explain her rigidity and the cat's screaming? But no; Lee was in the same spot as I, and there could be no real doubt about it.

Who, then? The Roil? Was it alive somehow, or something in it, working on the minds in the ship? Was Maja nearby in a ship we had failed to detect?

I saw the first hint of features in the cold haze before me.

They were . . . they were . . . young! They were . . . of a child!

First I saw a small, well-shaped nose, and almost immediately a smooth forehead with a hint of snow-white hair. Then the rest of the face was revealed, a faintly freckled face with pouting lips and wide-open, black eyes that stared unblinking at the ceiling.

A girl, I thought suddenly. A girl, not more than eight or ten years old. A girl. . . .

The haze dropped below her ears, and I saw that her smooth chest had begun to rise and fall. And I felt a change in the mind touch, a quivering as if it were being subjected to great spasms of increasing strength, under a tight control so as not to harm. It hurt, and I saw Lee wince involuntarily as the mental hold lifted for an instant and then fell back upon her with a jolt. The cat screamed a shrill, ear-splitting shriek.

And then fell silent. The cat huddled shaking in the corner, and a great weight seemed to be lifting.

The girl sat up. The last of the haze disappeared into the bowels of the ship. Slowly the girl turned her dark eyes toward me, and I found myself looking into the blankness of some inner power. No expression crossed her features as she looked at me, but I felt the mind touch loosen and I was able to breathe again. Beyond the girl, Lee's arms fell back onto the armrests of the study chair.

The girl's head turned and regarded Lee, and then she saw the cat. From behind, I saw sway to her feet. She held out her arms and said; "Falon!"

The cat moved not. It sat on its haunches, no longer shaking, but looking suspiciously at everything around the cabin, as if something were about to leap out of the wall at it.

"Oh, Falon," the girl said, her reedy voice full kindness. "Poor kitty, that must have hurt you. I'm so sorry."

She eased toward the cat. She was dressed in a simple pullover tunic, rich in its simplicity, embroidered on the edges with something that glimmered softly in the starship light. Of one thing I was instantly aware, and that was that she knew cats. She fairly oozed over the floor toward it, making no sudden moves, her body crouched consolingly, arms out to give the animal a chance to sniff at her before the rest of her body came too close.

The cat sniffed, and looked up, and then rubbed a furry cheek over her fingers, and with a glad exclamation she gently scooped it up and, standing, held it upside down like a baby. From her shoulders, I guessed that she was scratching the beast's head and belly, and I could see the end of the tail, curling in relaxation over her arm.

The girl turned, smiling, and looked through me without seeing me, or if she did see me, without caring. The cabin floor was unbroken again, and she strode once across it and once back, cradling the cat and crooning softly to it. Then she stood in front of Lee, and Lee looked up at her with wonder and fear.

"I hope I didn't hurt him," the girl said apologetically, and I was completely aware that she was talking, not about me, but about the cat. "It's too hard to operate from stasis; all I could do was blanket the room, and how the kitty would react to my control I couldn't guess. That's why I put it off so long, until I had it worked out."

Her voice was clear and firm. It was the voice of authority. I knew it at once from all the bossy types I had defied and toadied up to over the years. It had some of the same cadences as that of Selah Maja.

"You . . ." came Lee's voice, hardly a more melodious croak than had the cat's. "You did all this . . . from stasis?" She was incredulous. I knew; I had enough incredulity for both of us.

"Sure," the girl said, scratching the cat, from whom a low purr reached my ears. "But it's so slow, my lady! I hate working out of stasis. It takes me simply hours and days, just to work out an easy command. I've been working weeks on this one. And when the ship's in interspace, I can't execute anything; it's so tiresome."

The girl glanced over her shoulder and looked at me, friendliness absent from her eyes.

"So this is the one that caused all the trouble," she said softly. "And, my lady, I guess he kidnapped you too. It's a good thing I was here."

"Who . . . are . . . you?" my voice came then, and with a start I perceived that I was able to say it at all.

"Quiet!" the girl snapped, and my mouth and nose

closed up as if someone had stuffed it with rags. A moment passed, and I began to heave for air, haze forming before my sight. I could feel my eyes popping forward from my head.

"Stop," I heard Lee's voice saying desperately.

"You would save him then?" the girl inquired without emotion.

"Yes, please . . ." Lee said. "Please. . . ."

"As you wish, my lady," the girl said indifferently, and I felt air rush into tortured lungs. I breathed in great heaves, and my eyes began to clear.

The girl had turned back to Lee and was speaking to her.

"Just make sure he asks for permission to speak, that's all," she said. "I can't abide pushy men."

Pushy men—this girl is no more than ten years old!

"You want to come with me?" the girl was asking astoundedly. The two females were having some kind of hidden dialogue that was mostly escaping me.

"Yes," Lee said. "The Roil . . ."

"The Roil!" the girl exclaimed, and whirled toward the screen. "You mean that's it? We've come in time?"

She looked at the screen, eyes shining. "This is why I was sent, and Maja's not even here. Ship, report on our position please."

The ship did so, and while it did so the girl finished scratching Falon and put him gently down. She listened to the computer intently, comprehending jargon that would have baffled an interspatial engineer.

"But why?" she said. "You!" She suddenly pointed at me, who had crawled to a sitting position. "What evil plan did you have for taking the ship? Answer me, accursed unbeliever!"

I felt the menace in her voice, and hastily opened my mouth.

"Never mind," she said. "I can find out better, like this!"

And suddenly I felt my mind open and I began babbling, and to my horror-stricken soul somewhere inside, it seemed to me that I was speaking so fast that no one could possibly understand.

"Stop," Lee said. "Stop! It's horrible; what are you doing to him? Please. . . ."

The girl made an impatient gesture.

"It's not hurting him; I just have to link his voice with the thoughts. It's funny how unreadable a mind is when it's not making words."

For a good ten minutes I babbled, and after a time I could follow my own thoughts and see that she was pulling out of me the entire story from my first sight of Lee, through the capture of the four-seater to that very moment.

It was one of the strangest moments of my life, I can tell you, this forced baring of my soul on the deck of that golden ship. Never before had I been so emptied; never had I realized that I noticed so many things from moment to moment and filed them away in memory, virtually all never to be used again. And never had my own behavior sounded so crass, my attitudes so brutally vacuous.

At last I wound down and she said: "So! You shot the hand of a Wholeth Sub-Governor and stole a Lord's ship, and then froze the Sub-Governor without my desire. Ship! Resurrect Pod One."

Then I made the connection. Pod One was where I had placed Kalil, and the ship had told me that Pods Two through Six were empty. And so they were, I thought. But the deceptively numbered Pod Zero! And even honestly numbered, I thought, the ship would not have told me.

"Please," Lee said for about the fourteenth time. The girl turned toward her.

A panel slid open on the dark starship floor.

"What is it?" the girl said.

"He did it for me . . ." Lee trailed off, and then said again. "You heard what he said? You know why we're here?"

"The little that I believe the pirate," the girl said dramatically.

"Read my mind, please," Lee said pleadingly. "Get the whole story."

The knobby form covering Restor Kalil shuddered to a stop, halfway out of the floor. The girl stared at Lee. I wondered: was it common for the Wholeth paranormal women to be invited into each other's mind?

"All right, my lady," the little girl said quietly.

And then Lee began to babble, and I saw where the horror had come from when she had watched me before. Her eyes were half-closed, pupils turned backward and up, and her lips moved so fast that I wondered if there were such a thing as sprain of the mouth. And her voice: it was high pitched and frantic, the words tumbling over themselves, the vowels almost entirely lost in the flood of consonants. I could not follow it, and I tried to shut out the ghastliness of it.

When Lee had stopped, the girl just stood there for long moments. Lee sat back, exhausted, and I saw her exquisite jawline with a pang, even in this monstrous situation.

The girl stiffened.

"He," she said, making the word sound like "scum," "is thinking of you in . . . a . . ." She faltered. Intelligence flooded into Lee's violet eyes, and she said: "Dirty? A dirty way?"

"Yes," the girl shouted. "Shall he die, my lady?"

"No," Lee said, groping for words to present to

this child. "He has no control. Forgive him; he's a barbarian. What is your name, dear?"

The girl seemed dissatisfied, and looked again at me, contempt and distaste in her face.

"My lady, I stay out of your mind as a matter of courtesy, but him I'll watch every minute, and if he thinks anything filthy I'll . . ."

"He can't help it," Lee said, a bit of hysteria in her voice. "Let me be responsible, please. Don't . . . er . . . don't pollute your own mind by watching his."

"Yes, my lady," the little girl said. I felt something draw back, and for the first time since the mind touch began I felt that I was no longer naked.

The girl regarded the knobby lump of Restor Kalil, halfway out of the floor.

"Faargh," she said, or at least that's what it sounded like to me. "He's another one, and one is enough." She spoke to the shipcom. With a jerk, the knobby mass began to descend into the floor again. I breathed.

"Shall I freeze the other one, my lady?" I stopped breathing.

Lee looked startled. "Stasis? No, dear. Perhaps later. Please . . . who are you? What is your name?"

Finally, the change of subject worked.

"Allia," the girl said. "I am pleased to meet you, my lady."

The girl bowed toward Lee, who hesitated a bare second, and then bowed in return.

"You, my lady," the girl said, "have my gracious permission to move about my starship. But you," she growled at me, "can sit right there and don't you move, or I'll get you."

"Yes, Miss Allia," I said humbly.

"Silence!" she yelled.

She glared at me, and then moved to the wall and

called up a cold fruit drink, and some food for the cat.

She was a bizarre mixture of little girl and courtly lady and tyrant, and as I dictate this she rules the Wholeth Empire with ruthless efficiency. But as I saw her then, as a little girl, I knew only that she was one of the paranormal females of the Whole, and a very powerful one. But why should she be aboard Maja's golden ship? And why in stasis?

I could make an educated guess. Her Lordship might be willing to send a daughter against the black planet and the Roil, but she was not going to be foolhardy about it. Want to keep her as safe as possible? Order her to remain in stasis until her peculiar talents were needed. No one could target her if they didn't know she was there.

At that moment the ship spoke in Maja's voice.

"Stand to!" it ordered. The girl looked up happily.

"Maja!" she exclaimed. "Ship, let her come on in. I'll be so glad to see her!"

I won't, I thought. So the half-fleet was here already.

"Ship, evade . . ." I never finished the sentence. An invisible fist rammed into my solar plexus, and breath exploded out of me. I bent double on the floor and heaved. Lee looked at me in a sort of dazed terror.

The girl didn't bother to pursue the problem further. She had us, and she knew it. And her voice took priority over everyone else in the universe save one, she believed.

Nearly an hour passed, but I didn't sense much of it, for I had made the mistake of venturing a verbal observation. My consciousness was only just returning, and I was just catching my breath again when a clang rang through the little ship and the hatch in the corner of the floor suddenly dilated. And in climbed Governor Selah Maja, the Stead Lamonte at her heels.

"Maja," the girl shrieked, and flung herself into her arms.

"Little Lordship!" Maja said happily. Behind her, Lamonte kneeled, and I thought dumbly; *Little Lordship?*

Chapter 21

Her Little Lordship.

Maja, in hugging the girl, had carried her a little forward into the golden ship. Lamonte rose hesitantly to his feet and took a step forward, and behind him climbed two soldiers through the hatch. Then, in a rigid convulsive movement, Lamonte collapsed to his knees again and touched his forehead to the floor, short blond hair bristling.

"Send the soldiers away," Maja said without looking around.

Lamonte said nothing, and there was no sign that he had heard. But the soldiers had, and they scurried down as fast as they could shuffle, the port easing shut behind them.

Lee was still in her study seat, face twisted with, as I saw immediately, consternation. She had received some of the Little Lord's purpose from the mental link that they had enjoyed. But now, with Maja there, she was guessing that the girl had no need for another woman aboard.

Lee hissed at Maja.

"You are . . ?"

"The Little Lord's Protector," Maja said calmly,

the girl's face buried in her shoulder. "And Her Lordship's spy."

On the floor, Lamonte quivered. The Little Lord gasped and pulled away from Maja, staring aghast at Lamonte. Maja turned toward Lamonte slowly, and her manicured hand rose past her belt, easing a blaster out and pointing until it was steady at Lamonte's body.

"Rise," she said.

The Stead looked up and saw the blaster, and his pale face went suddenly paler. He climbed unsteadily onto his feet and staggered back a step until his back was against the wall, fear ending for all time the arrogant demeanor on his aristocratic face.

The Little Lord looked on impassively, making no move to interfere. I became acutely aware that a political drama, the depths of which I did not fully understand, was underway before me.

As for Maja, she had spent nearly two fortnights with the Stead as they sought the golden ship. He had believed that judgement would be in the hands of the Lordship Herself, whom he thought valued him. He had not grasped that the daughter might carry nearly equal authority, that her decision in the field would override any speculation as to what the Lord would do were she there. And he in his arrogance, had not perceived the depth of Maja's loathing as she used him to seek the golden ship.

It had been a thirty-six days that would live with her for the remainder of her life, a fountainhead of self-loathing and shame. This was the payoff. Never again, she thought, would he do to anyone what he had done to her.

"You see what is about to happen," Maja grated, addressing the Little Lord. "Do I have your approval to proceed?"

"Yes," the little girl said clearly, anticipation in her stance, her reedy voice.

"Your mother . . ." Lamonte ventured desperately, and his throat was strangled shut by the Little Lord's mind.

"My mother," she hammered as he sought for air, "is not here."

Lamonte's face suffused, and his tongue began to distend, and Maja said: "For blaspheming against the Lord in international diplomacy," voice strong and savage. "This."

Her face suddenly tensed and her eyes seemed to shoot out.

Lamonte was plastered against the port. He tried to scream, but could not; even had his esophagus been available to him, something had emptied inside and no sound could have come.

For a long moment of exquisite agony Maja held him that way. Only when she was in some way satiated did her voice come again.

"And for what you did with me," she said savagely, "*This*." And she blew a neat little hole in the forehead of the Stead Lamonte, her dampened blaster burping in an electronic spasm. Lamonte's body jerked once and his eyes fell upwards and back and then, his stiff body slowly relaxing, he slid downward to sit almost naturally on the cabin floor, back against the wall, backside on the dilated hatch.

I quailed, expecting the wall to burst outward into space and suck us all to our deaths. But again, the golden ship fooled me. Where his head had been there was a blat on the wall, a thin streak of blood smearing downward from it. The bolt had dissipated somehow in the weird alloy out of which the ship was made.

Lee had one fist against her mouth, the other hand digging into her thigh, knuckles white. The Little Lord, back to me, was relaxed and impassive. Maja slowly allowed the weapon to drop, until once again it slid gently into its little holster on her tooled and ornate belt.

Grimly, almost unwillingly, I pointed the little finger of my left hand, one of those with a blaster crystal, at the Little Lord. It was my last chance, went the thought through my mind. Perhaps I could take them both out with the crystals I had left.

But I hesitated. In theory, I should have done it. Everything I had believed about myself up to that point told me that it was my life that counted, and no other, except perhaps Lee's. I should disregard this savage woman and ruthless little girl, I thought. If I might live, they must die.

I think I did it. I think I sent out the nerve impulse to that deadly finger. Or maybe it was the little girl's sudden awareness of my thoughts, and her whirling at me, and the jolt of fear that shot through me, that set the crystal off. I don't know, but the Little Lord did whirl, and from her eyes there leaped something that caught the blaster bolt midway between us and spent it in a crackle of ozone and smoke. Maja twisted, her blaster in her hand again, and I jerked my bleeding hand backwards against my body and braced myself for the bolt from her weapon or the blast from the Little Lord's mind.

Nothing came. I feared the little girl most of all, for she was presumably inexperienced in these things, unlike Maja's lightning-quick control. And I believed now the little girl to be vindictive, self-indulgent, capricious.

I saw in the girl's face indecision; but in Maja's face I saw a deadly purpose. Once again I braced myself to die.

"Now," said Maja coldly, almost gloatingly. She smiled thinly. I recalled calling her "promiscuous" to goad her, and regretted it sincerely. I vowed in my mind that I would never insult a woman again.

"How true," Maja smiled.

She raised the blaster slightly.

"You will stop," said the Little Lord. Maja froze.

"But your Little Lordship," she said through gritted teeth. "This offal has stolen a Wholeth ship, interfered with Wholeth diplomacy, and kidnapped yourself." She seemed about to go on, but stopped abruptly.

The Little Lord was looking at her.

"Also he has insulted you in a way that you cannot bear," she said to Maja. "I have seen it already, and it is ugly, but it is revealed now, and you can say it if you wish."

"Yes," Maja said, and there was a crack in her voice. Absolute zero could not have been colder. "In the most base, verminous, obscene way he insulted me. And *he must pay*." Her finger whitened on the blaster. Across the room, Lee's eyebrows rose. Then she opened her mouth to scream.

"STOP!" the Little Lord shouted. The finger paused, then incredibly it bent backwards, an invisible grip forcing it away from the button on the blaster.

I noted the Little Lord's face. I saw no tensing, no concentration at all. Little effort was being expended.

Maja resisted until her finger was near cracking. Then suddenly she let the weapon clatter to the floor, and in a single collapsing movement she fell on her face before the Little Lord.

"Forgive me," her voice came, a sob lurking in it. "Please forgive my momentary resistance to your will. He offended me so deeply. Your forbearance toward him is so holy that I cannot begin to understand."

The Little Lord regarded her without expression, which was, I thought, something eerie in a little girl. Apparently she had seen this sort of behavior before.

"No lord, neither myself nor my mother, would

doubt your loyal soul," she said at last. "Were the anomaly not almost upon us, perhaps; but these two must stay with us now. You will rise and understand."

Maja rose. She looked haggard and bewildered. Her glance wandered toward Lee and back again to me. The venom had vanished somewhere.

"You will know why," the Little Lord said. "It is not for him." The last word was a mouthful of dirt. "He is nothing, less than nothing, but still something that *she* values."

She pointed a finger at Lee.

"Not for him, but for her," the girl said. "She may have come with this man in a stolen Wholeth ship, but all things are forgiven when you understand why. You see. . . ."

Maja's eyes widened as the reason came.

"She seeks to find her mother!"

Chapter 22

The Little Lord destroyed the remaining crystals in my fingers. I don't know the exact mechanism she used, but I think all she did was to reach in with her mind and crush them. I know I felt a sudden stab of pain, one jolt merging with the other, and that was that; they were sore for the next week. It hurt less than if I had fired them.

I had left the sonic shoes on the black planet, and now the crystals were gone. I was left with hands and feet and nothing else, against a hypermind so powerful that it could work from cryogenic stasis, and Maja's lesser, but still significant, psionics.

We had separated from Lamonte's flagship. We were orbiting the Roil, shipcom programmed to position us who knew when at who knew where.

Maja was striding agitatedly around the cabin; the Little Lord sat calmly on the floor, petting Falon with studied concentration. Lee still sat in her study chair, her mood rising and falling on the Wholeth words being exchanged. I, against the wall, was thinking that the Little Lord would not have bothered to verbalize if Maja had been more competent at the Wholeth skill. It was something to remember, and perhaps to use.

"May I respectfully remind Your Little Lordship," Maja said, not looking her way, "that there is no need now to penetrate the Roil. We know that Polarian technology is inadequate to deal with it." I exchanged a significant glance with Lee, but hers was dismissive. I felt a pang of horror. She would have tried the descent even with 99 percent certainty that she would fail.

"We know that this one, and her lover Kellem," and she pointed at Lee abstractedly while I squirmed, "had no secret means of pulling a Polarian ship out of the Roil, and never did, that she was merely pursuing a thoughtless compulsion covering some kind of continuing guilt, and can no more represent a threat to us than any other neurotic could."

Lee winced almost imperceptively, her face already twisted by whatever was going on inside.

The Little Lord said nothing, and after a moment Maja went on.

"She knows nothing more than her government knows, and it's not enough, not even close to enough. I have to admit to you, Your Little Lordship, that the motive of Her Lordship for sending you out here is obscure to me. I did not understand it in the beginning, although the reason given was plausible, I suppose. You needed independence, tempering, and you needed to employ your power against the enemy in its own territory. But surely you have now experienced enough danger and exposure to the Polarians for a lifetime. You wandered their research facility at will, and despite the precautions the Lord took to protect you, the airtight security and cryogenic stasis and the distraction of the fleet, and the presence of me and Kalil, you performed beyond even her expec-

tations. Surely that is enough; there is no point in
continuing to . . ."

"You ramble," the Little Lordship retorted. "Your
conscious mind is aware that the mission is not complete until the death or erasure of the spies is certain. We know they derived the secret; we know
that it is possible to survive ten years in a starship
equipped with a food reprocessor. If they are dead,
then it is our mission to destroy their ship and all
its memories. If they live, their ship dies, and their
minds die too. Unless we accomplish that, the mission is incomplete."

Lee was as pale as unbaked dough. I felt my bowels tighten; this crazy infant was insisting that we
plunge into the Roil. I felt my future sinking like an
anvil.

"Please," I said, and the Little Lord shot me a
dangerous glance. "Please, Your Little Lordship, I
most humbly beg for permission to speak for a few
moments only."

The girl regarded me penetratingly, her fair face
only faintly disgusted.

"You are not entirely sincere in your humility,"
she said finally. I cast about in my mind, aware that
the girl probably knew every detail there.

"I am as sincere as my knowledge permits," I said
at length, very carefully. "You can see my background and, er, inherited character. I see you as
honestly as I can at this moment, and I very much
respect your abilities as well you know."

The Little Lord smiled slightly.

"Honest, at least," she said. "All right, speak, but
be short." She turned her back deliberately and
called to the cat.

"I thank you most humbly," I began, and the Little Lord strangled the next words in my throat.

"You must," she said, her back still and quiet,

snowy hair a halo around her, "struggle against your tendency toward sarcastic thought."

She released me, and I drew a deep breath.

"Continue," she said. I looked at her back uncertainly, and concluded that she wished me to annoy Selah Maja with my questions, rather than her royal visage.

So I turned to the scowling face of the Governor of the Outer Archipelago.

"The Polar Cloud has no interest in the Roil," I said. "You took the mind of the only man who cared at all, aside from this woman before you, who seeks her mother."

Maja spat, and the Little Lord frowned. I went on hastily. "If it is death to go in, or if they cannot emerge, then the issue is closed; the secret you seek to suppress is suppressed, and nothing can bring it forth, save some technological advance that is unguessed, unresearched, and unlikely."

I stopped. That was my argument in a nutshell. I, for both Lee's and my sake, wanted to stay out of the Roil. Selah Maja nodded her head.

"Yet," the Little Lord said quietly, and all at once I heard not a little girl, but a mature mind aware of the implications of the profoundest thought. "Yet, such advances are commonplace. We make them all the time. You make them too; you achieved one-way shielding only a few months after we did, and you will soon be able to place minigrav cannon on your smallest ships. Knowledge radiates through the universe like a beacon, and we detect it and you detect it at almost the same time, whether consciously or not."

I kept my jaw locked in place, not daring to break into her reedy immature voice.

"You may discover power enough to penetrate the Roil at any time; therefore, I must ensure that when you achieve it, you find nothing there. Anyone still alive within must die or be excised. That is the instruction of my mother, and of her mother before her, and of her mother before that."

Falon! The girl looked at the cat, and I tried to suppress my consciousness.

"And only now do we of the Whole possess the requisite power," she rasped. "The golden ship, one-way shielding, and me."

Maja moved as if to protest, and the girl waved for silence.

"The anomaly is almost upon us," she said. "I must prepare myself. Maja . . ."

"But then," I broke in, shrill, in desperation. "We will master the art of psionic genetics too. If knowledge radiates . . ."

"You would have had it by now," the girl said angrily. "But you do not. We had it twelve hundred years ago. We received it from the Onn."

The Onn? That alien fable that the Whole waved before us like a bogeyman? But we had never discovered living alien intelligence in all our wanderings throughout the galaxy, and its shroud stars and clusters and satellite galaxies.

"Aye," she said, facing me now, in her black eyes the agate of triumph. "Knowledge spreads throughout a species in single waves. The Chinese discovered gunpowder about the same time that the West did, though the church suppressed it. The Copernican universe was divined all over the world within a single century, and cross-cultural contact does not explain it. Atomic power emerged in four different countries within a decade. Interspatial mechanics hit two worlds separately within a single standard year. So did tachyonic holography. The species is sent a message, and it runs with it. But the message is species-specific; other species are at other stages. We of the Whole encountered the Onn; and we have absorbed some of their specific messages, and you, lacking such contact, did not."

I groaned. "Then we will approach the Onn," I said.

She laughed, her back to me, her voice a tinkly elven-tongue. But Maja spoke, for it was her thoughts that the little one was reflecting. "They are dead, the Onn." said Selah Maja. "When we destroyed Sigma Radidiani, we had no further need of them. The Onn are millennia dead, their only legacy a burntout world within the Wholeth domain. Yet records there are, and records we have translated. Secrets of another species are ours alone now, and can never be yours. There is no more simultaneity in human space."

"The One and Glorious Whole," I spat before I could stop myself. Maja's beautiful round face snarled, and the Little Lord shook out of her abstraction to call: "Remember what I said about sarcasm, man!"

"They possessed the same secret that has brought about the Wholeth Empire," I went on, greatly daring, "and all that is left of them is a burnt-out world? Is that what you are trying to tell me? Either it's fantasyland, or you too will . . ."

The Little Lord looked at me then, and I saw in her face that I was treading on extremely dangerous ground. Immediately I directed my thoughts into other channels, bowing slightly to her, but ending the train of thought with: "Even if true, the knowledge offers no real advantage to me or the Polarians."

The Little Lord had picked that thought up, I could see, and she seemed to be considering it, a frown on her face. And then she turned away, and I breathed yet another sigh.

"And now, sir, you have polluted the air enough," Maja said. I opened my mouth to expostulate, and

caught the expression on the Little Lord's face.
Instantly I clamped my jaw shut again.

Males among the Wholeth aristocracy, I thought,
must lead a difficult life.

Maja recommenced her pacing, and after an inter-
val began the one-sided argument again. The Little
Lord had brought a chair out of the floor and sat,
stroking the vibrating cat on her lap.

"Your Little Lordship," she said. "We have accomplished our mission. Let's go home, now. I tire of
Polarian company and cramped starships and the
emptiness in this region of space." She paused. "I
want to be back where there is a whole galaxy of
bright stars in the sky, and where worship can proceed without the, not unwelcome . . ." She grew
hesitant, and the girl's smile returned. "Er . . ." said
Maja, ". . . circumstances have forced us to be
so. . . ."

"Close?" the Little Lordship asked, and eased the
cat from her lap. Rising, she moved over and threw
her arms around Maja. "Don't fear the closeness,
dear Maja," she said. "You are blessed by it, and I
am comforted by it. You are strong and loyal, and I
love you so."

Maja's hands trembled as she eased them around
the little girl and hugged, and tears streamed down
her cheeks and mingled with the auburn hair of the
little girl.

Lee and I, awed, looked on. What was it like, I
wondered, to be hugged by your god?

"But we are staying," came the muffled voice of
the girl, face buried in the fabric of Maja's dress.
"We have not yet finished."

When they separated a little later, Maja wiped her
face dry and sat down again.

"I don't understand," she said shakily.

The little girl had the forward screen on now, and was looking out at the surface of the Roil.

"My mother coached me about this," she said. "Should events bring me this close to the solution. Look, Selah. They are somewhere in there, and as long as they are the problem is not really solved, even if this particular group of Polarians cannot reach them."

Lee's face was alight now.

"I don't think even this ship would survive, though," the girl went on, thinking aloud. "It's not strong enough to get out again, I'm guessing. Even from here, without trying, I can feel the chaos there; it tugs at me and pulls from side to side.

"Dear Maja, you should see; cast your mind down and feel it. Someday the Cloud will build a ship that can go in, and then maybe they'll find them or their corpses and get the secret. And that we cannot have."

Lee's tongue flickered nervously over dry, half-parted lips.

"No, there's only one way to end the problem for all time, and that's to go in and either take them out ourselves . . ." Lee moved restlessly. ". . . Or make certain that there is nothing left to find."

Lee was on her feet, rigid with fear and, I saw, hope.

"You can do it?" she croaked.

"I don't know," the little girl said seriously.

"Your Little Lordship, no!" Maja said. "It's too much of a risk. Your power is too untried."

"Please don't kill them," Lee wailed, sinking to her knees, hands folded in front of her.

"Eleven," the girl mused. Lee looked up sharply. "I can feel it stir, down there. It's strong, and its time has come again."

"Eleven," Lee breathed.

"Eleven?" I said stupidly, forgetting that I was not supposed to speak.

"Eleven years from anomaly to anomaly, the key that everyone missed, save Kel Kellem, lady," the girl said, looking at Lee, "and my mother's minds. And eleven has come again." She faced the screen again. "Full holography," she said, and the walls of the cabin disappeared around us, and we felt as if we were almost standing on the surface of the Roil, that terrible frozen seething surface that looked as if light had become congealed and lumpy with a ghastly coagulation.

"Yes, I feel it," the girl's voice came, and I saw the top half of her, outlined against the filtered light. Image, black on white, black arm raising slowly, pointing. . . .

"There," she said. "THERE!"

And there, where she pointed, the Roil opened up.

Chapter 23

"And the Roil opened up its mouth and swallowed them." So the Wholeth scriptures later would say.

I could think of no clearer image to explain the power that was pulling at us, the insanity then revealed. Like a gaping jaw the Roil opened up, and in a mad instant the golden ship went from dead stillness to incredible hurtling speed. Only the internal gravity saved us all from being dashed into droplets against the bulkhead.

I saw the little girl, standing black on white, arm still extended and pointing invisibly at the awful stygian maw before us. Already below the visible surface, a tunnel seemed to wrap itself around us, a tunnel of knobby light filtered from incandescence by the ship. It sped by at unbelievable speed, planet-sized globules of superheated gas and dust, glowing in something that was only just more than vacuum, that looked as solid as red-hot rock. I felt Lee's body somewhere behind me, pressing against the cabin wall, palms flat against it, lips apart, watching almost against her will, her eyes skewed to one side, looking out of the corners of them at the dizzying kaleidoscope hurtling past.

As for Maja, she held a gentle hand on the shoulder of the girl, as if, now committed, she supported the girl's decision and prayed for the both of them.

There were colors, I saw, whites and oranges and ocher, black streaks and valleys, pink swirls and golden flares. Beauty and nausea. Dizziness and awe. How fast, I wondered, how incredibly fast, rushing down a well, falling into a pit of light.

It was long. It seemed as if there were no end. Static blasted from the ship's speakers, flares dazzled and cleared again, tornadoes of fire appeared and vanished. Spots and waves and mountains of light appeared before us. Giant prominences grew and fell as they approached and then hurled by.

Vision became distorted and confused. Ears hissed with white noise. The skin felt hot; the psyche feared incineration, and quailed back before it, in a starship that would have remained comfortable for a time in the skin of a red giant.

It ended. Two hours. More? I could not tell. Long enough, longer than I would ever want to bear again.

The static. I commanded the ship to shut up. It ignored me. The people in it ignored me.

The maw was gone. In its place was . . . something. A swirl, sort of. A stirring, nearly frozen to the eye by the speed of it, lumps of vivid ice sherbet humping crazily in dazzling rainbow colors, shapes of geometrical perfection, rising and falling, bulging and receding, elliptical solidities around a central madness. Two thirds of the horizon was taken up before us, moving so rapidly that I could barely see the movement, but of a complexity that I could only guess was planet-sized or larger, and that around that crazy something we were falling into a violent orbit.

I looked around. It was as if the whirl before us had sucked the sky clear for light minutes. We seemed to sit inside a sphere of wispy light, fuzzily knobbed and twisting in the same direction as the whirl.

And then I felt shock. Back the way we had come, there was nothing other than the light of super-heated gas. The hole was gone.

Now for the first time I began to reason clearly, and listened to the muttering readouts of the ship-com's analysis. Eleven years, the girl had said, a cycle that came and went with precise regularity, triggered somehow by that dizzy chaos before us. A gravitational cycle of some kind, an aligning of forces into linear strength, or perhaps a gap which allowed the power inside to escape, creating a complexity beyond technology's power to simulate, a complexity born of forty neutron stars and hundreds of planets and singularities and the dust and chaos of the Roil, and captured by a central mystery that bled in and out of the universe like two bellows, nozzles linked, pushing, sucking, pushing, sucking. And there was the cycle that had brought us in, that came and went every eleventh year, a periodicity like the sunspot cycle of most G-type stars, but here opening up a trough in space-time, a well of gravitation that grabbed anything around it and inhaled it into the hot belly of the Roil.

No, I decided, not the belly. Hardly even the skin. We had fallen long and deep according to my human senses, but the time had not been long enough for the golden ship to have been drawn even a sixteenth of the way in. The Roil was too big for that.

Not its belly, but its skin, a pustule erupting every eleventh year.

And there, far below them at the center of it all, hung a massive seething thing, around which the stars and other matter of the Roil swung in erratic, looping orbits of blinding speed. No wonder the sci-entists had never figured it out, from the outside, I thought as I regarded the screen and listened to the readouts with the others, thoughts of enmity drowned in awe. It was something that had captured stars and planets and dust and everything else in its path in its ages-long sweep through space, maybe capturing several things like itself to grow more massive and then smaller and more dense. Something out of the era of the Big Bang itself, and scientists did not even half understand its gigantic cousins, sitting billions of years in the past outside the galactic bubbles and radiating energy beyond present understanding. If they did not yet understand quasars, how could they understand this thing at the heart of the Roil?

It was not a quasar, though, for quasars radiate the force of millions of galaxies, and this thing's brightness came from the excited molecules around it, not the thing itself. The object pulsed in and out of a point source, in and out of a singularity, like a balloon pushed through a keyhole, squeezed back and forth, a million times a second. The fragment of a collapsed quasar, call it, something torn loose from one and nearly frozen in time, belching in and out of real space like a supermassive bubble of . . . what? And what was on the other side of that pinpoint keyhole? Interspace itself? Another realm entirely?

My thoughts moved in another direction. She had said she felt it stirring, that its time had come. What was "it"? The incredible thought flashed into my mind. The Roil . . . was it somehow alive?

"No." The Little Lord's voice came to me over the static hiss. She ordered the speakers dead then, and stopped the holography. Like a closing trap the walls of the ship snapped into view around us, and the outside scene contracted and condensed to lie at last flattened on the viewing screen above the control console.

All of the people in that little ship relaxed, visibly

or not, as the psychologically familiar starship walls replaced the strangeness that had surrounded us but a moment before. I reached up and felt my forehead; it was slippery with sweat. Then I saw blood, and stared at my last ruined fingertip. The pain was there somewhere, from the crystal blast at the Little Lord.

"No," the girl said again, turning to look contemptuously at me, the cabin's lights revealing her again. "Not alive, as your muddy thought suggests. I feel no mind, no volition, nothing on the thought scale. Except, of course, for the Polarian spies ahead."

Lee pushed away from the wall and flung her arms toward the girl in a mute plea.

"Yes," the girl said, turning her cold stare at her. "I feel them. They live."

Lee uttered a broken sob and fell to her knees, and held her tortured face up for all to see, tears streaming from her eyes, too much emotion there to even want to conceal. I moved as if to comfort her, and the Little Lord stopped me with a blow to my brain that left me dazed for minutes, forgetting what I had intended to do. I leaned against the wall, shaking my head slowly from side to side, hearing but not comprehending the dialogue that had begun in the cabin.

"Lady," the Little Lord said coldly. "Do not blaspheme by praying to another god in my presence, if you please. Your emotion gets the better of you."

Lee bowed her head.

Maja was still staring at the screen.

"Your Little Lordship," she said at last. "You sense them, somewhere in front of us? It would be beyond my power, I can see, as I feel nothing but confusion from outside the ship. But it's been eleven years! How could they survive for such a time, here?"

The cat appeared from somewhere and jumped onto Lee's inclined lap. She started, and the cat leaped indignantly away. It walked up to Maja and the girl, and rubbed itself sinuously around their legs, one after the other.

"They survive," the girl said flatly. "We speed not nearly fast enough that time is changed. The force from the fragment is strong; it spins us around like a yo-yo on a string." She leaned down absently and touched the cat, who leaned his head up to be scratched between the ears. "Theirs are the only thoughts I sense, out there. It would seem that Crestor Falon is dead."

Maja's voice exclaimed something incoherent, then said; "Falon?" The cat looked up, hearing its name.

"Oh, yes, dear Maja, Falon is somewhere out there too. But even with the speed we go, it is not enough; time here in the skin of the Roil is almost identical with that outside. My mother hoped, I think, that there was a chance for him, despite what her physicists told her. She had revenge to take, passed down from her mother's mother. I know now that it has been too long."

I shuddered. From what I had heard, Falon had been a lecher and a fool, but to sit in a starship while the air and water fail, trapped in a ball of light . . .

"If you had found him alive?" Maja asked tentatively.

"He would have died," the girl said. "Killing a man is not so difficult; you have done it yourself." She paused, thoughtful, her little girl's mind struggling with the dimly understood motivations of the adults who had instructed her. "But I would have taken him, and reserved the pleasure for my mother. The masses may have adulated him, but my mother was told by her mother what he had done, and it was everything that could be expected from a man." The bitterness in her voice was tangible, squeezed through the puritanism of the Whole in which she had been raised, and overlaid with the passed-down

memory of an infidelity hideous to its victim, and
the careless cruelty of a child.

Idiot that I was, to let such thoughts arise, still
struggling with the effects of her earlier mental blow.
Pity for her came suddenly unbidden to my mind,
and I quailed inside. Slowly she turned and looked
at me, and I left the universe.

I recovered my senses an indefinite time later,
and found that the ship was underway, and knew
then that during its long, mad rush into the Roil it
had used no power at all, except for shielding, hadn't
even tried to fight the force that was upon it. I saw,
glancing from my vantage point on the floor toward
the visible controls, and hearing the endless shipboard commentary by the computer, that it was
working on overtaking the spy ship, forcing itself
higher in the tightly wound orbit.

The first impulse of Lee's parents would have
been to try to fly out, I realized. But if they had
fired their inertialess engine, their shields would
have fallen, and they would have fried like bacon on
a skillet in the midst of that awful radiation from the
Roil. And even if they could have employed it, they
lacked the power to break free. They would have
known it, and they would have broadcast mayday
on tachholo, radio, and up and down the spectrum,
sending forth their secrets and crying and pleading,
and would have been greeted by enough static to
deafen them, for there was no signal in the universe
that could have departed the swept-out interior of
the Roil.

I looked over toward Lee, who was resting tensely
in her study chair, staring at the screen, and frustration came over me for about the twentieth time.
How I wanted to speak to her, encourage her, comfort her, hug her; and yet the Little Lord would
permit no such display of vulgar Polarian affection.

All I could do, I thought in my stupid romantic soul, was stare at her, try to catch her eye, make her see in some way that I was still with her, that I understood the turmoil that had been in her for all that time. But she seemed to avoid my eyes, hers being fixed intently on the screen, her face now showing no overt emotion. It troubled me, and self-doubt flared again, and I began to analyze my history with her again, while knowing at the same time that I would have run out on her before we had climbed aboard the OB, if I had known what I was in for. Yet now I loved her, G-d help me.

"And now," the Little Lord announced, "I believe that I will revive Restor Kalil."

My head jerked up. The Little Lord was watching me, a grim humor on her little pale face.

The floor of the cabin moved apart, and a mottled grey blob moved upward, much larger than the last one I had seen, but with cold mist swirling off in the same way.

"He is a jerk," Selah Maja observed quietly to the little girl.

"Of course," she said, implying "Aren't they all?" "But we don't know what abilities the spies still have. One more soldier may be important in that which lies before us this day."

Quickly now, the grey solidity hazed over and sublimated away. The rotund belly of the Sub-Governor appeared at the same time as the nose. The florid face came into view, eyes still closed as the mist faded down his body, sucked into the floor.

At length he lay sprawled there, his chest moving as breathing came, hand still bandaged in the regeneration sac that would now once again begin to work.

Slowly Kalil passed his free hand over his eyes and groaned. Then he rolled over and sat up groggily, digging at his eyes with both hands, then jerking with pain as the regeneration sac was disturbed.

The pain seemed to clear him, and he opened his eyes.

The first thing he saw was me.

A snarl and his good hand leaped for his holster, but it was empty. Then with surprising speed he clawed his way to his feet, hatred bringing what was almost intelligence into his eyes.

Desperately I shot a glance at Maja and the little girl, but they were sitting by, humor playing over both of their tight-lipped mouths. Then I looked back toward Kalil in time to avoid by inches a groin kick.

I wondered what the Little Lord would do if I smashed Kalil down, and then wondered that I could wonder, rather than be in the blue funk that true conflict had always heretofore put me in. But despite my untoward mental calmness, I was conscious of the limitations imposed by the bandaged hands. So I jumped forward and clinched with Kalil, and hissed into his ear: "No, you dumb ox. Not in front of Her Little Lordship."

Kalil froze and glanced with horror toward Maja and the little girl. After a long second, I released him and backed away, barely in time to avoid being dragged down as Kalil fell heavily to his knees, recognition in his eyes.

"Your Little Lordship," he croaked, forehead touching the deck. "Your Little Lordship. . . ."

"No, you don't deserve the honor," the Little Lord said haughtily, reading his thoughts, "and if I did not know about your rampant stupidity when you were fooled by this Polarian dog," she indicated me, "I do now by your own thought. Arise and get a chair and sit quietly and don't disturb me by word or thought."

Kalil rose hastily and pulled out a chair. I wondered with amazement how he could grovel and fawn at the same time. After a moment of bovine worshipfulness, the Sub-Governor allowed his eyes to dart confusedly around the cabin, coming at rest finally on the screen. Immediately the oddness caught his starship pilot's eyes, and he stared at it for long moments, wondering.

"Don't just sit there like a corpse," Maja snapped at him. She tossed him a stunner. "Cover Sangre but don't shoot him unless he makes a move. He . . . er . . . amuses the Little Lord."

Amuses? I thought.

Kalil looked toward me, hatred coming back into his eyes.

"Sangre, is it?" he hissed. "So. I'll . . ."

"And shut up," the Little Lord rasped. Kalil jumped.

"Yes, Your Lordship, yes. . . ."

She shot a baleful glance at him.

"Your *Little* Lordship," she said.

"Yes, my Lord . . . er, Your . . ."

"Silence!" the Little Lord shrieked.

"Let's freeze them both," Maja urged.

"The spy ship is signalling," the computer broke in without emotion. Lee leaned forward.

"No reply," the Little Lord said shortly, and then to Maja. "No, I'll not freeze them yet," she said. "The lady's guilt would confuse the mental flow. Let the Polarian soak in the helplessness that I feel in him; it's good for the cocky creep."

By now used to the insults, I ignored them and thought: *Guilt? Did Lee feel so guilty that she had brought me into this? Well, she damn well should!*

"That's only partly it, not even by half," the Little Lord said nastily.

Damn again, I thought; I can't get used to the idea that she can read my every thought. But what did she mean this time? What other guilt could there be?

"Just this," the Little Lord said cruelly. "She . . ."

"No," Lee's voice came suddenly. The girl looked at her.

"It must come sometime," she said.

"Not yet," said Lee.

Chapter 24

We watched as the golden ship accelerated along the orbit that the anomaly had brought it to, an orbit around the central something that so baffled the science of our day. Shipcom could detect the presence of separate stellar objects, planetary masses, and debris of all sorts, wildly gyrating around the central object; all we could see through the intensely filtered screens was a pulsation in the center of our universe and whirling lines like planetary rings around it—objects revolving so fast that they appeared solid. And covering it all, as if we were the filling inside a bun, was the phosphorescent shell of the Roil, excited particles that had not yet made the plunge inward, or had filled out from jet streams of material outward from the violence at the center.

We were in a region that had been swept clear by the objects rotating around the center of the Roil. Our orbit was dizzyingly fast, as would that of anything sucked down by the eleven year anomaly; yet time still stood as it did outside, to our limited perception. It would have taken a speed 90 percent that of light for us to notice the dilation when, or if, we finally emerged into the larger universe; we were going fast, but not that fast.

Here, in this hollow shell, had fallen every object caught by the Roil's space-twisting anomaly during its millennial history. Here, inside this empty space, there spun the astronomer's son, a desiccated corpse in a ship whose automatics were probably still scanning space-time for tachholo or other electromagnetic intelligence. Somewhere too was Crestor Falon, his ship newer and more aware, but the lover of the long-dead Wholeth Lord dead himself these many years. And somewhere too, nearby, there revolved the spy ship of the parents of Celia D'Ame. But here not only was the shipcom alive, but living beings within, though only the Little Lord and Maja could detect it.

There came a muted clang as the two ships touched. The port appeared silently in its place on the deck. We looked at it. On Lee's face, an expression of starved hope; on Kalil's, one of puzzled watchfulness. Maja's square, intense face looked square and intense; the Little Lord's shocking white hair matched her eyes, turned inward now, only the whites showing. I kept myself blank as several emotions chased each other around me.

"Do you feel it?" the Little Lord breathed.

"Aye," Maja said, some kind of apprehension distorting her tone. "Aye. This I did not expect."

"Nor I," the Little Lord said. "But they are young, without training. They are weak."

Then the attack came and the cat yowled. I felt it as a wave of panic that smote me from somewhere else, an emotional chaos that lasted only a split second, yet which shook me to the roots. I saw Lee flinch as her expression of eager expectation passed into horror and out again. Kalil staggered, pain clear in his face. Maja flinched not at all. The Little Lord closed her eyes.

"There," she said, and opened them again. The panic left me as quickly as it had come. "They are asleep now," she said. "Come, Maja, let us open the port and see what lies behind."

"Are they dead?" Maja said. Lee froze, fear fleeing and hatred rushing to its place.

"No, of course not," the Little Lord said, casting a glance of annoyance upon Selah Maja. "They are like us; I would not kill them."

The port dilated and they, as one, piled down inside, a fetid stench hitting us. I hesitantly looked through the hatch after them. Could I close it on them and escape? No way, I thought, not with Lee down there.

Her mother looked like Lee in angular natural, mature beauty. The man was grey-haired, and I saw Lee in the way he carried himself, in the expression on his face rather than in any single physical feature.

But it was the deck of the spy ship that caught my attention. There, stretched out all around the two adults, lay five children in various postures of peaceful sleep, scattered as they had fallen. From perhaps five years to one, in yearly increments. Five children with auburn hair and angular faces and, I saw with amazement, all girls.

Even as I cast about for some explanation, the woman raised her blaster shakily and pointed it at us. Kalil snarled and raised his stunner, but the Little Lord waved him back.

"No," she said quietly, almost kindly. "It will not activate." And she stepped toward the woman, Maja close upon her heels.

"Mother!" The cry came from Lee as she flung herself forward. The woman took a step backward and her finger seemed tightened upon the blaster stud. But nothing happened and Lee wrapped her arms around her. The man looked, recognition in his eyes.

After a moment the older woman, a frown on her face, disengaged herself.

"And who," she said matter-of-factly, "might you be?" She stared at Lee, a puzzled look of half-comprehension in her green eyes.

"Lee," the man said, moving forward, voice thick.

"Daddy!" And there was another hug, and the mother, realizing the truth, came to them hesitantly.

"But," the woman said, "It's been only eleven years. How . . ?" Then she caught herself. Lee's face—what had eleven years of obsession done to it? It had always seemed more than acceptable to me. But there were lines around her eyes, and a downturned cast to her mouth, and her cheekbones were prominent and strained, I saw in a moment of clarity.

Lee reached out and pulled her forward.

The Little Lord had bent down and touched the first of the children lying in her path.

"They are beautiful," she said in her little girl voice. "Maja . . ."

The Governor was right behind her. "I understand," she said. "Kalil," she commanded. "Take them inside and put them into stasis."

"No," Lee's father said, head swivelling around and body craning suddenly forward.

"Stop," the Little Lord said, almost disdainfully. The man stopped. I looked as if I didn't want to, but somehow had to.

"They are ours," the Little Lord said. "You bred them with your Polarian germ, but they are ours nevertheless. Don't you think that I can feel the presence of a sister, can sense the aura of their holy souls?"

Lee's mother held Lee at arm's length while looking queerly at the little girl.

"They are my children," she said simply. The Little Lord stared at her, baffled, but in her stance, in

her eyes, in her soul, there was some faint understanding at least.

"Lee," Teelya D'ame said finally, as her man quivered with suppressed pain. "Why do you come with
a Wholeth Lord?"

The five children were placed into stasis. Maja
herded us all back into the golden ship, which was
now becoming crowded. Kalil held a stunner on us,
a ferocious scowl of loyalty on his face.

The mother, arm around Lee's shoulder, watched
the Little Lord.

"I can only guess at what you've been going
through," the mother said quietly. "But . . ."

There was confusion in Lee's face, pain. Guilt. I
wanted to reach out to her, but was inhibited by the
presence of the Little Lord.

"Eleven years," the man said to himself. "One
more year, maybe two, and the air would have run
out, and we would have risked it then. The children
might have been old enough to bring us out. And
now we must lose them?" His voice became queru-
lous. A tear rolled out of one eye and down a handsome cheek.

"And I had assumed," Lee said to them, voice
breaking, "that you would have merely survived all
these years. I should have guessed, I really should,
that you might have put to work the secret that you
had stolen."

The father glanced at her through angry tears.
"And you destroy . . ." he said. His wife stopped
him, sadness filling her face. She spoke quietly.
"What would you have done? We knew that we
would die; the ship was not nearly strong enough to
pull us out even if we could drop the shields, but
we could not do even that. But maybe, just maybe,
with paranormals aboard . . ."

"They could not have done it," the Little Lord

said flatly. "They were too untrained. There is skill involved."

"I don't believe that," the man said. "It would have been a simple exercise of Wholeth mind-skill over particle and photon, and an easing of the gravitational trough. I was teaching them what they would face. They could have done it."

"You deceive yourself into hope," the Little Lord said. "You were among us long enough to know: skill is formed both by genetics and by technique; the one must come before, but the other must follow. They have native skill, but I am god-born, and have been trained from infancy."

The man apparently knew his Wholeth lords, for he did not pursue the subject even, apparently, in his overt mind.

"Oh, Lee," her mother cried. "We might have made it! We had the secret! And now they'll take the children, and they'll take the secret too." Lee clung to her, seeming not conscious of the indictment implied by her mother's words.

"You strain her sanity," Maja said to the older woman. The latter seemed to tense, and then looked toward her daughter, sadness again on her face. Her face altered, and she held her tightly against her, stroking her long auburn hair.

"It's all right," she almost crooned. Tears began in the corners of Lee's eyes. "It's all right. . . ."

"But you are correct on one point," Maja pursued in her relentless way. "We will take the secret away." Then I noticed that the Little Lord's face was intent, an expression I had seen before. I cast my eyes around, and saw the victim.

Lee's father had his mouth open and eyes closed. His mouth was moving rapidly, frantically. Silent words were pouring out. The others became aware of it, and Lee's mother, in some kind of mental agony, made as if to intervene.

"Do not," the Little Lord said, teeth clenched, eyes on the man.

"You may injure him if you interfere," Maja interposed hastily to Teelya D'ame.

After a time, the Little Lord said; "Three hiding places on the ship, aside from the computer banks themselves."

"Where?" Maja said crisply. The Little Lord told her.

"Watch them," Maja snapped to Kalil, and moved back into the other ship.

"And now you will forget," the Little Lord said, almost cruelly, as the father stood there, his mouth open, a vacancy in his eyes.

And then his head jerked forward as if something had been yanked from it. Lee's mother gave a cry and reached for me, and he fell against her shoulder, weak tears on his face.

"Oh, Teelya, oh Teelya," his shaky voice came. "There, there," she said, and then turned her gaze upon the Little Lord. For, she knew with crystal precision, it was her turn.

The Little Lord pulled it all out of her, but in a manner much more deliberate and kindly than that which she had used on the man. She permitted Lee's mother to speak aloud in an almost normal voice, telling of the long lonely days after their capture by the Roil, days during which each had, despite themselves but inevitably, palled upon the other. They had tried tachyonic holography, and had been greeted by a roar of Roil-induced static.

After a long time, they grew desperate as no one responded. Perhaps, they thought, someone would hear their transmission, response or not. While the secret of the Wholeth genetics was vital to the Cloud, it did no one any good while trapped in the Roil. And so they had, at last, broadcast the secret into the hissing ether. And of course, there was no reply.

Nothing, neither electromagnetic nor tachyonic, could escape the Roil in coherent form.

The desperate realization had born down upon them, that they had only one chance, and that it had meant the procreation of other lives which might then be lost in the failing air and food. The Wholeth process, the conceptions, the birthings, the child rearing with all its joys and sorrows and fatigue. The attempt to understand the paranormal powers of the children, the attempt to train them when the parents themselves did not know how. The struggle, sometimes vicious, to keep the children from blasting each other and their parents too, as rivalries came and went and raw mental power unsteadied the innocent minds.

And then, the unexpected. The golden ship had come. And they had made their hasty defense, for the other ship was Wholeth. And the five children grouped for a single, concentrated mental blast, similar to something they had practiced in the past. And . . . failure.

Struggle, desperation, hopelessness and hope. It was all mirrored in the eyes and face of Lee's mother.

"It hurt so much to leave you," she said at one point to Lee. "To go on a mission that was more than likely fatal for us. And we succeeded, but how we had to go about it, Lee. It hurts even now to think about it, even after all this time. The Wholeth women, and men, were as much animals as . . ."

The Little Lord cut her off there, with anger in her features. And after that the mother's words came in silence, increasing to a whispered babble. And finally, more gently, that jerk forward as the information was withdrawn.

*   *   *

"They remember no more, as to how the children came to be, as to how to make more," the Little Lord told Lee a little later as Lee cradled her two parents on the deck, a head resting on each of her thighs. "This way they will be happier. They will remember in an abstract sort of way, but the agony will be gone. The children, naturally, will remember nothing."

Maja appeared through the hatch, a smoking blaster in her hand. "It is done," she said. "The hiding places are destroyed, the databanks erased."

"Then we have finished," the Little Lord said. "The mission is at last accomplished. The secret is ours again."

We all looked at her, I with hatred, Lee with baffled self-doubt, Kalil with awe and Maja with affection. The parents on the floor stirred, as if the thought disturbed them in their sleep.

We cast off the spy ship; it would have been a drag rather than a boost, had we used a maglink. We spun mutely around the Roil, the lovely, terrible colors all around.

And then the Little Lord tensed and closed her eyes. And the golden ship paused in its mad orbit, paused and seemed to stand on its tail, and then, with the modern power of its engines, protected by one-way shields, driven forward and enhanced by the future Wholeth Lord, it leaped outward and away from the Roil of stars in a maneuver that would have killed everything aboard a lesser ship.

The golden cone tore through the sphere that surrounded us. This time there was no tunnel, no gravitational anomaly to direct us. We simply raged through the fabric of the Roil, ripping through a vacuum of superheated gas, the ship's sensors weaving around the occasional rock and dust grain in our path.

It took a little longer, this time, going in than coming out. The screen showed an almost changeless redness which rippled occasionally with flickers of other colors, oranges and yellows and sometimes blacks, always just an instant, come and gone again.

I thought I saw my chance. The Little Lord's face was screwed shut in the first real intensity that I had seen there. Immense power was being directed and expended, I saw. She was being tested to her limit. And, I guessed, she had no time to watch what was going on around her.

It wasn't patriotism that motivated me, I don't think. It wasn't love for Lee, or self-preservation, this time. If I can pin it down after all these years, I have to say that it was disgust. The idea of living under the aegis of someone such as the Little Lord disgusted me. Perhaps that is patriotism, I don't know. Certainly I wouldn't have done it a year before; then I would have whined and begged-your-pleasure, ma'am. But now I was action-honed, suicidal perhaps. Perhaps I sensed what could come under the Wholeth empire, with a paranormal precognition of my own.

The speakers roared with the random hiss of the Roil, and in a single step I reached Kalil and chopped down on the hand that held the stunner. Kalil, bemused by the scene on the screen, cried in sudden pain and anger. I backhanded him, pain shooting through me from my injured fingers, and bent to pick up the stunner.

And then Maja caught me in a mental blast that sent me reeling against the wall. My mind cleared just in time to see Restor Kalil's hamlike fist coming at me, too close for any reaction. It caught me on the cheek and split the skin, blood splattering into one eye. I moved aside clumsily, trying to shake off Maja's mental attack. Kalil moved in on me with surprising agility, and his knee struck me a glancing blow on the ribs, sending me to the deck. But even as I rolled back onto my feet, I thought that I saw a way to stop Maja at least.

Deliberately I brought into my mind a vision of sex, of man and woman, wrapped in each other, the passion, the taste, the graphic joy of it. And at once I felt Maja's mind jerk away. I laid it on, with relish, thrusting image after image at her with all the force of my consciousness. I saw Maja shudder, and felt her mind fall away from mine, and felt a moment of victory.

And then I felt Restor Kalil's foot in my solar plexus. The old soldier was as well-trained as any recruit in the Cloud. My breath went in a whoosh, the sound lost in the hissing static. And then the Sub-Governor's good fist came at me again, and I could not avoid it. I tried to pull back, to lessen it, and my head struck the cabin wall and rebounded forward, and Kalil's fist hit and rammed my head against the wall again, driving all thought out of my mind like a rock exploding into fragments.

At long last I came to. I was still in the golden ship. The hissing was gone. On the screen, the Roil rolled below us like a knobby golf ball. The port was open, and beyond it I saw the muted light of the Wholeth flagship.

Selah Maja was speaking. I saw then that I was in a chair, slumped against a wall. Standing around me were Lee, her face a mask; her father, silent, still possessed of a residual, now unfocused anger; and Teelya, her mother, a little sad.

". . . it will drop you on the black planet. Do not try to keep it there; it will only explode and kill someone. Just disembark, and it will seal and take off again."

The Little Lord came in, and saw that I was

awake. I looked around; but the cat was apparently gone.

"Come, Maja," the girl said shortly. She glanced again at me, and I saw an extra satisfaction in her eyes.

"Soon you will know," she said, white hair wild.

For a moment I was confused, and then I caught Lee looking at me with an expression of intense . . .

Guilt.

And then I did know, and a pain came into me that was like nothing before, all the worse for the fact that I had ignored the signs, or tried to. I hadn't wanted to face it, but now I had to.

The Little Lord took a step backward, shock darkening her face. I looked at it and laughed. It was a terrible laugh, a thing of pain and shame, shaking my shoulders and rasping at my throat.

"It hurts, doesn't it, Your Lordship? Even the echo of it that you can feel, hurts."

"Your Little Lordship," the girl said mechanically, but I was not going to stop this time until someone forced me.

"Maybe men have real feelings too, little terrible one. Maybe there's hope for you yet when you can feel it and it bothers you." There were tears in my eyes now, and I let them come and virtually shouted at the little girl. "Look around you, Little Lord, get away from your Wholeth harems and get out to the people and find out what human beings are like, not what power-mad twisted abnormal souls like Selah Maja are." Maja took a step forward, and the Little Lord restrained her. "Find out what it's like when you're not rich or powerful or comfortable. You'll never really be in charge . . ." A sob shook me, and I said, "until you *feel.*"

Lee was at my side then, and the Little Lord was standing there, puzzlement and something else on her freckled face. She seemed to hesitate, and hesitation was a thing foreign to her. and then Maja stepped in and took her arm and they turned away, and the last thing I saw were the unsettled eyes of the little girl.

"I'm sorry," Lee said clumsily then. I fought for control.

"I somehow knew," I said, agony still in my eyes as I looked at her exquisite face. "But I hoped. I loved you so, Lee. I really did."

"I know," Lee said. Her parents looked on, making no move to interfere.

"But," Lee said, looking away, her head bowed, auburn hair tangled. "I would have used anyone at all, Ryne. I had no wish to hurt you, but I had to."

"You strung me along . . ."

"Yes," she interrupted dully. "And I would do it again."

I looked at her in mute suffering, wanting her and knowing that I would never, never have her again.

She moved off toward her parents.

Epilogue

First Chief Anselm J. Dooty slammed us into his repaired brig after ascertaining that we all had normal fingers. Then Palla Belanger showed up like a bad penny, and debriefing began. I had mourned over Lee for the eighteen days it took the golden ship to reach the Institute, and the three days we were there, and for two more days while the newly appointed Fleet Admiral took us to what was left of Sigma Radidiani.

I saw Lee for the last time when we disembarked there. She didn't look at me, and I couldn't look at her, until she had turned away. Watching her erect body walking with her parents toward a waiting groundcar is a vision seared into my soul. Palla Belanger was watching me, and she got all the satisfaction she would have wanted from it.

I divined later that Lee and her parents had been turned inside out by Polarian Intelligence, but that they could reveal nothing useful to the Cloud. The parents had residual memories of the children they had raised under the awful conditions of the spy ship, but emotion for them, and of course the knowledge of the techniques of genetic manipulation, had been driven from their brains by the Little Lord.

Lee's memory had not been tampered with, but she knew nothing that was of any use. The admiralty thanked her for her role in recovering the spies, erased the blots on her record, and sent her home with her parents to Aryeh, an obscure backwater world near the center of the Polar Cloud. There she raised children, after a time, though I have not been able to identify who her husband, or whatever, was.

It wasn't Jame Torrester, who survived the Sigma Radidiani attack and went on to distinguish himself as a leader of fighter pilots; I had changed my subliminals several times, by the way, and they were beginning to sound like his. Randy Slader was dead; so were Claire Hevel, Rik O'Rourke, and Vice-Admiral Oul Chester, among the eighty thousand. Cassia Glane is back on Spandor, insofar as I can tell without drawing attention to my researches. Once this is published in the public on-line files, I'll be gone, and then I won't care anymore whether Cassia's thugs come after me.

I demanded a public trial. Already an idea was percolating in my brain. I had despaired of survival after the spies' secret had been erased, and hadn't cared much about surviving anyway, the situation with Lee being what it was. But then I began to consider, and some of my old cravenness emerged, thank G-d, though I was heartened to discover that it was much diminished. Lee had changed me in a number of ways.

Fleet Admiral Palla Belanger might have executed me out of hand, but the public notoriety I had brought through my transmission from the golden ship now served me well. Public opinion had been highly critical after my apparent escape from the black planet and destruction of the dreadnought, but now all that mattered was that I, rogue pilot, was an item of interest again in the on-line news. Reporters clamored to see me. I clamored to see them.

A week prior to the trial, I demanded to see Fleet Admiral Belanger. Two days later she strode in, fine body, shovel face, and all.

"What do you want?" she grated. I felt as if my ears had been clawed.

"I want you to call off the trial," I said. She snorted, staring at me from her speckled eyes as if I were berserk.

"If you think that what you did to Kitty could lead me to pity you, you should think the opposite," she barked. "Castrating you in public would be what I would prefer." I winced. If Kitty had been trying to reach me, my jailers had let me have no knowledge of it.

"I know," I told her, "how to save the Polar Cloud."

She snorted. She'd been having a bad time of it since her elevation to Fleet Admiral. She had to sit in council with the other fleet admirals of the Cloud, and it galled her to have to argue her militant point of view, over and over again, rather than to simply act. The worst thing about it was submitting to the civilian authority on Tyghe's Planet. She had no use for anyone not ready to kill a million people out of hand. Only later did she achieve true power, and then the cataclysms came.

"If you did," she rasped, "the Wholeth harpies would have erased your brain. You know nothing."

"I knew nothing *then*," I said. "I hadn't put it together; no one had. Now I am telling you that I know how to win this war over the Whole, or at least a way of bringing it to a standstill."

She snorted again, but in her eyes now was the glitter of interest.

"Tell me," she said.

"I'll tell in open court," I said, "with fifteen trillion

citizens watching. Of course, once the secret is out, it won't be much good. But the citizens of the Cloud will know at least that Ryne Sangre was a loyal soldier and could have saved them, if the pigheaded admiralty hadn't been in such a hurry to kill him."

"Loyal soldier!" She hooted. "Don't make me laugh." She laughed.

"Or," I said, "you can drop the charges and admit that I was on special assignment, deep cover, call it what you want. Tell the Cloud that it was the ship, not me, that destroyed the dreadnought. As for the rest, say nothing; secret spy mission, etc. In return, I'll win the war for you."

She walked up to the bars and stared in, eyes trying to kill.

"I will have you drugged, and drag out whatever fantasy that pea brain has inside it. Then I'll see you tried and shot, no matter what you've got."

"I don't think so," I told her, meeting her eye for eye, though I have to admit that my bowels were water. "I offer not only salvation in the war, Ms. Fleet Admiral, which you know as well as I cannot be won; the Whole is too numerous and just far enough beyond us in technology, not to mention the paranormals among them. All they'll have to do, eventually, is infiltrate more and more of those into the Cloud, and we're done, and you know it."

"Enough of this," she growled. "I will listen to no such defeatist talk. If you have nothing else, then good-bye and be damned. I'll see you at the trial, what's left of you."

"You don't have to drug me, Fleet Admiral," I said. "I am willing to give you two things. The first I have already said."

"And the second?" she hissed impatiently.

I took a deep breath.

"The second," I said. "The second is more personal. I would be willing, if our arrangements are concluded . . ."

"Well?" she said. "Get on with it."

"I would be willing," I said, "to marry Kitty."

I thought the top of her head would burst open and smoke pour out. Her face flushed so deep a red that I feared for her heart.

But I had worked this out in my mind, that great machine of self-preservation. Most of it was guesswork, but I was pretty sure it was solid. I had been imagining what it was like to be Palla Belanger, with a pregnant daughter yammering at her while she tried to lead the Cloud into aggressive warfare. What had Kitty been saying, I had wondered? Had she wept and wailed over her lover's fate, and the fate of her coming child, and the fate of her poor self, over and over and over in her mother's ear?

One thing I had known ever since our interview on the black planet: Palla Belanger valued her daughter. She would deny it and fight it and it would bedevil her, but she valued Kitty. That would turn out to be as important for me, I fully believed, as the secret I carried to save a civilization.

"I will not speak further of this now," she finally was able to force out. "Later, when I am more settled. . . ."

"Take all the time you need," I said airily. "Mom."

She went purple and raised her left hand, hesitated, then dropped it and turned away with a frustrated snarl. Only later did I remember that she, too, was a fighter pilot, with crystals in her fingers.

Fifty-five years passed.

On the Wholeth side, the Little Lord, no longer little, had succeeded to the throne, well-served by her able, aging adjutant, the Stead named Selah Maja. The war with the Polar Cloud was going well, from their point of view. The Whole kept to its one-planet-per-month schedule, and nearly seven hundred planets were gone. There were epic battles in space, but the Wholeth technical superiority prevailed again and again, even when the Cloud was able finally to meet the design of the golden ship and more. The Cloud was weak, riddled by internal bickering, fractionalized by growing conversions to the Wholeth religion, its government lacking the iron paranormal hand which the Whole enjoyed. And paranormal spies from the Whole soon held the Cloud in a tight intelligence network, made irresistible by psionic power.

Word occasionally came regarding the Onn. The Whole still dredged up the shibboleth of alien invasion, despite what the Little Lord had denied and revealed. There was a flurry of such claims around the thirty-third year, the rumor flying that the Whole had identified an infiltration network from the aliens it had considered long extinct. Nothing came of it, though; unless the rumors were true, and the aliens themselves suppressed them. I found out the truth on one of the suicidal missions Palla Belanger forced me into, but that's not a part of this story.

That was the year that the black planet Institute finally sent another mission to the Roil, this time in a new class of starship whose power was, it was believed, more than enough to overcome the intensity of the gravitational chaos. It was a mission driven by a Polarian desperation, a clutching at straws for any chance, any wedge to use against the Whole. It was also, though few knew it, a mission brought about by the secret that I had revealed to Palla Belanger, an inference I had made, a connecting of disparate facts.

The Little Lord or Maja might have thought of it if they had tried, but they had been too confident in their psionics, too dismissive of what the spies had done. Now, as the mission went out, they in their empire in the galactic arm were aware of some of the desperate thinking behind the mission; what we let them know. Knowing as they did the events of Lee and my time, they simply looked on, amused. The spy ship had been cleaned out, as their Lord well knew.

And so the Roil opened up and swallowed the Institute ship, and only a few paid any real attention. Soon the shipful of the finest male scientists the Cloud could muster—male to avoid any possibility of a paranormal Wholeth spy aboard—found itself in wild orbit around the central peculiarity.

They reached the spy ship, and their disappointment was great. Hoping against hope that the Little Lord had left something behind, they found nothing, not in the ship's databanks, not in any secret hiding place inside or on her skin, though they virtually took the vessel apart. The ship had been wiped as clean as a newborn baby.

But the Polarian ship went on; why not? There was nothing to lose. They overtook and studied the ship of Crestor Falon; and they even reached the dusty hulk of the astronomer's son, *The Defiant*, whose age had brought it closer than any of the others to the deadly rings sweeping the sky.

And from that point, the expedition dropped from the ken of the Cloud and of the Whole. Both believed for a long time, one officially and the other absolutely, that the ship had been lost, as those before it, in the Roil of stars.

But in fact, something quite otherwise had occurred. The scientists had found all three ships functional when it came to their electronics, hard though time had been upon the people who had died inside. All ships were still sucking power out of the light around them. All had automatics turned on. All three shipcoms, two of them for centuries, had been monitoring the channels, electromagnetic and tachholo, analyzing and rejecting the constant roar of static that the Roil threw between them and the outside universe.

And two of them had caught the desperate transmission that the third had made when Lee's parents had despaired of surviving the grip of the Roil. Had caught, and recorded, the full details of paranormal genetics. After all, there was no Roil between them and the spy ship's transmission; they were in the same swept-clean, closed-in space.

The scientists, well aware of the Wholeth intelligence network and on admiralty instructions, took a chance with their new and powerful ship and, emerging from the Roil in another direction from their entry, sped away to an uncolonized planet which the Cloud had preselected, one of the few known, lying far out on the rearmost fringes of the Cloud, too remote to have attracted settlers as yet. And there highly screened wives and lovers joined them, and they took the information that Lee's parents had forgotten, and used it.

And twenty years later, the Whole became aware that its spy network was no longer as reliable as it once had been. The pace of conquest slowed. There was paranormal interference coming from somewhere. But where. . . ?

AN OFFER HE COULDN'T REFUSE

They were functional fangs, not just decorative, set in a protruding jaw, with long lips and a wide mouth; yet the total effect was lupine rather than simian. Hair a dark matted mess. And yes, fully eight feet tall, a rangy, tense-muscled body.

She clawed her wild hair away from her face and stared at him with renewed fierceness. Her eyes were a strange light hazel, adding to the wolfish effect. "What are you *really* doing here?"

"I came for you. I'd heard of you. I'm . . . recruiting. Or I was. Things went wrong and now I'm escaping. But if you came with me, you could join the Dendarii Mercenaries. A top outfit—always looking for a few good men, or whatever. I have this master-sergeant who . . . who *needs* a recruit like you." Sgt. Dyeb was infamous for his sour attitude about women soldiers, insisting that they were too soft . . .

"Very funny," she said coldly. "But I'm not even human. Or hadn't you heard?"

"Human is as human does." He forced himself to reach out and touch her damp cheek. "Animals don't weep."

She jerked, as from an electric shock. "Animals don't lie. Humans do. All the time."

"Not *all* the time."

"Prove it." She tilted her head as she sat cross-legged. "Take off your clothes."

". . . what?"

"Take off your clothes and lie down with me as *humans* do. Men and women." Her hand reached out to touch his throat.

The pressing claws made little wells in his flesh. "Blrp?" choked Miles. His eyes felt wide as saucers. A little more pressure, and those wells would spring forth red fountains. *I am about to die. . . .*

I can't believe this. Trapped on Jackson's Whole with a sex-starved teenage werewolf. There was nothing about this in any of my Imperial Academy training manuals. . . .

BORDERS OF INFINITY by LOIS McMASTER BUJOLD
69841-9 • $3.95